BLUE
FLAME

Praise for *Blue Flame*

'With this gorgeously and intricately braided novel, the first
in the Perfect Fire trilogy, K. M. Grant provides a top-notch
tale of star-crossed lovers, court intrigue, twisted religious
hatreds and the mystical power of landscape.'   *FT*

'Grant certainly knows how to tell a story . . . she handles
suspense well, and her main characters are believable – even
the dog . . . She has woven such a gripping plot that I shall
certainly be lining up to read Book Two. I hope she doesn't
keep us waiting too long.'   *Guardian*

'A rich surrounding cast of fully fleshed characters. Indeed,
by the end of this first volume of a trilogy, my heart was in
my mouth.'   *Bookbag*

D1151340

K. M. Grant is an author, journalist and broadcaster. She currently writes for the Scottish *Daily Mail*.

Her first book, *Blood Red Horse*, was a Booklist Top Ten Historical Fiction for Youth and a USBBY-CBC Outstanding International Book for 2006. The sequel, *Green Jasper*, was shortlisted for the Scottish *Royal Mail* Children's Book Award and *How the Hangman Lost His Heart* was an Ottakar's Book of the Month and a *Sunday Times* Children's Book of the Week.

BLUE FLAME

K. M. GRANT

Quercus

First published in Great Britain in 2008 by Quercus

This paperback edition published in 2008 by

Quercus
21 Bloomsbury Square
London
WC1A 2NS

A CIP catalogue reference for this book is available
from the British Library.

ISBN 978 1 84724 528 1

10 9 8 7 6 5 4 3 2 1

Designed and typeset by Rook Books, London
Printed and bound in England by Clays Ltd, St Ives plc.

For Alice, in good times and in bad, with love

THE GREETING

Last night, I thought I saw them again: Raimon, throwing out his arms to the wind; Yolanda, delighting in the clear water running between her toes; and Parsifal, sitting near Yolanda, polishing his father's sword. I'm sure he was humming.

And I did see them, I'm certain of that, for a place never forgets those who have loved it, and I am a place with a longer memory than most. I am the Amouroix — that's pronounced a-more-rwa (the x is silent, which is of no importance except to me) — set deep within the broader lands that roll off the mountains now separating France from Spain. That broader land is still known to some as the Occitan, or Occitania. That cc is pronounced x, making it ox-i-tan-ia. So I am A-more-rwa in Ox-i-tan-ia. A pretty name, don't you think.

A map would be both useful and useless, for no map could show the Amouroix-in-Occitania that Raimon and Yolanda knew, and Parsifal, of course. Maps have no interest in the winter ice and spring torrents, the sun-spangled noons and crisp evening chills, the engulfing cloud and the sharp, new-washed air that were my essence. No map salutes the stonemasons who, with rope and windlass, muscle and sweat, dotted my high crags with peerless, peering castles. Yet that's the Amouroix that those who loved me carried in their hearts. It's what matters.

And then there is the Blue Flame. What map could tell of that? It is hard even for me to tell. Occitanians knew of it through stories handed down. They heard that it contained the soul of their land within itself and would one day appear. But though Occitanians sang of it and some even longed for it, they also had a certain fear of it, for when it came, if it was not used rightly, so the story went, it would exact a revenge. Who was to say what was right?

I'm drifting, now, back to my town of Castelneuf, perched on a lumpy hill like a crown on the head of a tipsy lady. Raimon and Yolanda are there, and they are running. Raimon has lost Yolanda's hand. Parsifal is there too, though he is very pale. There is a dog and there is smoke. But wait. If I am to tell my tale as it should be told, I must drift further back and further north, out of the Occitan at least for a moment, to show how the Flame came home, and what came with it.

Chalus Chabrol, in the Limousin, 1199

They were never going to give in quietly. Even as the knights fled into the round keep, their last refuge, they were shouting defiance. Even as they should have been praying, they were dragging heavy armour up the stone stairs with a clanking that should have raised the devil. Even as they passed through the chilly, cheerless chapel and crossed themselves in front of the dainty filigree box no bigger than a small candle-holder, they were counting arrows. If Richard the Lionheart, King of England, Duke of Normandy and Aquitaine, would not accept the terms of surrender they had offered, then blast him to hell, even if he was a heroic crusader. Their terms were unconditional, as befitted the terms of Occitanian knights, although, in the end, the terms were of course pointless, for whatever the knights said, whatever they did, it was quite certain that Richard would take the garrison. How could the ramshackle castle at Chalus Chabrol, in which they had taken refuge, withstand siege machinery built to reduce the very walls of

Jerusalem to rubble? But the company, though it consisted only of fifteen knights, two archers and a child, would make certain the Lionheart remembered it to his dying day.

Only one knight, though brave as the rest, was not shouting. Instead, Bernard de Maurand was speaking to his son, and the little boy's cheery responses, even in the face of what he knew was to come, made the other knights smile their doomed smiles. What a knight Parsifal would have made had his mother not died and Bernard given away his lands in a grand gesture to take the Crusader's Cross, leaving his son in the care of a monastery. It showed such spirit that the boy had refused to stay there when he heard rumours of his father's return, and had come instead, kicking on the fat pony which was his special pet, to see if the rumours were true.

'Well I'm *glad* King Richard has refused our surrender,' Parsifal's voice chirruped, echoing up the steps and then suddenly flattening out as he and his father reached the top platform of the tower, open to the skies. 'He'll have to take us now, Father, and I'll be in a real fight.'

His father was torn between shaking his son and kissing him. Perhaps it was as well that the boy had never seen a man hung, never seen the indignity of knights dying not in battle, using the full force of their strength, but lining up like beggars, their possessions reduced to the rope that would choke them. If Richard did spare Parsifal, as Bernard had reason to think he might, for the king's reputation, though bloody, did not include child-killing, he hoped the boy would be sent away before the executions began.

A brother knight, an elderly fellow, had other concerns.

Sending Parsifal to find an archer, he spoke gravely. 'What are we to do, Bernard?'

Bernard knew at once that his comrade-at-arms was not speaking of the child. It was not by chance that King Richard had journeyed at such speed into the Limousin, straight to this insignificant place, even though he had other, greater, battles to fight. Somebody had blabbed. Somebody had told him that the Occitanian treasure was on its way home. The identity of the traitor was of no import now. God would judge him soon enough. The only thing that mattered to Bernard and his companions was whether to destroy the precious thing they had brought all the way from Jerusalem, or give it up. 'Bernard!' said the other knight urgently, even as he clumsily pulled on his armour, for his squire had fled, 'we have so little time. I am resigned to dying, but if we are to give our treasure to Richard, let's do so as men and not have it torn from us like babies.'

Bernard looked through the battlements. Richard's camp was well set up, pennants flapping joyously over the tents as if victory was already theirs. Under thick, arrow-proof canopies, men were oiling the joints of the siege engines ready for the next bombardment, a bombardment they clearly expected to be the last judging by the few stones lying about in careless heaps. They were not replenishing their stock.

The besiegers' warhorses were unsaddled and grazing, Sir Bernard's horses amongst them, for they had been taken by King Richard's men as booty. Only Parsifal's pony was standing loyally at the bottom of the keep. The besiegers had not wanted him. Parsifal had felt very insulted.

On a hillock pushing up through low trees, they could see

Richard mounted on a fine bay stallion and surrounded by a gaggle of starstruck pages. He was personally supervising the erection of a line of gallows and Bernard found his palms growing sticky. Only a fool or a saint can look at gallows meant for himself without his skin prickling and Bernard was neither. He turned back to his friend. 'But if we do hand it over, Arnaud, will the Occitan survive?' Nobody could answer that question.

Parsifal had wandered off, and was now engaged in conversation with the arbalester, who, for want of anything better to do, had handed over his crossbow and was teaching the boy to shoot a bolt. 'Now crank up the ratchet,' he was saying. Bernard could hear Parsifal grunting with effort and found himself praying. 'Dear God, spare my boy. Please spare my boy.' And as he prayed, he suddenly knew what to do. He turned back to Arnaud. 'We'll destroy it,' he said. 'How can we let Richard have it? It would be like handing over not just the soul of the Occitan but our own souls too.'

Arnaud held his helmet more firmly. 'Shall I come with you?'

'No. Wait here. I'll be back before Parsifal notices.'

'What does he know?'

'Nothing.'

Arnaud nodded. 'Good, that's good,' he said. 'What he doesn't know, he can't tell. If the boy's spared, even after our deaths Richard will be left guessing what has happened to the prize he wanted so badly.' He laughed. 'It will drive him mad,' he said. 'What sweet revenge.'

Bernard gave a grim smile, touched his friend's hand, and descended into the keep again. He reached the chapel and could now clearly hear the rumble of wheels three floors below. Two men were calling to each other. At ground level, on the other side of the door of thick French oak, an iron-capped battering ram was being put in place, ready for tomorrow. No wonder King Richard was so successful. Everything was pre-prepared. Nothing was left to chance, nothing to the last minute.

Bernard turned to the treasure and, as was his habit, knelt before it. He was not a man much affected by beauty but he had to admit that the wood of the filigree box was so finely carved it was difficult to imagine fingers delicate enough to have wielded the chisel. Then he rose and picked it up. The box was not heavy, for the treasure it contained had no substance whatsoever. It was simply a Flame, a perfectly ordinary-looking Flame, except that it burnt the most glorious shades of blue, and in it Bernard could see reflected all the hope of the land of his fathers.

Now that he had hold of the box, he gripped it, wanting to crush it quickly for he could not but feel it was a terrible thing he was doing. However, when the oil tipped in its fragile silver bowl and the Flame drew itself up, thin as a heron's leg, he hesitated and missed the moment. At once, he cupped the box in both hands and carried it out of the chapel, determined to drop it on the steps and stamp on it. He began to mount the steps. This one. Then perhaps this one. But still he held the box, with the Flame now shaped like a question mark. *Better to throw it from the top of the keep*, he told himself by way of an excuse. It would be some consolation if all Richard could gather up was matchwood.

Bernard climbed the steps more carefully now and when

he reached the top, he walked over to the battlements, breathing hard. He held the box between his fingers, poised. But before he had quite let go, he heard a wild roar and, above it, a short, sharp squeal, like a falcon taken by surprise. The box rocked, the Flame wavered and turned turquoise, but Bernard stayed his hand. The arbalester came running. 'Parsifal!' he cried. 'Parsifal!'

Bernard was turned to stone.

'Sir,' the archer was grinning so widely that his face nearly split. 'Sir, Parsifal has shot the king!'

Bernard dropped the box, which was caught by Arnaud, ran to his son and followed Parsifal's eyes downwards. The king, unmistakable in his surcoat of white and red, was still on his horse, but sat decidedly lopsided. Even from up here, it was easy to see the crossbow bolt now lodged between neck and hunching shoulder. Bernard seized his son's arm. 'Did you do that?'

'I didn't mean to, Father,' the boy's lips were trembling. 'I never meant to hit the king. I've missed everything up to now.'

'He has, he has,' nodded the arbalester, 'but that was a sure shot if ever I saw one.'

Parsifal could hardly take it in. 'What will happen, Father?'

Bernard regarded his son as his world shifted on its axis, and then he held him as close as his hauberk would allow. It was a long moment before he let go and looked over the parapet again, leaning right out to get a better view. 'You've not killed him, Parsifal. Look! He's still riding. He's just injured.' Bernard's relief was palpable. To kill a king was a terrible thing indeed for a boy to have on his conscience. He and Parsifal watched together until they saw Richard order the panicking sentries back to their posts. Then, as he was attempting to pull the crossbolt out, he inadvertently snapped off the shaft.

Only now did Bernard gasp and his knuckles turned white. For knights well versed in injury, that snap of the shaft was like the crack of doom. The snap meant that the bolt-head was still embedded in the flesh, and though nothing in Richard's demeanour had changed, it sent a gangrenous shiver into Bernard's stomach. The bolt-head would work like poison. Short of a miracle, the king would die. When he spoke again, his voice was quite different, almost as if he and his son were strangers. 'Now, you listen to me, Parsifal. Listen and obey. Don't argue, just promise me, on your mother's life, to do exactly as I say.'

'I don't –' Parsifal was still trying to look at the king.

Bernard shook him. 'Never mind the king. Look at me.' There was no warmth at all in Bernard's eyes. The boy was terrified but Bernard did not relax his grip. 'If the king dies, the fate of the man who shot the bolt will be beyond imagining and I won't, under any circumstances, allow that fate to be yours. When you have a son, you will know why.'

'But you said –'

'Never mind what I said.' Bernard peered over the battlements again, more cautiously this time. Richard, swaying slightly, had dismounted and was retreating to his tent. Bernard could see the apothecary hurrying over, and the farrier with pliers, and they could all hear the young pages squawking like chickens. At news of the king's plight, everything else was forgotten. Stacks of spears were unguarded, piles of shields uncovered and tent flaps were open. The grooms had left the warhorses, who moved uneasily on their tethers. Even the pack animals, sensing calamity, raised their heads from their endless eating. Only Parsifal's pony took no notice. It simply looked up at the tower and whinnied, as it had been doing since daybreak. It was missing Parsifal's treat-filled pouch.

Bernard was still holding his son when Arnaud appeared. Both men were thinking the same thing. 'It might be possible,' Bernard murmured. Arnaud nodded. 'We must try.'

Bernard put one hand on each of Parsifal's shoulders. The boy could feel the weight, as if his father's whole presence was pressing down on him. 'My son,' Bernard said, and his voice was even deeper than usual, 'I'm going to tell you something of very great importance, but before I do, I want you to promise me something.'

'Anything, Father,' the boy whispered. It seemed the right thing to say.

'Very well then. You must promise me that whatever happens, if anybody asks, anybody at all, you will say that it was I who shot Richard, not you. That is what you say. You say that I, Sir Bernard de Maurand, your unfortunate father, fired the crossbolt that hit the king. Do you understand?' His grip was tight as a vulture's. He repeated again, 'I took the crossbow from our archer friend here, and I shot it. Now you repeat that. Repeat it, I order you.'

Parsifal did not want to, but the weight of his father was too much. It came out as a breath.

'Not good enough. Repeat it again, louder.'

Parsifal repeated it again.

Bernard's hands were a vice for a moment longer, then they gentled. 'Dear Parsifal,' he said, 'now for the other thing. It's very important. It's also dangerous, but the king's injury makes it perhaps possible. I think you could get out of here and there's something you must take with you.'

'But if I can get out, couldn't we all?'

'We couldn't, my son. A small boy might get through Richard's camp in this confusion, but not a knight. So you see this is a mission I can entrust to nobody else but you.' The father knew just how to appeal to the son and even in his fear, Parsifal felt a thrill. A mission! He would be like King Arthur of old. He stood taller under the weight of his father's confidence. 'What is it, sir?'

Bernard let go of his son's shoulders, walked swiftly away and returned with the box. 'This,' he said.

Parsifal looked very disappointed. 'That old box?'

'This old box, as you call it –' he stopped. How could he thrust such a responsibility onto a boy not yet even big enough to carry a sword? He had to collect himself before he carried on. 'This box contains the Blue Flame of the Occitan.'

Parsifal peered at the box from all sides. 'But the Blue Flame is supposed to be big. It can't be inside there.'

'Look,' said Bernard, and he knelt so that his son could see.

Parsifal peered into the box again, and when, at last, he raised his face to his father's again, his voice had almost vanished. 'The Blue Flame of the Occitan! Can it really be?' he whispered.

'It is.' Bernard was patient. This was too important to hurry. 'We were taking it home.'

'But I thought it lived in Jerusalem, in the tomb where Jesus was buried, so that he would remember the Occitan and God would give us his special protection.'

'It has been in the tomb, Parsifal, for many years. When the first Occitanian knights went on crusade, they took it with them and we have been guarding it in Jerusalem ever since. But I was asked to bring it back, for the Occitan has caught the eye of the King of France. Even now, his armies are rolling towards her.' He paused. 'The Flame must go home to save our lands and somebody must take it there.'

Parsifal was quite cheerful again. 'I'll come with you.'

Sir Bernard shook his head gently. 'I shall not be going now. My son, the journey is yours. You must take it.'

Parsifal paled. 'Alone?' The Flame's blue eye seemed to wink at him not warmly, as a friend, but coldly, like his grandmother used to when he forgot to kneel with her serving dish. It was not going to be a comfortable companion. 'Why can't I stay here and somebody at home could light another one?'

'Parsifal, Parsifal,' his father admonished. 'Could your hero King Arthur use just any sword?'

'No.'

'We cannot have just any Flame. This Flame was lit specially for us at the moment of Christ's death, when the veil of the Temple was rent in two. You know how it came to us.'

'Through Christ's mother. She brought it.' He could still hear his mother's voice, telling him the story, though her voice was fainter now. She had been dead for too many years. He looked at the Flame again but it did not seem motherly to him. It seemed to be eyeing him up, assessing him, judging him. It was a relief to turn back to his father.

'Tonight,' Bernard was saying, 'Richard's men will be focussed on his wound so it will be easier to leave and once we've got you out of this keep, you must ride home as fast as you can.'

'I can't! I can't go by myself!' Parsifal quailed.

Bernard looked at his son, and his heart was filled with foreboding. He looked at Arnaud, who shrugged. 'We have to try,' he said.

Bernard stiffened his voice. 'You must be brave,' he said. 'You must find the right leader to whom to give the Flame, somebody who will keep the Occitan free in the paths of righteousness.' He wanted to say something more, but his voice choked.

Parsifal wanted to help him. 'Couldn't we –' he said.

Bernard shook his head. 'No more. I will join you if I can, otherwise we will meet again in heaven.'

Parsifal cried out, 'Heaven is so far away!'

'Yes,' Bernard said, 'but far away from suffering, too. I shall be happy there. Come now. That fat pony of yours may be useful yet.'

The other knights slowly gathered round, dead men walking. 'God bless you and God keep the Occitan,' said Arnaud sincerely, and kissed the boy, and all the other knights did likewise. Lastly, Parsifal shook hands with the arbalester.

Then he walked with his father back down the steps, right into the fetid damp of the foundations. Counting the steps all the time, for the only light came from the box, Bernard at last stopped and pushed open a trap door just large enough for a badger or a small boy. He held his son again for a moment, but awkwardly, almost overcome.

Parsifal tried to say something, but his father interrupted.

He did not want to prolong this parting. 'God speed,' he said and pushed the box containing the Blue Flame out first and Parsifal after it.

'Father,' he heard the boy whisper, poised on the edge of darkness.

He could not remain silent. 'Yes?'

'When we meet again, can I have a proper sword? I should like to name mine Unbent, after yours.'

'I expect so, if you deserve it.'

It was the traditional response of a father to a son and it made them both smile fleetingly. There was more scrabbling, then Parsifal's voice came again, muffled this time.

'Father?'

'Yes, my son.'

'Nothing. I just wanted to hear your voice again.'

Bernard was glad Parsifal could not see his tears. 'Go now, Parsifal, and may God go with you.'

He waited, sealing his son in his heart, as Parsifal made his final scramble and emerged in the shadow of a buttress. There was no clamour, and Bernard felt his way up the steps to the ground floor. After checking the heavy bars slotted across the main entrance, bars which would be no match for Richard's battering ram, he began to climb again.

At the top of the keep, Arnaud was watching as the pony wound its way into the forest. The guards were not interested in a small boy not even big enough for a wolf's dinner. If they thought about him at all, they thought he must be somebody's page collecting leaves for his bed.

On his way past the camp, Parsifal picked up one of the lanterns that were loosely gathered together in a pile, and once he was out of sight, he removed the ordinary wick and placed the tiny box inside instead. The flame shone, a pinprick of midnight blue on the end of a pole. Bernard held his breath. The colour was a beacon. Why had he not told Parsifal to cover it? But the boy was not stupid. He saw the danger at once. The light wobbled and then turned an odd shade of yellow. By flattening some leaves against the box's sides, the colour was completely disguised. Bernard gave muttered thanks and only when the light had disappeared entirely did he stop looking.

Eleven days later, Richard the Lionheart, King of England, Duke of Normandy and Aquitaine, died. He had left quite specific instructions that the man who had loosed the deadly crossbow bolt was not to be harmed. His orders were disobeyed.

And Parsifal? He began with such good intentions. He made a proper pocket from thin animal skin so that the Flame's blueness could always be disguised from curious eyes and kicked his fat pony south. But he found what he did not expect: the Occitan was already filled with flames. These flames were red and carried above them the sign of the cross.

How had this happened? Two ways of worshipping God in the Occitan and neither sect willing to countenance the other. On one side, the supremely powerful Catholics, and on the other, the Cathars, whom the Catholics designated 'heretics', fewer in number but just as fanatical, each convinced that God was on their side and their side only. It was the Catholics who lit the funeral pyres and the Cathar heretics who offered themselves as martyrs to the flames, both sides joyfully grasping at these most unholy deaths as a sign of their own righteousness. And the worst of it? Each side claimed the helpless Occitan for themselves.

What was Parsifal, still so young and with nobody to guide him except his fat pony and a Flame, to do? What would you have done? He did what came naturally. He hid. He wanted to be heroic. He dreamed of being heroic. He dreamed of saving the Occitan. But he had no idea how to go about it. To which faction did the Flame belong? He didn't know and the Flame wasn't saying.

At last, almost starving, he was taken in by an exhausted widow, who sold the pony to pay for his keep and put him to work. Parsifal thought his heart would break as his pet was led away. But the Flame, sympathetic for once, dried his tears and kept him alive when he ran off into the freezing mists of the Pyrenees. It was the Flame who led him to the old Moslem shepherd with whom he found solace.

It was no life for a knight, but then Parsifal, although now of an age for knighthood, with no armour, no squire and not even a pony any more, could hardly count himself as special although, curiously, his hands remained unblemished by wind and weather. The old man was kind and Parsifal made himself useful, helping to guide the flocks over the passes into Catalonia for the winter, and back into the Occitan for the summer. Soon, just like his shepherd master, he could tell, just by sniffing, from which valley the wind was gathering strength. The shepherd had no cause for complaint and asked few questions. His only interest was sheep. He noted Parsifal's curious hands, and the box from which strange colours emanated, sometimes in sparks, sometimes in small tongues. But the boy's hands were quick and deft and the shepherd respected secrets, and besides, whatever it was that the box contained kept away the bears and wolves better than any guard dog. Its mystery, like most mysteries involving Christians, bothered him as little as the rain or the cold.

Forty years passed. The Cathars and the Catholics bickered and fought. The armies of France rolled to and from the Occitan, never extinguishing it, never leaving it alone, the French kings eyeing it up as a man eyes up a sliver of sugar for his breakfast table. People spoke of the Blue Flame, wondered about it, but it never appeared.

The old Moslem died and Parsifal lost all sense of himself and the boy he had been. He turned vagrant, wandering after flocks of sheep that were not in his charge, stealing food and, occasionally, when a shepherd was idle or asleep, secretly helping a ewe to lamb or saving a cow in a stream. He was quite aimless but still the Flame burned on.

Every now and again he fell in with knights who had turned bandit, dispossessed by stronger forces than their own, or those who had returned from foreign wars and found their castles overrun. He heard them sing the Song of the Flame that Occitanians loved to sing. Sometimes he would sing with them. But though these knights, as their voices rose in chorus, pledged allegiance to the territories they thought of as their own, their conversation was less uplifting. Most wanted to use the Flame as an instrument of revenge against those they felt had wronged them. Parsifal did not linger long with these knights. None of them, it seemed to him, had much interest in the paths of right-eousness.

Only once did he show the Blue Flame in public. It was in Foix after he had helped another shepherd drive the flock down to sell. He had seen some knights taking their ease outside a tavern. These knights were not bandits, they were simply old and battle-wearied. One had lost an eye. Another had a wound that would not heal. Yet they were joking gently together, loyal companions-in-arms who had seen each other at their best and at their worst. Parsifal crept close to them. These men had the kind of companionship for which he himself longed. His throat knotted with shame at his tattered appearance and tattered dreams. He left the knights and ran back into the market place, pulling the Blue Flame right out of its pouch. It seemed annoyed, sinking down until less than a pinprick, but Parsifal shook it until it glittered, even in the sunlight, and then held it up over his head. 'Who loves the Occitan? Who will lead her in the paths of righteousness?' he called out, above the hurly-burly of the market.

What did he expect? That a selfless hero would rush across the street and claim it?

Of course people stared at him. The Flame in the possession of a madman with pale hands and a beard as thick as a blackberry bush was too much to take in. It must be a hoax. Only not everybody thought so. When Parsifal turned, he found himself directly in the path of three Inquisitors. These stern-faced, white-robed Dominican friars were the Catholics' most lethal weapons against the Cathars. It was the Dominicans who claimed to be purifying the Occitan for God and themselves by burning at the stake everybody who disagreed with them. From where do such ideas spring? From some thick, black sediment at the bottom of men's stomachs.

The leading Inquisitor saw the Blue Flame straight away and his eyes almost doubled in size. He gripped his hands together and came to an abrupt halt, his whole attention glued to the tiny slice of colour. He shook his head. This could not really be *that* Flame, not really the Flame of the Occitan. And yet he catapulted forward, his hand thrust out.

Parsifal was never sure how he escaped. He only knew that he ran faster than he had ever run, and once off the main road, he scrambled and climbed, crept and crawled over hill after rocky hill and through valley after silken valley, until he could no longer feel the Inquisitor's breath on his back. Only then did he sleep, enfolded in a crag that protected him, like a shield.

He remained hidden for weeks, getting up only when forced to by hunger or thirst, whilst the Flame, more agitated now than it had ever been, both comforted and taunted him, for whilst it reminded him of his father, it also reminded him of duty unfulfilled.

It was weeks before he found the strength to emerge, and it was on this day, as the French armies were once again rumbling south, determined in one last, grinding attempt to wear the Occitan down, that a lumpy, shaggy dog appeared, its tail wagging and its mouth full of rabbit. The dog and Parsifal regarded each other, and when the dog dropped the rabbit and licked those pale hands, Parsifal chose to take this as a kind of sign. Men clutch at anything when the map of their life has fragmented. The dog, on the other hand, whose life did not depend on a map, quickly regretted the rabbit and when the pale hands did not give it back, gave Parsifal a very old-fashioned look and yawned.

Near the Town of Castelneuf, Amouroix

Now we are in the spring of 1242, and by the time Brees – for that was the name of the dog – returned and flopped down in his original position, Yolanda and Raimon were lying on their backs in a patch of scrub amid the trees that rose in an uneven, tufty carpet above a small lake into which water from the mountain flowed, sometimes in a trickle, sometimes in a torrent, according to the seasons. The seasons are a comfort when trouble comes, don't you think? They remind us that everything passes, not that Yolanda, at this moment, wanted anything to pass.

April, when the lake swelled with snowmelt, was the time of year she loved best. Her birthday party was just over a month away and as she and Raimon lazily spotted the butter-flies beginning to flutter in nervous green and orange clouds above the grass, they were discussing, as they did every year, what the entertainments should be. 'Jugglers and fire-eaters,' Yolanda was saying, 'and perhaps, since I'll be fourteen, we might have a mock tournament and dancing until after dawn. I'll get to lead the Song of the Flame and then I expect Gui and Guerau will have new romances for us to hear –'

'All about you, naturally,' Raimon glanced sideways at her, his irises encircled by rims so thickly black that there was only a sliver of deep hazel between them and the pupils in which Yolanda's reflection shone. He was going to dig her in the ribs, but didn't. Instead, he raised his arm to pull gently at Brees's long tan fringe. This dog was not a beauty. An unintended mixture of savage alaunt – a burly, broadheaded greyhound type, bred for gripping prey and pulling it down – and a shorter-legged speckled running hound, he was all untidy limbs and matted fur. When he panted, as he was doing now, his tongue flipped sideways as though he was permanently licking something just out of reach. 'We should teach Brees to howl a birthday tune.' Raimon avoided the tongue, leapt to his feet and threw back his head so that his slick of dark hair cascaded down his back. 'Yawoooooool,' he cried, and laughed when Brees threw back his own head and joined in. Raimon's laughter was not just a response to Brees's attempt at a duet. He laughed also because where once Yolanda's presence had been as unremarkable to him as trout in the stream or purple orchids in the meadows, now it made him jumpy as a lynx. Brees was a very useful diversion.

Though they had scarcely spent a day apart since Yolanda had learnt to walk, Raimon had, over this last long winter, during which he had celebrated his fifteenth birthday in rather less grand style than was planned for Yolanda's, become aware of her in quite new ways. He could not pinpoint when this awareness had begun. He only knew that instead of Yolanda just being a friend, his greatest friend, who happened to be a girl, a person so close to him he could no more describe her than describe his own hand, he now noticed the cleft in her chin, the shape of the freckled arc that bridged her nose, the way she scrunched up her legs when she was listening to a sad story and the sudden creasing of her top lip when her brother Aimery teased her in a way she did not like. This was quite unlike the way it creased when she smiled and the edges of her eyes, brown and slightly speckled, slanted downwards, giving her smile, however happy its genesis, an unexpected wistfulness.

Raimon had not looked for these things. He never even described them to himself. It was just that this year, by the time his father had thrown open the doors of the weaving shed to let out the stale winter air, he knew she had become an astonishment to him, and half longed and half dreaded that she would notice.

'Don't,' she was saying now, rolling over and catching at his legs. 'You'll scare the sheep.' She shook herself like a wild pony, her hair a tawny, billowing mane, as uncombed as her dress was unwashed.

'Too late,' said Raimon, although he did stop howling and Brees, finding himself howling solo, soon lost interest and began to sniff for more rabbits. Raimon and Yolanda climbed onto an outcrop of rock and together looked down over the treetops. There, sure enough, were the sheep, running towards the lake in an uneven snowy tide.

'Peter will be cross with us,' said Yolanda. It was a statement rather than a regret. The shepherd was always cross, particularly if Brees appeared. He disliked Yolanda's dog intensely, for Brees was not reliable with the flock. It was not that he ever meant to kill the sheep, it was just that sometimes, particularly if out alone and the flock was bleating, a red mist would descend and his pulse would quicken in response. Then he was hunter and the sheep were prey and he heard nothing but roar of the chase in his ears and tasted sweet blood on his tongue.

Twice Yolanda had had to beg for his life when he had appeared, tell-tale bits of fleece still sticking to his teeth. Twice her father, Count Berengar, lord of all my land, had reprieved him. The third time, when Yolanda knew that there would be no more indulgence, Raimon had hidden the sheep's body and, shortly after dusk, had taken Brees out and tied him to a ram. All night long, the dog had been buffeted and butted and Raimon had sat and watched as the lesson was painfully learnt. In the morning, it was a chastened Brees who, after Raimon had tended to his bruises, was returned to his mistress. He had not chased the sheep since although the instinct still lurked. However, Brees also seemed to know that in some odd way Raimon had saved his life, and in the great hall, if Raimon was serving the count, as he sometimes did when Aimery was away, he would often lie at his saviour's feet, staring up at him with ardent eyes. This amused Yolanda very much and she would whisper to Raimon, tickling his ear with herby breath, that it was a good thing the dog could not speak, or he would surely give their secret away. His eyes would crinkle, and hers would crinkle in return. Both pairs of feet would seek Brees under the table. The dog would splay himself out. This was his heaven.

Today, however, the sheep were running of their own

accord, too far away for the dog to give them more than a nostalgic passing thought and anyway, at this moment, there was another smell on the wind.

Raimon, alerted by Brees standing solid and four square, turned to inspect the horizon himself. The weather was clear, so he could see not just the near hills but the far as well. At first he could see nothing unusual, then, below the horizon but at the top of one of the gorges where I, the Amouroix, melt into my neighbour, a small plume of grey rose before thinning out and vanishing. He frowned. It was surely nothing, just farmers burning timbers from winter storm damage. The spring saw many such fires. But as he watched, plumes continued to rise and then it was not their increasing number that bothered him so much as the smell – just tiny snatches of it carried over. Surely it wasn't possible to smell anything at all from here? He shifted and put his hand on the dog's neck. Brees was bristling. He could smell it too. The smell was real and it was foul. Raimon had smelled it before, six years ago, when he and his father had been walking home from his grandmother's funeral. When his father would not tell him what the smell was, Raimon had known that it was not burning wood.

'Come, Yolanda,' he said, rather more abruptly than he meant to. 'It's time we went back.'

But Yolanda was also looking to the west. 'That's a lot of smoke.' Clouds of it were forming. She, too, was sniffing, but without fear. 'It's not in Amouroix, and even if it is, it's a long way from Castelneuf.'

'Quite a long way.'

She nudged him. 'Well, whatever it is, it needn't trouble us, need it?' That was another thing he had begun to notice about her, the way she often deferred to him, as if he knew better than she did. How long had she been doing that? He didn't know but hoped she would never stop. He gave a grunt, which she took for agreement, just as he meant her to. He didn't want to alarm her and anyway, it was probably nothing to do with the new rebellion against French King Louis, and anyway, even if it was, there was no need for concern. There had been so many rebellions against the greedy French, and none had ever touched the Amouroix. What was more, everybody said that Raymond of Toulouse, who had inherited the mantle of leadership for the whole Occitan, could weather the latest storm.

Yolanda turned her back to the smoke. 'I wonder if we could get that famous fortune-teller from Poitiers to come.' She was still mentally organising her party. A shadow now stippled Raimon's face that was nothing to do with King Louis. He did not like it when Yolanda mentioned Poitiers. To him, Castelneuf was enough. Why did Yolanda even have to mention other towns, miles away? What could they offer which was not better found here?

Yolanda watched him. She could follow his thoughts quite easily even when he didn't speak. It was always funny to her when, afterwards, he felt he must explain himself. She never told him there was no need, and anyway, just lately, she, too, had felt the new jumpiness between them. She knew it alarmed him, and she hugged this knowledge to herself, for it did not alarm her at all, it just made her blood run quicker, her legs run faster and the world seem full of new possibilities.

And anyway, how could Raimon think that she'd really

prefer anything to the excitement of clinging together on the back of one of her father's packhorses, his legs curled round warm flanks, hers curled round his, with the wind whipping their eyes. Under Raimon's light hands and her lark's voice, the animal would lose itself in their makebelieve and become a destrier, tossing its mane and arching its neck, with Brees providing some doggy heavy infantry in its wake. Sometimes they pretended to be the saviours of the Amouroix, beating back a French king, or an ogre – they were interchangeable since neither seemed very real. Sometimes they were the King and Queen of the Occitan. In the summer, they would find a spot where they believed no other humans had ever trodden and, sinking down on a cushion of scented blossom, Raimon would turn the clouds into fantastical animals, or they would lie together on green stones behind the heavy curtain of a waterfall, gloriously deafened by the thunder until they could stand the noise and slime and chill no longer. And they danced. How they danced. When they danced, they never spoke because they didn't need to. If she liked to wonder about Poitiers, or even Paris, it was only because she was naturally curious about other lives, other halls, other music, whole other worlds completely different to mine, worlds of which she sometimes got a glimpse when visiting knights passed through.

She began to run and her belt, which actually belonged to another dress, finally frayed in two and dropped off. She didn't bother to retrieve it. 'Let's swim,' she yelled. She knew that would wash away the shadows and the smoke.

'The water'll still be freezing.' Raimon was grinning again. 'Even Brees'll yelp.'

'It's never stopped us before and we can't say it's really spring till we swim. Come on.' They linked arms and rushed along full pelt, hopping and tripping as they pushed their way through branches sticky with buds until the stream broadened out into a spot perfect for their first dip of the year. Yolanda tossed off her shoes, dipped a toe in and gave a little scream. 'It IS freezing.' She hopped about. Two years ago, or perhaps even last year, she'd not have cared about the cold, but this year it pricked her like needles and, for the first time in her life, she hesitated.

'I told you so.' Raimon laughed like a bell at the dismay on her face, the smoke not forgotten but crowded out. There was no hesitation from him. He stripped off his shirt, the belt in which he slotted his knife, and chucked away his boots. The freezing needles from which Yolanda shrank were just what he wanted. She skipped along the bank as he plunged in, exulting in the crash of his heart as the water hit his chest. The stream was a miracle of cleanliness and purity. He stood quite still, pretending he was a dagger of silver. Then, when he could bear to be still no longer, he doused his whole head before rising up, a thin, pale nymph under a dark dripping mop, flailing his arms and splashing her. Hitching up her skirts, she fled, then returned, and thus they made their way along, Raimon almost blue, shouting with glee and threatening that since he wouldn't get out until she got in, he would shortly freeze to death and it would be all her fault and she, pretending that swimming had been all his idea. 'Madness,' she yelled. 'Coward!' he answered. They both lost sight of Brees as they teased each other, revelling in the sun and the water.

At last, when it was clear that despite ever more fantastic threats, Yolanda really wasn't going to swim, Raimon forged his way back to find his shirt. Yolanda was there before him, whipped the shirt up and began to run into the trees again.

'Yolanda! Bring it back at once!' Raimon was half laughing, half annoyed as he grabbed his belt and knife and stumbled off in pursuit, one boot half on and his teeth chattering. It really had been freezing. He caught her back in the clearing, where she was standing with the light pouring in behind her. *Why*, he thought, forgetting all his discomforts, *her hair is shot through with copper*, and for some reason he could not and did not want to explain, this fascinated him. Yolanda was holding out his shirt and as he took it and their fingers met, his so icy that hers felt like fire, he forgot everything but the fact that her face was tilted towards him and on top of the patchy grime on her cheeks a spray of diamond drops dazzled. He would have done nothing had she not stopped breathing at exactly the same time as he did, and had her eyes not met his with something more than her usual mischief. There was a challenge there, and something more than that. He could not help himself. 'Yolanda,' he thought he said, although he actually said nothing at all as he leant forward and kissed her.

Her reaction was immediate and not at all what he expected. She jumped, rather as if he had turned green or grown two heads, and he, who believed they had moved together as one, found himself floundering alone. Then she laughed.

Now it was his turn to jump, tripping right over for his boots were still not properly on. He did not recognise her laughter for what it was — a mirror image of his own, earlier: nervous, a little brittle, a reaction she could not control. Though she had lived this moment in her dreams a hundred times, had longed for it, she had never imagined it would come when Raimon was dripping wet with his boots half on and a shirt clutched between them. In her mind, their first kiss would be, well, at a special moment, when everything was perfect. Her friend Beatrice, who was to be married in the summer, had told her what such a moment should be. Her bailiff-fiancé had shown her. When he had taken his first kiss, he had held Beatrice's hand and gazed soulfully at it, recited a few lines of poetry in a theatrical style, then coughed, closed his eyes and pouted his lips. That was how it was done, according to Beatrice, although when Yolanda had pressed her as to what it actually felt like, she was less forthcoming. She did not want to tell Yolanda that she had had to keep her eyes open to remind herself that she was kissing a man, not a fish. 'It is a very important time for a girl,' she had quickly intoned, crossing her plump legs. 'You mustn't let it come just any old how as you do other things, Yolanda.' Yet that's just what Yolanda had done and she laughed because she didn't know what else to do.

Raimon turned his back, hoping she would not see the flush he knew was spreading from his neck. He felt just as he had a year ago, when Aimery had crowed over him, having floored him during a bout of boxing. It was a humiliation.

'Raimon,' Yolanda said, angry with herself, 'I didn't mean –'
'It doesn't matter.'

She ran in front of him, wanting to brush away the hurt from his lips but they were set and she was nervous to touch them now. It was hardly like brushing away a crumb. 'But it does,' she said. He pulled his shirt over his head. 'I don't know why I laughed. It was just the cold, and your shirt, and I don't know. I suppose I imagined it would be different.'

'Different?' He tied his boots. 'Better, you mean?' Though Yolanda's laughter had quite disappeared, he could still hear it in his head.

She tried again, rubbing her palms on her dress. 'No, not better, just different. Can't you understand?'

'No, can't *you* understand?'

He began to walk away, now angry with himself for being angry with her. It was not her fault that it had begun to trouble him, and trouble him very much, that though they could always flip trout and sit crammed like sardines in the hearth listening to the Castelneuf troubadours, in reality they had little chance of a future together. The granite indifference of my silver mountains might be a constant lesson in humility for everybody, from knight to pauper, but he could make no presumption. She was the count's daughter. That was a fact. And just because Count Berengar's ways were not grand, his château was crumbling and there was little deference or ceremony except when Aimery demanded it – and fortunately Aimery was away at present – this did not mean that Raimon could expect Yolanda not to laugh if he kissed her. If she dreamed of Paris, she might also dream of another future in which she had more than a weaver's ring on her finger. And there was something else. Raimon's family were not Catholics as Yolanda's were, they were Cathars. This had never mattered before. In my peaceful lands nobody seemed to care how you worshipped God. But in Raimon's new, raw state, everything seemed to matter. Just as he was noticing her, he was losing her.

He began to walk more quickly until he heard Yolanda's voice, high with anxiety: 'Oh, no! Brees! He's in the sheep.' At once, they were running together.

The dog had wandered amongst the ewes, so much more tempting with lambs at foot. It was strange how like a snake he could look for a heavy, ungraceful creature, his long back a mottled smudge in the chalky white. The mothers were bundling together, their voices raised in a fury of fear. 'He hasn't, has he, Raimon?' Yolanda could hardly bear to look. Brees raised his head. He had something floppy in his mouth.

'He wouldn't,' Raimon tried to reassure, 'not with us here.' His words were more certain than his voice. The lesson with the ram was long past. He shouted for Brees to come to him, and the dog might have returned without further incident had Peter not chosen that moment to hurl a rock, which hit him smartly between the eyes. He yelped, dropped his burden, headed up the ride cut into the trees and vanished over the hill.

Raimon and Yolanda at once changed direction, Raimon easily outstripping Yolanda up the slope. Over the crest, the landscape altered and between thick strips of forest a path of rough scree descended into a small sunless depression pitted with four or five damp caves. The scree had formed natural barriers at the mouths of the caves and though they were always chilly, they were also good for shelter during the frequent storms. Raimon called the dog's name again and again, climbing into one cave after another. He could hear Yolanda searching about fifty yards to his right.

It was thus that Parsifal and Raimon came face to face, not in bright sunlight, but in flat, rather sinister grey. They stared at each other, Parsifal's eyes, though almost invisible under eyebrows thickened with age, the saddest Raimon had ever seen, and Raimon's dark as coal. Parsifal had his hand on Brees's collar and would have made some kind of exclamation had the noise not got stuck in his throat.

Raimon immediately reached for his knife. 'Let go of the dog.'

Parsifal's hand shot up. Raimon was surprised by its pale appearance. It didn't seem to go at all with the rest of the scarecrow figure. But Brees was free. Raimon began to edge away but found Parsifal moving towards him and when he got close, Raimon struck out rather harder than he might have done had Yolanda not laughed when he had kissed her. It felt good to hit something. However, the untidy stranger was niftier than Raimon supposed and suddenly Raimon was on the floor himself, face first in the ashes of an old fire. When he rolled over again, the stranger had vanished.

He could hear Yolanda scolding Brees. 'You foolish dog, what on earth were you thinking? Peter could have killed you! Look, it was only a rabbit. Thank goodness. Come on, let's get back into the sun.' It was only then that she saw Raimon had flakes of white in his hair. 'What happened to you?'

'There was a man,' Raimon said. 'Didn't you see him? He must have run almost straight past you.'

'I didn't see anybody.'

'He caught Brees and then he knocked me over. He must have run past.'

'Are you sure? I saw nothing.'

'Of course I'm sure.'

'Well maybe he's in one of the other caves.'

Raimon ran back and searched. All the caves were empty.'

'What did he look like?'

He answered without thinking. 'He looked as Merlin the Magician would look if he'd been buried under a tree for a thousand years, except for his hands, which were, I don't know, just not a thousand years old.'

'I see.' She couldn't help it if her voice was a little disbelieving. It was three Christmases since they had become obsessed with the story of Arthur, first sung in the winter firelight by Guerau, the younger of the Castelneuf troubadours, a barrel of a man whose tight curls made him an eternal youth but whose voice transformed him by turns into Lancelot the Sad, Gawaine the Burly, Galahad the Sinless, Bors the Steadfast and Tristan the Lover. As he acted out their deaths, Guerau could make his voice rise like a soul in final ecstasy or whisper like one of the sorrowful damned. Even Aimery's cheeks would not be dry by the end. And, being an Occitanian, Guerau had naturally changed the tale to suit his audience. Instead of searching for the Holy Grail, Arthur's knights were on a quest to find the Blue Flame, which they would deliver to whichever Castelneuf knight had Guerau's particular favour at that moment, usually the one who had tossed him a jewel or coin. The knight would then be Arthur for the night. At the end of each ballad, Guerau would act out the moment when King Louis himself would come face to face with the Flame. Then the troubadour would scream most horribly, and crumple, much to the delight of all, before being carried off by the château servants, dressed appropriately for their part as avenging angels.

'Well, if he was Merlin, he's gone now,' Yolanda said. She saw that Raimon was shivering and noticed too, now that she was looking properly, how tightly his skin was drawn over his cheekbones. She remembered that his mother was ill and suddenly wondered if he was getting enough to eat.

'And I do believe you,' she said gently, although she still wasn't sure. 'Let's call him the Knight Magician of the Breeze, because he looked like Merlin and it was Brees who found him.'

Raimon didn't want to be humoured. 'I shouldn't have said Merlin and he looked more like a bear than a knight.'

Yolanda didn't want to give in completely. 'He could be a brigand knight,' she said, and though she was hardly conscious of it, her voice grew a little dreamy. When she was little, during the dull sermons of Simon Crampcross, a man with jowls like a walrus and a high regard for his position as the town's Catholic priest, she had often imagined such men. They lived wild lives and though their reputations were brutal and their faces locked under iron helmets, she knew that they were always handsome. Sometimes, even now, she still imagined herself swept up behind one on a white horse with a foaming mouth and emerald trappings. The knight would introduce himself as Sir Brigand of the Four Winds and would declare her more beautiful than Arthur's Queen Guinevere. When they got to his castle, she would tame him, but not too much, and they would sail towards a hazy but glorious future in a spangled barge drawn by swans. She knew she was too old for such things, and anyway, galloping with Raimon was far better than any swan-drawn barge. But she remembered.

Raimon shook his head at her. Bandit knights did not merit dreams or dreamy voices. If such men did sweep girls up behind them, it was not to crown them queen but to tether them with dirty rope until their families ransomed them back. He frowned, remembering the smoke. 'I'll have to see you home,' he said.

'See me home? But I don't want to go home yet.'

'I really think we should go. Come on.' He began to walk briskly and, sighing, she followed. Both put their hands on Brees's collar but their hands did not touch.

Right at the back of the largest cave, where a perfect screen was provided by an almost impenetrable fringe of flapping treeroots, Parsifal heard their voices fade. How he envied them their companionship. 'I just have you,' he croaked at the Flame, which prinked at him, 'and you are no conversationalist.' He gathered his things together and went to look outside. Perhaps he should move on.

He climbed up the scree. Over the horizon the smoke was still rising, but now in small gasps rather than plumes, and the strange smell had vanished. As he watched, however, the wind changed and instead of flighting upwards, the smoke bent over the gorge towards Castelneuf. He frowned and rubbed his stubbled chin. Then he went back into the cave. Inside its pouch, the Flame's wick was darkly solid at the centre of the oily pool. 'I'm now the Knight Magician of the Breeze,' Parsifal told it. 'Should I stay and defend my title?'

The question was a wistful joke, but it seemed to him that the Flame did him the honour, almost for the first time, of taking him seriously. Spreading itself over its salver, it hissed and when Parsifal bent towards it, it hissed again. 'Not much of an answer,' he remarked, but after all these years of silence, he was cheered that there had been an answer at all.

IN THE CHÂTEAU

Just over an hour later, Raimon and Yolanda crossed the river bridge and began to climb up towards the thick, castellated walls of Yolanda's home. Though its perch looked highly precarious, with the stones of its foundations hewn unevenly from the mountainside itself, the château offered at least a semblance of protection. Underneath, as if queuing for a place under its shadow, the paths and houses wound their way toward it in tiers. Raimon could have left Yolanda here quite safely but he did not, and not just because he didn't really want to leave her at all.

You see, though the appearance of the Knight Magician and the smoke might be entirely coincidental, Raimon felt a tinge of true uneasiness. It occurred to him that the Knight Magician might not be a bandit knight at all. He thought once again of that journey with his father from Limoux. What if the man and the smoke were related? What if the man was a Perfectus, one of those Cathar high priests his parents held in such high regard that they bowed from the waist when they even thought about them? Raimon had never knowingly seen a Perfectus, but he knew they often hid in the hills, waiting to be summoned to perform the last rites for those Cathars who lay dying. Occasionally, his father's weaving shed would have more men in it than usual. Raimon had never asked who the extra men were, but he had suspected. He felt a cold knot in his stomach because even the rumour of one in the district might be enough to draw in the Inquisitors. He had never met an Inquisitor either — none had ever thought me worth a visit — but everybody knew what they did. Then again, if the French king really was pushing south, maybe the man was a scout, although he certainly hadn't looked as Raimon imagined a scout to look. It was unnerving meeting someone he couldn't place. He urged Yolanda on.

She followed him without argument although they had to slow once they got further into the town. A mule train had passed along the towpath on the river and people were pouring out, then staggering in, intent on exchanging bolts of cloth and fine leatherwork for carpets and dyes, fancy baskets and spices. Many were gossiping their way home with bulging bundles, their children more overburdened than donkeys. Reluctant oxen lowered their heads under the whip and shrugged their bony shoulders. Raimon cursed, but half-heartedly. The busy, familiar scene settled him a little and it was almost comforting when the oxen took no notice of his prods. They were not fussed by anything. They would take the hill in their own time and Raimon would just have to wait.

As they were forced to halt, Yolanda spied Beatrice and sang out her name. Usually the girl would have been as burdened as an ox herself, but today she appeared to be carrying nothing but her purse, a wide beaming smile and a great deal of dignity. She kept the dignity for a while then couldn't resist. Pulling up her satin skirts to display unlovely ankles, she leapt over three new cauldrons and a sack of salt dumped in the road for later collection. 'Look what I've got!' Glowing and giggling, she opened her purse to reveal a tiny phial. Yolanda stopped.

'Perfume! Oh, Bea!' she exclaimed, 'can I smell it?'

Beatrice laughed, closed her purse and donned her dignity once more. 'Don't be silly!' she said, settling her skirts. 'That would be a complete waste. The only scent you like is dog!'

'It is not!'

But Beatrice only laughed some more. 'Dog and dung, Yolanda. That's you! Don't you agree, Raimon?' She flashed her eyes at him, hoping for an admiring look. 'Dog and dung. That's Yolanda's scent.'

Raimon gave her a look. It was not admiring. 'I like the smell of dog,' he said carefully.

'That's because you're still a boy,' retorted Beatrice, preening, but also looking from Raimon to Yolanda, back and forth, her small round eyes missing nothing. 'My bailiff has a man's nose.'

'Is that why it's so big?' Yolanda made a shape with her fingers. Beatrice flushed. The size of her future husband's nose was something she tried not to think about. Raimon grinned and pulled Yolanda on. She was happy to be pulled. Bea was never cross for long and she was a good sort, really. Soon they would spend an evening surrounded by silks and linens, wedding head-dresses and glosses for eyes, cheeks and lips. It was not an evening Yolanda would discuss afterwards with Raimon, particularly as Yolanda happened to know that

Beatrice's mother had bought the wedding shoes from Paris. The north was their enemy, but had fashions no girl could resist.

They caught up with Brees, his head almost submerged in the horse trough as he drank. On impulse, Yolanda dunked her own head beside her dog's and set to, scrubbing at her face and hands. When she stood up, sniffing at her fingers, her cheeks were pink and streaked. 'Do I really smell of dog?' she asked.

'You smell of Brees,' Raimon replied. She had a tiny chip in a front tooth he'd not seen before. It gave a very particular tenderness to her mouth.

'Is it horrible?'

His lips twitched. 'Well, that depends. There's wet Brees and dry Brees, and Brees after he's rolled on a dead fish, and Brees when he's been lying by the baking oven. Some Brees is nice, some –' he made a hideous face and took a deep breath. 'Do you know what you really smell like, Yolanda?'

'No.' Her irises were mottled pearls in the bright light.

'You smell like the sky.'

She was slow to respond this time although she never took her eyes from his. 'The sky doesn't smell.'

'It does to me.'

She gave a smile that began somewhere deep in her chest and pursed her bottom lip so that her chin wrinkled and the cleft became very pronounced. He saw the chip in her tooth again and quickly bent to pat Brees. They walked on.

The château's fortifications, which seemed mighty from below, were, in fact, more decorative than functional for the land which to its original builders had seemed quite solid had begun to slide away. As the stones worked loose and caused minor collapses, the townspeople came quietly and gathered them into barrows to shore up their own houses. Stone could not protect them against the unwanted attentions of roistering men-at-arms drunken in victory or the pitiless predations of retreating soldiers bitter in defeat, but at least if your house was of stone, when soldiers threw fireballs something would remain. Since there had been no roistering soldiers in Castelneuf for fifty years or more, the solidity of the houses and the collapse of the château ran in natural, almost organised tandem, much to the townsfolk's satisfaction.

As they neared the gate, unconsciously reverting to a habit of their early childhood, Yolanda and Raimon tailored their steps to the rhythmic clangs from the farrier's forge. It had always been their custom that if you missed a clang, you had to eat a spoonful of pig swillings from the kitchen bucket. Raimon wondered if Yolanda was remembering the time Aimery had deliberately tripped her up and then made her honour the forfeit. How he had felt for her, even as he watched her gag and retch, for Aimery would not be thwarted. Yolanda was not remembering. She had chosen to forget. Instead, she was wondering, as she paced herself, if Beatrice's perfume could possibly smell as nice as the sky.

A sleepy sentry opened the heavy gates for them and Brees bounded in causing the chickens to squawk like twittery nursemaids when an armed man appears. Yolanda ran after him, growling in her throat. Brees shut his mouth but resented it. Those chickens were enough to tempt a saint. One day he would come in here alone and teach them a lesson.

All three made their way over to the wooden steps beside the armoury, climbed up to the small plateau on which the small, bedraggled kitchen garden rambled, and then up again until they reached the outside steps leading into the great hall. These steps were now so cracked that Raimon felt justified in virtually lifting Yolanda up the final three. She could feel his arms, tight as wire, around her and when he set her down, they were close enough for his breath to warm her cheek. 'I'm sorry about laughing,' she said quietly.

'I know.'

They were easy again and Yolanda happily reached into his hair to pick out a twig. She had to use both hands, for his hair was thick as a meadow before the hay harvest. He did not object, but when he felt her fingers so deft on his scalp, he swallowed hard, and quickly pushed her inside.

They were plunged at once into powdery darkness. Below thin lancet windows too narrow to let in anything but two crescent-shaped slivers of sun, the hall had only two torches lit, and they were at the far end where the count was peering, with some despair, at a long parchment on which columns and columns of figures had been drawn. When he saw Yolanda, he opened his arms. 'Daughter!' He did not see Raimon at once, for Raimon hung back as she ran for her welcome.

The count kept Yolanda close for slightly longer than usual. Tall of stature, slightly bent about the shoulders, he walked with the deliberate gait of a man who has carried full armour, even though he had seldom carried it out of necessity. His face was craggy, as befitted his age, yet had he shaved off his curly beard, once golden but now faded to no colour at all, his character would have been evident in his chin. This was a poor, receding affair, which the cleft he had passed on so attractively to Yolanda made poorer still. His position as count had come through accident of birth rather than feat of arms, the accident having made him the oldest of three brothers when either of the other two would have done a better job. And he had been unfortunate. His first wife, Aimery and Yolanda's mother, a French woman who loved him, had died five years before. Two wives had followed in quick succession but neither had lasted. One, quickly and unmourned, followed his first wife to the grave. The next Aimery saw off after she had confined Yolanda to her room for a week, without Brees, for saving a litter of unwanted kittens from the drowning barrel. This, incidentally, was why Yolanda glossed over the pigswill. Aimery's kindnesses were arbitrary and few, but since they mainly involved his sister, she forgave him much. The count, however, was frightened of his son. What had once been a small boy's charming knack for getting his own way had turned, after their mother's death, into something rather less charming.

The count's long embrace was not lost on Raimon. It troubled him. It was the kind of embrace his mother gave him when the weaving shed held more men than usual. It was a parent's reaction to something troubling. He moved into the light. 'Ah, Raimon,' the count said, 'Aimery's on his way home.'

Raimon did not pretend to share Yolanda's pleasure. The only time Raimon felt like an intruder at the count's table was when Aimery was around. Yet he understood her excitement. It was natural for her to love a brother who reminded her of a time when their family was whole.

'And he's bringing a friend,' the count added.

There was a less neutral silence from Raimon.

'What friend?' Yolanda asked.

'A friend he's made on his travels,' said the count vaguely, but uncomfortably. 'Sir Hugh of Somewhere and he's got a new squire, Alain something. I've ordered sixteen ducks, a goose and a sheep to be slaughtered. Will that be enough for the homecoming feast, do you think? Will Aimery think so?' He plucked at his beard.

'Plenty, I should think,' Yolanda told him. 'When will they arrive?'

'Before sunset tomorrow. Do you really think that's enough? Oh! I've forgotten about fish. We must have fish. Should we have fish?'

'There'll be enough with the meat and fowl,' said Yolanda again, stroking her father's arm. She hated his nerves. They made her nervous.

'And we will dine on the dais.'

Yolanda paused in her stroking. They all knew what this meant. When Aimery was away, the count sat amongst his household, with only his special platter and being served first to distinguish him. At these times, Raimon carved the meat and sat at his ease next to or opposite Yolanda. This would now stop. If Raimon ate in the hall at all, it would be below Yolanda's feet.

Yolanda sent over a look of powerless regret, but the look returned to her was startlingly direct. Could she not see? Raimon saw at once. The reason the count was uncomfortable was perfectly clear. He already knew that Aimery's visit was not just a normal homecoming but was timed to coincide with Yolanda's birthday. After all, at nearly fourteen, she was already older than some of her married friends. This friend Aimery was bringing doubtless knew that too.

Raimon moved purposefully further into the light. If Yolanda felt about him the same way he felt about her, she must say so right now. He cursed himself for that clumsy kiss, but surely she understood? Surely he didn't have to spell it out? There was so much they never said because they didn't need to, like when they both avoided telling anybody where they were going because they just wanted to be together. She must know what he was thinking now, she *must*, and she must declare that whatever the intentions of her brother and whatever the hopes of this friend of his, her heart was already taken. This would not make things certain between them, of course, but it might make them possible. Her father would not want to see her unhappy. And her heart was taken, wasn't it? *Tell him*, Raimon urged silently. *Tell him.*

Yet though she felt his wordless pressure, Yolanda said nothing. It was not because she didn't want to be with him. It was because she couldn't help wondering, just for a second, if the love she felt for him was the deepest love she could ever feel. How could she tell since she had met so few others? Certainly, her love for Raimon was far deeper than anything Beatrice felt for her bailiff. It was deeper than the love she felt for Brees, or the brief flutter she had felt for Aimery's first squire. Yet something in her shied away from so important a declaration, standing in the unlit hall with Raimon glowering at her. She knew he wanted her to speak. She herself half wanted to speak. But once a declaration was made, she would be set down a path, probably the path she wanted, but nevertheless a path with boundaries as paths must have, and she was not quite ready for that yet.

So the moment passed. There was more conversation, but Raimon hardly heard it and when the count turned to domestic matters, asking Yolanda to scrub the dais table herself since whilst Aimery had been away the pages and grooms had been playing skittles on it using animal droppings for balls, he took his leave. Yolanda mouthed 'tomorrow' at him, but he did not reply.

He walked back to the lake alone, taking his time and kicking the stones. Why was he such a fool? How could he ever compete with a warrior in jewelled armour boasting a warhorse and a squire? This Sir Hugh of Somewhere would doubtless remain for Yolanda's party. What kind of present would he give her? A personal slave from Egypt? A milk-white pony from Arabia? He had nothing but new dance to offer. The future seemed suddenly bleak. Their time together was over. Very soon, Yolanda would forget his existence, or, worse, she would remember him with the same patronising affection that he now bestowed on the wooden dagger and shield his grandfather had whittled for him one winter when they were stuck in a snowdrift. How he had once loved that dagger and shield and sworn he would never be without it. Now it lay in a chest and he occasionally came across it, always with pleasure but without real interest. When he got to the fat end of the lake, he skimmed a flint across and when it sank his face was stony.

That night, although he was hungry, he didn't go home. He couldn't, he decided, for if he did, his mother would see at once that he was upset and he'd end up telling her why. It was not that he didn't want to, it was just that he didn't know how to. It would come out all wrong. She'd think he was ashamed of his home and he wasn't. And then she'd try and make him talk to his father. It was not that Sicart and Raimon did not get on, it was just Raimon had no interest in weaving and Sicart had no interest in much else, and as for his sister Adela, five years older than him, either she had been born ill-disposed or she had never forgiven her brother for surviving when all the girl babies had died. To her, Raimon was a chore, and worse than a chore, for they both knew that their mother loved him best. Not that Felippa ever said so. She didn't need to. It was obvious in the way she would sometimes just touch the top of Raimon's head, or catch his arm when he was humming and they would dance for a moment or two. There were no similar moments with Adela. How could there be, he asked himself with all the irritable guilt of the favourite, when she was always so quick to find fault with everything?

As he lay under the stars, however, the slight wind cooled his temper and blew in a little remorse. He should have gone home. His mother had been so poorly. But then she'd been better yesterday, in her chair, mending his cloak with her usual loving impatience at his carelessness. He would go home tomorrow and collect it. If he knew his mother at all, in the hem would be a poke of salt or a tiny horn bowl of paste for the cuts and bruises only she noticed. He rolled over, spreading out his limbs on the grass, wondering if she might have been well enough to bake.

THE FLAME

Parsifal saw Raimon return, his gait slow and disaffected, saw him angrily skim the flint and watched him settle for the night. He also saw something that Raimon, deep in his own thoughts, missed. There were new plumes of smoke, and they were not on the horizon. They had crept nearer and these did not fade away. Inside its box, the Flame curled over, hunched like a runner taking his marks. Parsifal scrutinised it closely. The Flame crinkled under his inspection, whether with amusement or worry, Parsifal simply didn't know.

He did not have a peaceful night, and just before dawn he gave up trying to sleep, left the cave and started to climb further up the hill.

He could see the smoke still hanging like a sultry flag and occasionally billowing in a random pre-dawn air current, but was glad that it seemed no nearer. As usual, he had the Flame in its pouch in a sling over his shoulders and he climbed for a further twenty minutes before he drew breath and looked over the shrouded valley with Castelneuf sleeping at its neck. Quite unexpectedly, he became conscious of a patch of heat, uncomfortably hot, on his back. He twisted round. In all the miles he had travelled, the pouch containing the Flame had never caused him any bother before and at first he wondered if he had packed it badly. He changed its position and carried on climbing, but very soon was obliged to stop and take off his bundle completely to find that not only was the sack hot, it was so scorched it seemed likely to combust at any moment. There seemed little else to do but undo it and pull out the Flame's box. Parsifal expected it to be blackened, but it was not. The delicate filigree was untouched, although not the leaves with which Parsifal disguised the Flame's colour. These were burnt to gossamer skeletons and Parsifal had to watch, with increasing alarm, as the red flames quickly turned to blue. He tried to shield the conflagration with his cloak but though tiny in size, the Flame seemed too big for that, and instead of being absorbed by the dusk, the blue began to swallow the dark itself, wholesale, until the dark became the Flame and the Flame became the dark and Parsifal could no more hide it than he could hide the sun. Helpless, he could see the blue spreading away from him like a huge ink spill, yet the colour was richer than any ink that even the best scriptorium would have in its store. It was a colour that could shimmer pale and deep at the same time. Parsifal suddenly recalled – or thought he recalled – a jewel his mother used to wear in the small hollow of her throat. His father had brought it back from a crusade and his mother had never taken it off. But it was not even that colour. It was no real colour, Parsifal thought, unless you could call it the colour of the Occitan.

He could not precisely say when the Flame sank back into

itself. One moment it was everywhere and everything, the next it was just a small tongue on a silver salver. Gingerly, he touched the box. It was cool, and when he folded up a new set of disguising leaves, they remained green and damp. But after a moment, Parsifal took the leaves out. They were not needed now. The Flame had chosen to show itself. It was not his place to hide it again.

Raimon was woken by the glare, as was the whole valley. He got up very slowly, partly because the colour seemed to thicken the air so he could hardly breathe, and partly because he was afraid that if he moved quickly, it would disappear. He was surprised to find himself unsurprised. It was as if the whole of the day before had been leading up to something odd: the smoke, the kiss, the Knight Magician. And just as a hound knows the hunting horn even if he has never heard it before, Raimon knew what the glare was.

At first it made him tremble, for as the blue curved round the hills and glanced over the water, he had never felt anything so demanding or irresistible. But Raimon did not want to call out, or even to run towards it, he wanted, and wanted urgently, to dance, and so he began, with no prelim-inaries, leaping and spinning, swooping and diving like an odd-shaped fish in an airy sea, every pore open to the blue, breathing it in and breathing it out. At his dance's height, he closed his eyes and could see Yolanda. In her arms she held a looped rope of flame which she flung out, making it arch like a bridge between them, not to burn them up but to weld them together. Then she began to dance too. Raimon's vision was so clear that when he crossed the fiery bridge and put out his hand to take Yolanda's and there was nothing there, he was caught off balance and fell over. Only then did he open his eyes. He had tripped on a tussock and the blue was vanishing, trailing its glory over the notched horizon like a comet. Then, quite suddenly, it was dark, much much darker than it had been before, as if the light of the world had gone out.

The boy stood for what seemed an eternity without moving a muscle, trying to cling to the colour, but though he could still feel it, it became harder and harder to imagine. He tried not to breathe and only when he knew, finally, that it was completely gone did he wipe his eyes and look around. The sheep were eating as if nothing had happened. Peter, though, was nowhere to be seen. Raimon looked to the horizon again. It was empty.

With the instincts of a shepherd who senses danger in the wind, Raimon went to the lake, gathered up the sheep and drove them before him to corrals by the river near the town cemeteries. Though he hurried, it took him well over an hour, and in that hour, though he imagined the whole world would have changed, he saw nothing unusual, except that those who had been sleeping were awake and through the clarity of the early morning air, he could hear shouts and exclamations where there was usually silence. The château, however, looked exactly the same; no strange knights came hurrying through; the sun was rising as usual and though he wondered if he might bump into him again, the Knight Magician of the Breeze was nowhere to be seen. When the sheep were safe, Raimon went back to the hill to see if he could discover any trace of the Flame, but found he couldn't quite remember now where it had been. Others joined him. Perhaps it had been miles away. Perhaps it had been very near. It was impossible to say.

It was noon before they gave up and returned to Castelneuf. The sheep were still corralled by the cemeteries and Peter was back with them. He'd attracted quite a crowd, telling them that the Flame had brought the sheep home and everybody was disappointed, or said they were, to find that it had, in fact, been Raimon. They exchanged nervous banter, then Raimon crossed the bridge and made his way up through the narrow ginnels towards his father's door.

Those people who had remained in the town were huddled about. In their songs and carnivals, when they often made replicas of the Flame either of turned wood or painted parchment, it was assumed that a dawn such as the one they had witnessed would be greeted with unadulterated joy. But now the initial amazement was giving way to something more edgy. Why here? Why now? What for?

Many were glad when the ordinary tasks of the day reminded them that however blue the dawn, the animals still needed tending, the rota for the mill organising and the crops weeding. It was a relief to hear the babies still crying and the old grumbling and when sceptics began to put it about that the blue had just been a trick of the light, they were not shouted down. In the privacy of their homes, husbands whispered to wives and wives to husbands that perhaps the Flame was best when in a song and not actually in the neighbourhood. If it was here, they might have to do something and I, the undemanding Amouroix, had never required them to stir themselves. Battles were fought elsewhere. Decisions were made by others. My people took their lead from the count: defied the French in song and then minded their own business and got on with living. That was how it was, how it had always been and how they wanted it to be. When old Nan Roquefort, the oldest inhabitant of Castelneuf, told them that if the Flame had come, it had now gone, they were quite happy to believe her.

THE WHITE WOLF

Adela was outside carrying water when Raimon reached his door. She dropped her buckets and seized his arm. 'Raimon! Stop! We didn't expect you.'

He shook her off. His mood had changed many times since the dawn and although he was not sure what it was any more, he knew he was not in the mood for her. He just wanted to see his mother. 'You don't have to expect me,' he said, pushing at the door. It was barred against him, so he banged on it loudly. There was a brisk scraping of chairs and a murmuring before Sicart's face appeared through a crack. 'Raimon.' He spoke his son's name without warmth. 'Has somebody sent you?'

'Of course not.' Raimon bent his head and barged.

Like the château hall, the kitchen was dark, but as far as Raimon could see, it looked quite normal. Neatly stacked cooking pots reflected the flames from the hearth and two large hams were hanging, as usual, from the rafters over the table. One thing, however, was quite different. His mother's chair, which always sat next to the hearth, had been exchanged for a truckle bed and there was no telltale smell of early baking. His mother had not been up.

He approached the cot and stretched up for the lamp on the shelf. His mother murmured and tried to shade her eyes as though the lantern, though barely glowing, was too bright. Raimon shaded it with his hand but could still see that her skin was dewy with sweat and the colour of an unwashed fleece.

He turned to find his father and Adela standing taut, as if he were the doctor who would pronounce the final verdict. 'She's much worse,' he said.

Sicart had his back against the door to the street. 'If you've come for a clean shirt, Raimon, take one and go,' he said. His cheeks were sunken and unshaven.

Raimon stared at him. 'Didn't you see the Flame?'

'Get him a shirt, Adela,' Sicart said abruptly, 'and cut the boy some ham. Then go, Raimon.'

'You must have seen the Flame!'

'Do you think we've been outside? Do you think we've been thinking about anything?' Adela, standing on a stool, dropped one of the hams onto the table with a thump. It rolled a little, then came to a halt. She got down and without another word began to unwrap it.

Raimon went to the bed. His mother's eyes were closed and now he dropped to his knees beside her. 'Mother, it's me!'

Her eyes fluttered. 'Raimon!'

'Ssssh! Don't talk. Did you see the Flame? Did they lift you up to see it? Just squeeze my hand.' A tiny squeeze. He bent close and began to whisper.

Adela interrupted. 'She doesn't want to hear your whispering now.' He ignored her until it became distressingly clear that Adela was actually right. His mother was not really listening. He thought she was tired and though disappointed because he had so much to say, he stood up again. But his mother seemed less tired than expectant. Her eyes rolled beyond him as if she was searching for something. 'What is it?' he asked her and then asked his father and sister, 'what is it?'

Neither of them moved. He was suddenly filled with suspicion. 'What's the great secret here? You're hiding something.' His father's eyes flickered towards the weaving shed. 'Or somebody.' Raimon bolted across the fireplace, towards the corner where the door to the shed was tightly shut. He thought at once of the Knight Magician. He had been right. The man was no magician, he had come for a more sinister purpose.

Sicart was there before him and would not let him pass. 'Please leave, Raimon.'

'I won't.'

Adela threw a parcel of ham in his direction. 'Do as Father says.'

Raimon let the parcel fall to the ground. 'I came to see Mother,' he said.

'You've seen her. Now go.'

Raimon was filled with angry panic. 'How dare you order me out? I'm just as much a member of this family as you are.'

'Are you?' Adela picked up the parcel and threw it back onto the table. 'I doubt that.'

'What on earth do you mean?'

'Can't you understand, Raimon? You're not one of us.'

He turned back to his father. 'One of us? One of *us*, Father?'

'What Adela means is that you don't believe what we believe.'

'I believe in the Flame. Didn't you see it? I can't believe you didn't.'

'Of course we did. That's why you've got to go.' His father's lips had a white dryness about them, but he came over to his son. 'Can't you see how things are changing? Don't you understand, Raimon? Do I really have to say it?' Raimon looked completely baffled.

'Tell him, Father.' Adela's voice was imperious.

'Be quiet, Adela. Look, I wish you hadn't come back, but as you're here, I must tell you that though you'll always be my son, you aren't really one of us any more.' He took a deep breath. 'Now is the time of the Cathars, Raimon, and you don't believe.'

Raimon almost laughed. 'You think the Flame has come just for Cathars? How could you? It hasn't come for you or for the Catholics or even for Castelneuf or for Amouroix. It's come for the whole of the Occitan, for all of us. We can't divide off into little groups. If King Louis really is coming, if that's what the Flame means, we've all got to fight together.'

Adela opened her mouth, but the voice that emerged was not hers. 'Oh, if only it were so simple,' it pronounced mildly.

From behind Sicart the shed door opened and a man appeared. He was not the Knight Magician. He was much taller with eyes the colour of slate under eyebrows that met in the middle. A pelt of prematurely pure white hair spread from his forehead to the nape of his neck and was finely complemented by a similarly white beard, carefully cut, soft as a swan's breast. Only his skin betrayed his age and his constant exposure to the weather. It was tinted and leathery, like the seat of a well-used saddle. Fit rather than thin, his lips, underneath the smooth hair, curled naturally into the kind of smile that invites you to smile back and he was dressed just like Raimon's father, in a buff-coloured tunic and leggings, a thick belt full of weavers' tools round his waist and sturdy shoes on his feet. In his hands he held a piece of cloth that he had apparently been checking for faults and his demeanour was that of a friendly uncle, slightly past middle age but who might still outpace you over a mountain pass. Sicart and Adela bowed deeply from the waist. Raimon remained upright.

The man acknowledged Sicart and Adela, then turned his attention to Raimon. 'Shall I introduce myself?' he asked easily. 'We should not be strangers, you and I. My name is Perfectus Prades Rives but I'm always known as the White Wolf.' He laughed, as if this nickname was the cosiest in the world.

Raimon's father gave a small growl although his tone was respectful. 'I thought we agreed that you would stay in the back when we had visitors.'

The White Wolf inclined his head. 'So we did, Sicart, but your son is hardly a visitor.' He turned back to Raimon. 'I've come to this house not because of the Flame, although it would seem that my arrival is more than timely, but because your mother wants to receive from my hands the blessed consolation that a Perfectus can offer. We must make her ready to take her place at God's side in heaven.'

'She's not dying.'

There was silence.

'As I say, Raimon, I've come at her request to give her the blessed consolation –'

'She's not dying, I tell you. Where's the apothecary? What does he say?' Raimon addressed his father.

The White Wolf noted everything. 'You're angry that your mother is leaving you, Raimon,' he said with careful sympathy, 'but that is selfish and wrong. Soon she'll be a spirit, far away from the material world that is nothing but filth and evil. Do you begrudge her that?' His words fell like petals. They always did, for that was his great gift, to make everything he said seem like a garden of flowers. It was hard to argue with flowers.

'She wants to get better,' Raimon said with some desperation. 'She doesn't want to leave us.' The White Wolf simply smiled. Raimon turned to his father. 'Don't you want her better, Father? Would you prefer just to let her die?'

It was the White Wolf who answered. 'I repeat, I am here at the request of your mother, Raimon, and I never refuse a request. You should be glad, for a Perfectus does his job without calculating the quality of his consolation on the amount of money slipped into his palm. I would have thought you would appreciate that, for you have a look of honour about you.' Raimon was suspicious of the compliment, but Adela seemed to appreciate the pointed reference to Simon Crampcross, who would barely lift his hands to grant the Catholic dying the Last Rites without the flash of a silver sou.

Raimon went back to his mother's bed. She was calmer now that she could hear the White Wolf's voice. It was very hard for him to watch the man take both her hands and

Felippa begin to whisper to him although she'd said not a word before. The Perfectus beckoned to them all. 'I think we are ready. Come. Stand beside the bed. Felippa would like you all here.'

Raimon moved back.

The White Wolf was calm as calm. 'Have you seen a Cathar consolation before, Raimon?' he asked. Silence. 'Then I'll explain. It's very simple. I shall ask if Felippa has ever done anything to harm our church, then spread out my cloth and place a copy of the Gospels on her head. If you want your mother to pass over without pain, you should place your hands on her head, along with the rest of us. If you don't, then stay back. It's entirely up to you.' He now turned and smiled his silken smile, then concentrated entirely on Felippa. When she had answered his list of questions satisfactorily, he placed a black cloth beside her, rested a small copy of the Gospels over her eyes and gestured. Adela and Sicart placed their hands on the book without hesitation. Raimon never moved.

The White Wolf turned with an inviting smile. 'Can you really not join us?'

'No.'

The White Wolf shrugged, but did not press him.

A prayer was said, then the Gospels were removed. The consolation was over. Felippa murmured something and the White Wolf shook his head. With an enormous effort, the fading woman pulled herself up. Sicart and Adela held her for though she was frail enough to break, she was determined. 'Come, come,' Sicart gestured to Raimon. 'Can't you see your mother's trying to speak to you? Come nearer!'

Raimon wanted more than anything to hear his mother's voice but now he dreaded what she might say. Nevertheless, he edged forward. How could he not? 'Raimon, dearest Raimon!' she whispered to him, the muscles round her lips straining to form the words. 'Just put your hands on my head with the Perfectus then I can die happy. Please, Raimon. It's such a small thing.'

Adela was breaking down. She loved her mother too. 'For goodness sake, Raimon. It's our mother's dying request. How can you be so cruel?'

'Your brother doesn't mean to be cruel.' The White Wolf was the steady voice of reason. 'He just cannot see what we see.'

Adela turned on him. 'Won't see, more likely.'

Felippa groaned, and in her desperation Adela seized her brother's hand and tried to force it onto the Gospel book still lying on the bed. 'It's that girl, isn't it?' she hissed as they tussled. 'That girl of yours has turned you into a Catholic. Count Berengar's daughter means more to you than your own mother.'

Raimon hated Adela's grasping fingers. 'This is nothing to do with Yolanda.'

'Isn't it?' She was almost beating Raimon.

'Adela, stop it.' Sicart tried to intervene. 'Show some respect.'

'Don't accuse me of disrespect, Father. I know just where respect is due. It's Raimon who needs a lesson.' Raimon shielded his head from her blows.

'Gently, gently, Adela,' the White Wolf broke in quickly.

'Don't defend him, Perfectus.' Adela could see tears falling from her mother's eyelids. 'Do you want her to die crying, Raimon? Do you?'

'Of course not, but you know I don't believe, Adela.' Everything was happening too fast. His mother couldn't be dying. Only yesterday he'd been a silver dagger in the stream and Yolanda had been planning her party.

'Oh, you and your beliefs. Just remind me what they are.'

Now Raimon was silent. To say that he only really believed in the Flame, the smell of the Occitanian soil and the way its music soaked into his skin didn't seem enough.

In the silence, Sicart saw his chance. He was sponging his wife's face and could see her lips move. He wished he were better with words, but he must try, for her sake. 'Look, my son, you must grow up a little. You know that King Louis is on the move, that the Amouroix can't stand apart any longer, and you must also know that for all your talk of Occitanians fighting against him together, in the days to come you'll have to be either a Catholic or a Cathar. There's no room for anything else.'

'But we're one people! The Occitan may have many parts, but it's just one place.'

'Oh, come on, Raimon! You know perfectly well that the way Catholics and Cathars in Amouroix live happily together is false. Under all their apparent friendliness, the Catholics are always waiting for a chance to burn us and if they get the Flame, that's just what they'll do. Do you think, for all his "good mornings", Simon Crampcross would hesitate to light the Castelneuf pyres himself? But they haven't got the Flame yet. This is our chance, don't you see? The Flame's come for us and once we've got it, we can rid the Occitan of King Louis and the Catholics all in one.'

'But Catholics are Occitanians too!'

'No, they're not, not really,' Adela insisted. She could feel her mother's pain. How could Raimon argue like this!

'They are! Count Berengar has never handed over Cathars to the Inquisitors. We've never even had an Inquisitor here.'

'Look,' Sicart said, 'why do you think the Flame has returned? It must be for us.'

'Why on earth should that be so?'

'The Perfectus has told us.'

Raimon turned on the White Wolf. 'You said you came for my mother.'

'And so I did, but I think it not a coincidence that the Flame came at the same time.' Adela began to berate Raimon again, and the White Wolf put up his hand. 'Adela, Adela, quietly please. Let's not get so excited. It's right that your brother says what he feels. There are too many who don't. I admire him.' Adela shook her head. 'Go back to your mother.' Adela, breathing heavily, obeyed.

The White Wolf sat on the chest where oats were stored. A half-eaten garlic pie was warming and he picked at it, for all the world as though it was his right. After he had eaten, he wiped his fingers delicately on the fine linen cloth that he kept tucked at his waist and only when he was satisfied that he was entirely clean did he speak again. 'You must make up your own mind about what you believe, Raimon, but you might like to remember this: that whilst all Cathars are good Occitanians, the same cannot be said of all Catholics. They have other allegiances: to the Pope and even,' he paused, 'to King Louis himself. So your father is right. In the troubles to come, there can be no middle ground. You will be either a Cathar or a Catholic, a full Occitanian or something rather less. Everybody will have to choose.' He went back to Felippa and took her hand. 'Which you choose is, naturally, entirely up to you.'

Raimon badly wanted to argue, but all he could see was his mother's hand held by a stranger when it should have been held by him. He ran to her. He couldn't stop himself.

She whispered to him, harsh whispers, for she had so little strength. 'Please, Raimon, I'm so afraid. If you love me – just lay your hands – please, Raimon, it would comfort – please.' She lay back exhausted.

Her agony was dreadful to him. He could see, in the spasms in her cheeks, the guilt she felt. His unbelief was her fault and God would hold her accountable. She should have tried harder. She was too tired to cry now but she seemed to be dissolving, swimming in grief.

And suddenly Raimon couldn't bear it. Why was he making such a fuss? What did it matter what he really believed? The thought that his mother might die with that look in her eyes would torture him always. And for what purpose? The White Wolf was no money-grubbing cleric. If, by putting his hand on her forehead and muttering a few words, Raimon could give comfort to the mother who had so often given comfort to him, should he deny her?

He watched Adela, tight-lipped, wash Felippa's face and Sicart stroke her hair. Only he was barred from this charmed circle. It was intolerable. 'I'll do it,' he said before he could have second thoughts. He spoke in such a low voice, he half hoped nobody would hear, but the White Wolf heard.

'You are a good son,' he said, quick as a flash, and his smile was full of understanding. 'You will be rewarded in heaven. It will not harm to do the consolation again.' Without waiting even for a second he placed the Gospel book back onto Felippa's head, and Raimon's hand too. When his mother felt it, she opened her eyes and this time, when she saw her son with his arm outstretched over her, murmuring the words of consolation after the Perfectus, the grief was washed away and her face filled with the beauty of joy completed. For that instant, Raimon was certain he had done the right thing. What did anything matter now, except that his mother knew he loved her and that she loved him again in return? As the White Wolf moved back so that Raimon could take his rightful place, a new kind of peace, descended over the whole household. There was no more talking. They just waited. The end could not be long.

Two hours passed and Felippa's breathing, far from growing more laboured, became easier. Her skin felt less waxy and the pulse in her neck beat more strongly. She still slept, but no longer the struggling sleep of the dying, and in a gesture so dearly familiar to all her family, she slowly put up her hand to push stray hairs from her face. It was as if she had opened a curtain. Quite suddenly, the ordinary sounds of the day intruded. Sicart, Raimon and Adela murmured. Only the White Wolf still sat in silence.

At last Adela got up, rattled the fire and began to prepare some soup, dropping an egg into it to give her mother strength. At the sight of smoke from the chimney, there was the occasional bang on the door as neighbours called, still exclaiming about the blue dawn but then to ask how things were.

Sicart sent them away. His relief gave way, once again, to tension. 'You should go back into the workshop,' he said to the Perfectus. 'People will talk if we don't let them in.'

Unhurried and unperturbed, the White Wolf took out his bit of working cloth. 'I am just a visiting weaver,' he said.

Sicart shook his head. 'That won't be disguise enough now. We've Catholic neighbours and, well –' he carefully didn't look at Raimon.

'Yes. I understand.' The White Wolf got up. 'What are you doing?' This was addressed to Adela, who had brought her mother a bowl.

She showed him the soup. He smoothly took it away from her and threw it in the fire. Adela gave a small cry as the logs spat.

'There should be no food after the consolation,' the Perfectus said. 'That is forbidden.'

'What do you mean?' demanded Sicart. 'Surely my wife can have a little soup? Perhaps no meat, just as you eat no meat. But soup?'

'There should be nothing.'

'Nothing?' Sicart could not take this in.

'Nothing.'

'Just for today?'

'No, nothing ever again.'

'You mean,' said Raimon slowly, hardly able to believe his ears, 'that she should starve?'

The question hung in the air only for a second before the White Wolf, smiling as always, dealt with it. 'No, no, not at all. It's not starving. It's like fasting, ready for the eternal feast. Your mother is in a very particular state of grace now. Only her soul is important, not her body.' He was standing over

Felippa and she was looking up at him, absolutely trusting. 'Yes, the eternal feast,' she whispered.

'But then she'll surely die.' Sicart still thought he had misunderstood.

'We'll all die one day,' said the White Wolf pleasantly, 'and we have become lax. The fast has fallen into disuse. But this is how it should be. Once you have received the consolation of a Perfectus such as myself, you divorce yourself from all the devil's works.'

'Food doesn't come from the devil,' Raimon said, breathing quickly, 'it comes from the earth.' For once, Adela did not contradict him.

'And everything on earth comes from the devil,' said the White Wolf, still so pleasant. 'That's what we Cathars believe because it's the truth.'

'But you eat,' Raimon did not care that his mother winced at the harshness in his voice.

'So that I can carry out my ministry,' the White Wolf replied. 'When I become too old to walk, preach and console, I shall eat nothing more. Then, like your mother, I'll wait for the eternal feast. I know it's not easy, this last bit, particularly when so much of life for a Cathar before consolation is quite ordinary. But this is our last preparation. Come, Adela, pray with me now, at the time of your mother's final struggle.' And he smiled still more reassuringly, his slate grey eyes looking full into hers.

However, Adela was still too horrified to go to him, and Raimon seized the opportunity. 'Don't pray with him! Please Adela, don't. Just think of our mother. If you love her, don't pray with him.'

'If you love her, you must pray with me.' The White Wolf never raised his voice. 'If you don't, your mother may never see salvation. She will be reborn, perhaps as an animal, and condemned to live out another life of servitude and corruption. Do you wish that?' How was it possible to say such things? Raimon could not imagine. But the White Wolf never let his eyes leave Adela's until her whole face was trembling and, seemingly against her will, but with awful obedience, she began to sink to her knees, the practised authority of the Perfectus bearing down on her like an iron cloak.

At once, the White Wolf knelt beside her, leaving not a parchment's space between them. If her voice faltered, his did not. Felippa closed her eyes.

'Get up! Get up at once! Father, make her!' Raimon tried to pull Adela to her feet, but she was a dead weight. He began to shout. Starving people was what despots and torturers did, he yelled. God could not possibly want good people who were dying in good faith to suffer in such a stupid way. He stopped shouting and tried to reason, to inject some sense into this senseless scene. Then he was shouting again and at last, Adela cracked, but only to stop her ears and beg him to be silent. 'We must do what the White Wolf says,' she cried. 'It can't be wrong if he says it's right. And look! Look! Even our mother agrees!' It was true. Felippa was nodding and when she looked at Raimon, her look was once again full of reproach.

Raimon ran to his father. He was not kneeling, which gave Raimon hope. 'You can't agree, Father. Stop all this. Stop it now.' But the White Wolf began to speak again, utterly persuasive and utterly implacable. Sicart began to sweat. The Perfectus was so sure. Who was he to contradict him?

The White Wolf did not ignore Raimon. That was not his way. 'Of course you are upset,' he said, 'and how can I blame you? But if you don't live as you believe God wants you to, what's the use of living at all?'

'But how can God want this?' Raimon cried.

'God wants what he wants,' said the White Wolf enigmatically, 'and only the foolish or the wicked don't understand that.'

Raimon made for the door. He wanted to slam it shut as if the slamming itself might crush the White Wolf, but something stopped him. Long afterwards, it was of some comfort to know that a slam was not the last sound his mother associated with him. Once he had clicked the latch, however, he ground his heels into the dirt as if crushing the Perfectus beneath them. He thought he heard Adela's voice crying after him, but once he had started down the road he never looked back. For miles he heard himself murmuring the words of the consolation. They taunted him. He wanted to take them back. But then he saw his mother's face, and for hours, all he could hear, as if it were real and beside him, was the drip drip drip of her life needlessly ebbing away.

SIR HUGH DES ARCIS

The following evening, two knights, conscious of the spectacle they made, clattered noisily through the town, eyeing up the girls who walked arm in arm in twos and threes. In the pearly light, even the ugly looked beautiful, particularly as many had rolled up their sleeves and loosed their hair as they whispered about the Flame and other, more personal affairs, in the lingering warmth. Thank God for spring, which made it possible to escape from the stifling mugginess of their parents' hearths where no gossip could ever be private. When they saw the knights, the girls giggled and clung closer together.

The knight riding on the right forged ahead and despite his hurry, bent down, paying fulsome compliments as he passed. He never liked to miss an opportunity. Then he returned to his companion. Though yesterday's blue dawn had dominated their conversation since reported by a breathless messenger, Aimery of Amouroix had another concern. Sent to assure Count Raymond of Toulouse, leader of the Occitan rebels, of his father's support against King Louis, he had also conducted some business of his own and part of this business involved his fellow traveller. 'I hope the homecoming feast will be to your liking,' he said. 'My father is not known for the excellence of his table and I wouldn't like you to think us inhospitable.' Sir Hugh des Arcis offered no reassurance. He just gave half a smile, which Aimery couldn't read at all. Aimery jabbed his spurs into his horse's sides and made it gallop up the final steepness to the château gate. 'Open up, this is Aimery of Amouroix,' he shouted rather unnecessarily. The porter, roused from sleep, gave a nervous squeak.

The first thing Aimery noticed as the gate swung back was that during his absence the château had become even more ramshackle. It could, of course, have been that absence sharpened his perceptions, but whatever it was, he now looked with open distaste at the mice foraging amid a sea of speedwell and storksbill and twisted weeds clambering unimpeded up the curtain wall. He kept talking, hoping to distract attention from the door to the armoury swinging crazily on one hinge, the pungent trickle round the bottom of the tower, the blackened scar from a kitchen conflagration and the small tree that seemed to be growing from the stable roof.

The count was waiting in the main courtyard, at the bottom of the steps to the great hall, with an urchin from the town hopping from foot to foot beside him. There would be a reward for being the first to tell the count that his son was almost home and as Aimery dismounted, he watched his father drop a coin into the boy's open hand, a coin so much more valuable than could ever have been expected that the urchin, biting it hard to test he was not being duped by base metal, scurried off without even saying thank you in case the count should realise his mistake and ask for it back.

Berengar, however, had eyes only for his son. 'Aimery!' he exclaimed, full of welcome, but no sooner had he embraced him than he began to scold. 'For goodness sake, child. Why aren't you armed? Have you no sense at all? Two knights riding back from Toulouse at a time like this and neither of you even wearing a hauberk? What were you thinking? Was it for nothing that I told you of the miserable death of King Richard the Lionheart, cut down in his prime through being careless with his armour? How many times must I remind you? If you had been kidnapped and held to ransom like your Uncle Peter –'

'Yes, yes, yes, it would ruin us, and we have Yola to marry off yet.' Though he flushed slightly, Aimery nevertheless finished his father's speech for him, as he had done so often in the past. Uncle Peter, now dead, and whom neither Aimery nor Yolanda had ever met, had become a figure of fun to them, so frequently did their father use him as a model either of good behaviour or bad, according to the needs of the moment. 'But nothing did happen to us, Father. Here we are. This is Sir Hugh des Arcis. He has been very kind to me.'

Hugh dismounted and bowed to the count. Before the count had a chance to nod in return, he was giving directions about his warhorse. Only then did he turn back. Nearly a decade older than Aimery, his face had that lived-in, battle-worn aura that women tried to copy onto heroic tapestries. His individual features, though not distinguished in themselves, fell together in that fortunate way features sometimes do, which implies, without any real reason or evidence, that the man who bears them is a man of great character. 'I am at your service, sir,' he said, with another of his half-smiles.

Berengar, already rendered nervous by Aimery's slightly dismissive tone, gave the worst possible impression. 'Oh no, I'm at *your* service, as is Castelneuf. Now, I should say what fine horses you have. Yes, fine horses indeed. I hope you and they will be comfortable although, well —' he waved a vague hand, saw Hugh's smile again, then took a deep breath. That was enough. He changed the subject. 'Now, Aimery, tell me at once. Was Raymond happy with the letter I sent?' Berengar had taken such pains over it, making it supportive but not too supportive in case King Louis should ever get to read it. Berengar hated trouble and most of his life had been designed to avoid it.

'Oh, I think so, Father.' Aimery could be vague too, when it suited him.

'Did you watch him read it?'

'I was there when he read it.' Aimery's soft blond beard, newly grown whilst he had been away, hid a smirk his father would not have liked. 'He sent you a message, though. He said it was good to know he had nobles on whom he could rely absolutely.'

The count's wrinkles bit a little deeper. The message seemed bland enough, but he knew that tone. Raymond had seen straight through him. 'Oh dear,' the count said.

'Who cares about the letter now,' Aimery said impatiently. 'Are people saying that the Flame really has come back?'

'People seem to want to believe it.'

'And do you believe it?'

Berengar sucked in his cheeks. 'I'm rather hoping not.'

Aimery stared at his father, somewhat despairing. How typical, he thought. Castelneuf could have been a stronghold and a fortress, sending men out to increase the family fortunes. By now I, the Amouroix, could have been rich, and Berengar, not Raymond of Toulouse, the most powerful leader in the Occitan. Instead, Castelneuf was a crumbling apology of a place where men danced instead of fought, sang of their ambitions instead of marching out to fulfil them, and I was a small county of which few people had ever heard, let alone taken any notice. Except that they would now. Whatever happened to Raymond and the Occitanian rebellion, whatever happened to his father, Aimery was not going to end up on the losing side. He would make sure of that. He felt a shiver of excitement at the thought of the Flame. What a piece of luck that it had appeared now. He would find it, and he knew just what to do with it. He glanced over at Hugh, noting the solid, expensive Parisian armour even now being unpacked from the baggage wagon and the glint of gold on each finger. What a catch! Yes, Aimery thought, under his guidance, Castelneuf had a shining future ahead.

They could hear singing.

In Occitan there hovers still
The grace of Arthur's table round.
Bright southern knights will yet fulfil
The quest to which they all are bound.
No foreign pennants —

A small tornado whipped out of the air from above. 'Aimery! Did you see the Flame?' Yolanda's pleasure was quite uninhibited. She threw herself off the top step, straight into his arms, trusting that he would catch her just as he always had. He did, but his pleasure was rather less than hers. 'Yola! Honestly! You're getting a bit big for this. Where's your dignity? And don't you know you could have killed yourself!'

'But I didn't,' she responded gaily, and, at the echo of their father's favourite exclamation and their favourite reply, Aimery gave a genuine laugh. He had not yet completely shaken off his boyhood.

'Now,' he said, setting her down, 'before anything else I want you to meet Sir Hugh des Arcis. We've become great friends. He tells stories as well as a troubadour. Gui and Guerau will have competition.'

Yolanda went directly over to Hugh, who bent his head in a low bow. 'Oh!' she exclaimed, and curtsied back. Aimery's friends usually ignored her. 'You're very welcome, sir.'

'It is entirely my privilege to be here.'

She attempted to smooth her rumpled skirt. 'Aimery says you are a fine storyteller. That will be a great pleasure.'

'It will be in your listening that my pleasure lies.'

She wondered if he was making a fool of her, with this over-elegant formality, but he seemed quite serious.

He went on, without hesitation. 'That was a fine song you were singing when we arrived. Would you like to sing a little –'

'No, she wouldn't,' said Aimery hastily.

Hugh gave another half-smile. 'Aimery here tells me you like the Knights of the Round Table. Which one do you like best?'

'Parsifal,' Yolanda said, at once. 'He has a heart on his shield which I think is the nicest device.'

'Hearts are always nice if they're in the right place,' Hugh replied, fixing her with a look. It was a line and a look he'd used many times before. He had never known it fail and it did not fail now. He recognised the signs – the slight flutter of the eyelids, the tightening at the corner of the lips, the unconscious straightening of the shoulders. Women were very predictable. Yet this one did seem to have something different about her. For a start, though Aimery had described his sister as a scruffy bird in need of a good grooming, Hugh's first impressions were more of a dryad: that hair, tumbling about like leaves in a gale! What would it look like, he wondered, if it were clean? Those almond eyes! What man would not seek his reflection in them? And though she was certainly a trifle rough about the edges, it would not have been wrong for Aimery to claim that his sister had the potential to be quite a beauty. True, her face was a little thin and her features sharp, but that only made her more mysterious, like a mural picked out in chalk before it is painted in, and as for her mouth, Aimery had said nothing about that, but it reminded Hugh of a summer rose. Like Raimon, he too noticed the tiny chip in the front tooth. How odd that that should add to her allure! But it did, and had Hugh been a dog and Yolanda a joint of meat, he would have licked his lips. He leant towards her and suddenly, it *was* dog he was smelling. Brees pushed in and his eyes were hostile. Hugh stepped back. It would be humiliating to be bitten. He eyed the dog but that smile still remained. 'I do know stories of Arthur and Merlin. I learnt them when I was a page.'

'Can we hear them tonight? You see, the Flame –'

'Daughter, daughter!' Berengar remonstrated. 'The poor man must be hungry and thirsty, we've a lot to discuss and you are already on about stories.' He patted the visitor's shoulder, glad that at least the man wasn't taller than him. 'My daughter is a little impatient,' he explained, 'and a little over-excited. Now, come, everybody. Eat! Drink! I hope it will be satisfactory.' He ushered them all inside, already knowing that he should have sent for the fish.

'I'm sure I can eat anything,' Hugh said, winking at Aimery and Alain as he threw his sword at his own squire for safe keeping.

Yolanda caught the wink and her smile grew uncertain. He could not, surely, be making fun of them? But then he tucked her arm under his and told her how he had looked up at the château from the valley and thought such a fairytale place must contain a beautiful sorceress, and that he had been right. She was charmed once more and proudly led him into the hall.

And she had reason to be proud. Usually, for lack of anybody bothering, the hall was dark, but now, under her guidance, for she had been hard at work since Raimon had left her, banks of thick candles revealed the château's glory: a curved vaulting roof resplendent with painted heroes slaying monstrous mythical beasts, their swords not steel grey but fabulous, impossible colours, and each sword reflecting the face of a maiden gazing over dewy mountains towards turreted castles beyond. Below flapped heavy tapestries on which hunting scenes had been painstakingly worked by generations of Castelneuf women, singing, dreaming and gossiping in the lamplight. Usually, Yolanda scarcely noticed them and her preparation of the hall for a visitor would have been perfunctory, but since yesterday's dawn, she had suddenly become aware of the details of her home, as if, like the Flame, it, too, might vanish. It was not just for Hugh's benefit that she had counted trenchers with care and sent to Simon Crampcross to borrow silver bowls to make the table look smart, just as it was not entirely for Hugh that she now picked up a candle to highlight some of the finer embroidery. She needed to see it too. It was, however, with some embarrassment that she noticed some of the hunters sporting a jaundiced look, for the colours were faded brownish yellow from the wood smoke, and at the bottom, amongst the embroidered ladies' skirts, generations of dogs had marked out their territory, often and repeatedly. There was a distinct smell of rot.

There was also quarrelling. As usual, Gui the Singer of Cavaillon and Guerau the Catalan were facing each other as if in the tournament lists, Gui brandishing his viol and Guerau waving his bladder pipe. They had been arguing all day about the exact meaning of the Blue Flame, and now, strutting like a pair of irritable peacocks, they were arguing about something else near to their hearts. 'I'm telling you, Guerau,' Gui, thin as a bowstring although not quite as bent, was insisting, 'when a girl is fourteen, she wants a song of some sophistication, not a ditty whose chorus, so far as I can tell, exhorts her to roll amongst the flowers like a pig in a barley field.' He flourished a final chord.

Guerau listened impolitely, then squeezed his pipe until it collapsed with the whining splurge that always made Yolanda and Raimon snort. 'Sophistication might suit other girls –' Guerau always spoke at full volume – 'but I write for Yolanda herself, just as she naturally is. She'd much rather roll around in the barley than sit like a nun on a misericord, as you would have her. But, my skinny friend, you've never had my talent for capturing character in a song. Perhaps it's just your age. We must make allowances.'

Gui bristled. He was five years older than Guerau and loathed to be reminded. 'Like all Catalans, you're quite deluded. Nobody wants to listen to a lot of random notes pouring out higgledy-piggledy in no particular order. There's no difference, so far as I can tell, between your songs and the mewlings of the cook's cat and what's more, you know nothing about women. What girl in her right mind wants to be seen as she naturally is? Girls want songs that show them as goddesses.'

This was not a new quarrel. Its beginnings were obscure and its end would never come. The two men had been quarrelling since their first meeting, many years before, at the court of the Count of Barcelona, and had continued to quarrel as they travelled together over the Pyrenees into the Occitan until quarrelling was what they did most comfortably, particularly at times of stress. Since the blue dawn, their quarrelling had been deafening, for each was anxious lest the other create the best new song about it first.

The count wagged his head in mock despair. 'Those two,' he said. 'Sometimes I think I should send one packing. The noise is intolerable. And that's just their arguing.'

'No change there, then,' Aimery murmured to Yolanda. Yolanda felt a little disloyal, but she laughed. Gui and Guerau could make her cry with their lays and odes, but they were also funny and Raimon did a marvellous imitation of Guerau in a huff. She heard Hugh laugh too, but also saw him nod to the musicians, acknowledging their place in the household. That pleased Yolanda. Hugh was nice, she decided, and Aimery himself seemed different from when he had last been home. Not his face which, even with his new beard, was a bit like one of cook's puddings, flat and slightly grainy, but he had a new sparkle to him. Perhaps it was because he was wearing a silk surcoat with double-coloured sleeves such as Yolanda had never seen before. Perhaps — and her chin dimpled — he had found himself a lady-love. She wondered if she might ask Hugh.

The table on the dais was sparkling clean, and sweet-smelling rushes had been strewn rather patchily under the trestles. Berengar sighed when Aimery said nothing about this, and only asked why, as the servants clattered platters of venison and mutton and boys ran in with chickens and ducks skewered from the spit, there was no fish. *I said we'd have enough with the meat,* Yolanda thought. Aimery was going to scold until he found Hugh congratulating her on being such a practical housekeeper and then he raised his tankard in her direction.

The evening went with a swing. It was much later when Aimery, who had not stinted on the wine, pointed to the moth-eaten bear's head hung over the double doors. Though it was long past its best, it was his father's proudest trophy. He leant over. 'Time for fresh blood,' he announced with pointed ambiguity. 'Don't you agree?'

Nobody really wanted to answer, and Hugh, noting Yolanda's unhappy gasp at her brother's unkindness, chose that moment to throw bones to the dogs. They all leapt up and in the fullblown war that followed, Aimery's remark was left hanging.

Yolanda, more glad than she could say of the interruption, launched into the fray with nothing more than a bucket of water. With trestles tipping and the servants shrieking, it was some time before order was restored, but finally, when most of the dogs had been hauled out, she called for Brees. He came reluctantly, a haunch of mutton still clamped between his jaws, and it was only with trembling unwillingness that he sat at her command and gave his treasure up. She took it, then returned it to him, reproaching him for his greed, and when she eventually sat down again, she found Hugh's eyes appraising her. When he raised his goblet, commending her for her bravery, she shrugged as if what she had done was little. But even though she told herself she cared nothing for what he thought, she couldn't stop her heart thumping giddily and her eyes shining brighter than the candles.

Aimery passed and bent down. 'You're flirting, Yola,' he whispered, 'and it suits you.'

'You must not be horrible to Father.' He made an apologetic face and she pretended to hit him. All of a sudden, she felt sharp and brilliant. It was the same feeling that once, when she was walking along a thin, high wall, had made her suddenly skip.

Aimery, back at his seat, delivered his news without any preliminaries, as if it were an observation about the weather.

'Girald is coming,' he said.

The count paled and dropped a duckbreast. 'Are you sure?'

'Brothers do visit each other,' said Aimery softly.

'But he's always so busy preaching.'

'He heard of the blue dawn and sent a messenger to me on the road.'

'Oh dear. Will he be staying long?' Berengar tried not to sound too anxious.

'I hope not,' whispered Yolanda to Hugh. 'My Uncle Girald is like an icy wind –' she drew an imaginary shawl round her, '– and my other uncle, Bernard, is like a great damp fog. Whenever either visits, everything is spoilt.' Hugh said nothing at first and Yolanda bit her lip. Perhaps that was what a child would have said. But then he was whispering in her ear. 'I think nothing could be spoilt if you are there.' The compliment was pretty, although its reception was a little spoiled when her hair, bundled into a great knot behind her head, worked loose and swung into the gravy. She wished now that she had at least combed it. To distract attention, she lambasted the steward, an old man who had been in service with her father as long as she could remember. 'Jean, we should have bowls of water for our fingers,' she exclaimed. 'Can you make sure we do in future? We are not savages here in Amouroix.' Jean opened his mouth to argue. Only yesterday, the young mistress had happily wiped her mouth on the hem of her skirt, just like everybody else. But he saw something new in her face, shut his mouth and shuffled off, grumbling.

Yolanda twinkled at Hugh, and as Aimery and others began to talk about rebellion and the Flame, and Aimery began to castigate his father for not having already dispatched teams of men to search for it, their guest began to chat exclusively to her, telling her of his home among the vineyards and of the great fairs, where bolts of wools and fine linens formed multi-coloured walls and where women exchanged patterns for fashionable gowns unseen as yet anywhere but Paris. 'But I am very dull at home in Champagne,' he said with a slow, self-deprecating sigh. 'You see, I've nobody for whom to buy trinkets and treasures.' He looked straight into her eyes. 'My wife is dead and none of my children reached their second birthdays.'

He saw her frown, but not about the deaths. 'Champagne? I thought Arcis would have been in the Occitan.' She glanced at Aimery, but he was deep in conversation.

Underneath his half-smile, Hugh's eyes were watchful, missing nothing. 'It's not, I'm afraid, and that's my misfortune.'

'You're French?'

There was a little pause whilst he filled her goblet with wine. 'Yes, I am, for my sins, although I know Raymond of Toulouse extremely well.' He took a sip of his own wine. 'I spend a great deal of time in Paris. Have you been there?'

Yolanda shook her head. Of course she hadn't been to Paris!

He went on smoothly, not rushing, his half-smile always present, as if it were the most normal thing in the world for him to be here. 'We don't have the glorious sky of the Amouroix, and we don't have the mountains. How fortunate you are! But we have a few compensations.' He began to talk, always comparing Paris unfavourably with the Occitan, but nevertheless painting a picture. Paris, he said, was a city of bells and arching stone, and boasted a river which was green and gold by day and blue and orange by night.

She should see the great processions and the gatherings where women wore clothes too fabulous for a simple knight like him to describe. Did she like books? Paris was full of books that told stories not just with words and music as the troubadours did, but also through delicate pictures painted with ground gemstones. She was soon hanging on his every word, her mouth slightly open. It was only when Hugh told her that it was a city fit for a southern sorceress and that if she came to visit, it would fall at her feet that she grew flustered. She wanted to retort that it couldn't be as marvellous as the Occitan, but the right words wouldn't come.

Hugh did not let the silence become awkward. He told her, in a matter-of-fact way, about the house he was having built, but in the middle of his description of the plumbing, she sprang up. 'Play something,' she ordered Gui and Guerau. 'Play something now.' Why was she bothering with words? This was how Hugh should learn of the Occitan, of me, the Amouroix, and of Castelneuf.

Gui needed no more encouragement. On a stool set amid the dogs, he tested his viol strings and then began to sing. He had a high, melancholy voice, well suited to his tale of glorious southern knights and their ladies, of sighs and favours, of unrequited love and a fallen world. He sang in time and in tune, and when he had finished, everybody applauded.

Guerau did not wait for silence before he kicked over his stool and was on the table, standing jauntily between two large candlesticks and pumping up his bladder-pipe. His song was an unashamedly lusty ballad of flowers coyly raising their heads through the frost, of lambs in the springtime and of sun on bare skin. His voice was lively as game soup with a kick like a peppercorn and he had a way of banging his foot that made every leg twitch. When his last chorus was finished, he raised his pipe to his lips and Yolanda, already strung tighter than an arrowstring, could contain herself no longer. Grabbing Aimery, she began to dance and when Aimery, self-conscious in front of his new friend, was slow to respond, she lost patience and danced alone.

To begin with, she danced as she usually did, with complete abandon, up and down the middle of the hall where the stone floor was free of its rushy carpet, her skirts twisting and her hair banging this way and that. But Guerau's music was different tonight. His pipe, so often such a joke, found a new voice, a breathy, wistful melody in a rope of blue smoke that might have curled from the Blue Flame itself. The rope did not tame Yolanda, but it bound her childish exuberance to its will. Now a different sort of abandon possessed her and she stretched out her arms for something or someone she could not yet see. The company fell silent and pressed their backs to the walls as she danced, for they thought she might burn them as she passed. Though the beat pulsed, nobody clapped and as the dance grew more intense, it was as if the Blue Flame itself was flaring in the hall.

Under his beard, Aimery smiled secretly at Hugh's expression. What a good choice he had made! Yolanda would have been too vital, too alive for many of the northern knights to whom he had considered offering her, but not this one. They would be well matched.

Yolanda herself was no longer aware of anybody. The music possessed her entirely and she knew nothing at all except that she could not stop her lonely dance until it let her go and that she must go where the music willed. Supple and light as a feather, she abandoned her shoes and leapt like a deer from trestle to water barrel, and water barrel to trestle, all the way round the room, knocking over nothing, disturbing nothing. She closed her eyes. She was no longer Yolanda: she was just a strand of that flame-shaped smoky rope which held her in its mystical grip. And then her dance was no longer lonely, for loneliness was banished by happiness, a kind of happiness she had not felt before, a happiness that by its very strength overwhelmed and frightened her, for whilst she could hardly bear to lose it, she knew it could not last.

The rope snapped and the pipe's music suddenly beat to an ordinary rhythm, jolting her back into the hall. Aimery began to clap as the spell broke and Yolanda staggered, breathing thinner air. She put out her arms, wanting Raimon, then, when she realised he was not there, dropped them again.

Hugh's eyes were narrowed to an arc as he gazed at her. Well! These Occitanian women really were shameless, but he had to admit that beside them, northern women, even city courtesans, were bloodless and flimsy. The thought of Yolanda dancing such a dance in Paris made his head spin. With her hair brushed and a clean face, she would be a sensation: his sensation.

Delighted with his sister's success, Aimery at last lost his inhibitions and caught her round the waist. Yolanda blinked and responded automatically, for the movements were in her sinews and bones, and when she next flung out her arms, it was an invitation for everybody to join in. In moments, the dance spread like a happy infection. The bolder servants grasped each other whilst others beat time with ladles on cauldrons or window ledges. Even the woven tapestry figures flapped to the rhythm and Berengar, though too old for capering himself, waved his fingers, remembering when his first countess used to dance like this.

Hugh tried, albeit unsuccessfully, to look as though tapping his feet came quite naturally. Even Yolanda could not persuade him to dance and Aimery had to do, even though he had grown heavier in his time away and the music never really possessed him. Dancing with Raimon, she thought to herself, was like dancing with a story whereas dancing with Aimery was like dancing with a dextrous bear. Nevertheless, Aimery was fine for tonight. She tossed her head in Hugh's direction. Once she had taught him, he would never refuse.

The music died down only when Guerau grew tired and at the first drooping note, Gui, who had danced in spite of himself, ran back to his seat and sat trimming his nails. Yolanda collapsed, laughing, no longer a dryad or a flame, just a hot girl. She took a long drink. The wine had never tasted so good. 'You will be here for my party, won't you, Aimery?' She glanced sideways at Hugh. 'And you too, Sir Hugh?'

'I'll stay if you ask me,' he said. 'Are you asking me?'

'Of course I'm asking you. We know how to be polite here in Castelneuf you know. Let's just pray that Uncle Girald doesn't stay long enough to spoil it.'

'But I am staying, little Yolanda, I am.' The voice was like stone crushing against stone and she swung round, feeling as though the hall fire had suddenly gone out. Her uncle had crept in behind her, his friar's robe the colour of dirty snow, his feet bare and bleeding and the pilgrim's scrip which contained all his worldly goods dangling from his staff. Thin and pale as a steel spike, he sucked all the joy out of the room.

'Uncle Girald,' she stammered. Even though he was so dirty himself, he made her feel dirtier. He had that capacity.

'Child.'

She felt her father at her side and squashed the urge to hold his hand.

'Girald,' Berengar's voice was high and reedy. Though he had spent most of the evening preparing for his brother's arrival, sternly lecturing himself that he was the count and therefore entitled to respect, he found himself, as always, amazed and disconcerted by his brother's inbuilt and unassailable aura not just of superiority, but of extreme importance. It was as if he breathed different air from everybody else, richer air, air that Berengar would never breathe, not even if King Louis were to hand him the crown of France. 'Yolanda meant no harm. You are very welcome. Have you eaten? Jean, Jean, more mutton.'

Girald turned on his brother. 'MUTTON, Berengar, MUTTON? Does nobody at Castelneuf observe the Lenten fast? Do the sufferings of the Lord Jesus mean nothing to you?' His voice carried far, though he never raised it.

Berengar put both hands to his forehead. 'Oh my Lord!' he exclaimed. 'Oh! The fish. I shall do penance, Brother. But come, sit. Have some water at least.'

Girald's feet, scraping over flag and rush, stamped out the dance and Yolanda edged away to the hearth and sat crammed up against the warm ashlar stones right inside the fireplace.

Brees was there at once, a great shaggy barrier, and Gui and Guerau squeezed in beside her, one on either side. When Girald came past, they breathed in but Brees growled, causing Girald to bend down. He inspected the dog from his nose to the tip of his tail but the thing that frightened Yolanda most was that although Brees's teeth were showing, Girald never flinched.

At last he passed on and drank from a barrel before allowing himself to sit down and accept a crust of bread. His teeth clicked as he chewed, for the bread was hard. Not that that mattered, for there was no pleasure in his eating. To him, food was not an evil, as it was to the White Wolf, but it was a weakness and in Lent was only to be consumed to keep a body upright. As soon as the crust had scraped down his throat, he wiped his mouth on his sleeve. 'You know why I'm here, Berengar.' His voice rasped and he pushed the thick gold band he wore on his fourth finger round and round. The ring was too tight, and as he turned it, it ground a groove, creating two swollen mounds of skin. He rejoiced in the pain. 'I am come, brother, to claim the Flame which has appeared in time to welcome me in my new role.' He paused. His stomach was not good, and he wanted it to settle. It would not, so he went on anyway. 'I come with God's blessing, for with the recommendation of the cardinals in Rome, I am named as Inquisitor for this area.'

Berengar froze. 'As Inquisitor?'

'Yes, brother. This time of laxity is past. The blue dawn tells us that those who profess to belong to the one true Catholic Church must now show their mettle. We can no longer tolerate the heretic Cathars in our midst. For the sake of the Occitan, we must find them and they must recant or they must die. If we do not, the Flame will abandon the Occitan, and we will all be lost.' There was silence. 'Have you nothing to say?' The ring ground round and round.

Berengar struggled, and finally recovered himself. 'It is an honour to have a brother chosen as Inquisitor, dear Girald, but I really feel that we are too small, here in the Amouroix, for your attentions. If what you say is true, you need a bigger, more important place than here. The city of Toulouse, perhaps? Or at least Foix or Pamiers?' He knew he sounded feeble. He wished Aimery would say something but Aimery said nothing.

Girald scrutinised his brother, then crumbled more bread. He wanted to eat it, but denied himself and dropped it onto the floor. No dog came near him to pick it up. 'No, indeed,' he said. 'The Flame has specifically chosen this place. It has chosen it because places like this need me most. You have allowed your people to grow careless, Berengar.' The servants who followed the Cathar creed began to sidle out and Girald raked each one with an eagle eye. 'Yes,' he said, 'you certainly need me and it should please you that I shall set up my court here in this château because by the time I am finished, Castelneuf and the whole of the Amouroix will be clean again. Won't that be a good thing?' He went back to the barrel and washed his hands in it, sullying the water.

Berengar was ashen-faced. 'Brother, really. We live in peace here.' It was the best he could do.

It was not good enough. Girald batted the objection aside as if Berengar, were a small, irritating gnat. 'I don't doubt that. But peace and cleanliness do not go together. Can you deny that there are Cathar heretics in this town? Even in this château? Even in this hall? Can you swear on the Bible that everybody under your charge is faithful to the correct teachings of our Lord Jesus Christ?' His eyes roamed the hall again. 'Do you not smell Cathars, brother, those distorters of the truth, for I surely do.' At this, the rest of the servants, whether Cathar or Catholic, made for the door. Girald gave a colourless smile. 'Guilt makes people run. But never mind. We shall dig out the dirt.' He scraped a long thumbnail into the wood of the table and his stomach rumbled.

Aimery stood up. Berengar's face lit with hope that was quickly dashed. 'It's hard, Father,' Aimery said, 'but we must accept what Girald says. We must think what's best for Castelneuf – and for the Occitan.' He avoided catching Hugh's eye. 'Even if it's difficult, we must surely do what's right.'

'But haven't we always?'

'No,' said Aimery. 'You've just muddled along, minding your own business.' The 'you' was very pointed.

'But we can do right without the Inquisitorial courts! I beg you, Girald.' Berengar at last stood up and faced his brother.

Girald stood too and fixed him with a special glare. 'Are you happy to allow heretics to lead innocent souls to perdition on land you inherited from our devout father?'

'Well, of course not, but –'

'And are you suggesting that I, an Inquisitor with the full weight of the one true Church behind me, do not know exactly what needs to be done, unpleasant and uncomfortable as that task may be?'

'I'm suggesting nothing but –'

'Berengar,' said Girald, very slowly. 'Are you denying an Inquisitor of the Church his God-given authority? Are you saying that in matters of faith you, an ordinary man who cannot get to heaven except through a priest, know better than me?' Girald faced his brother, forehead to forehead, eye to eye. 'Be very careful how you answer that.' Yolanda could scarcely breathe. 'I'm waiting.'

Guerau's bladder-pipe chose this moment to belch. It was a long, loud belch that trumpeted through the room in elephantine decibels. Who could have thought such a little bladder could make so much noise? But it cut through Girald's menaces like a clown through a funeral oration. Berengar's household began to shift. Somebody laughed, and when the bladder-pipe belched again, they all joined in. It was mainly release of tension, but it was a laugh all the same.

Girald pushed away from the table and grasped a torch. Pain stabbed his feet and legs as he walked swiftly back to the fireplace and thrust the torch so close in to Guerau's face that the troubadour's hair fizzed and frizzled. 'You scoff at me, sir?' He thrust the torch even closer, singeing Guerau's eyebrows as well and making Brees bark loudly. Yolanda pulled the dog back as far and as fast as she could. 'Ssssh,' she begged. She wished he was in the kennels. Girald should never have seen him.

Girald was conscious of Brees but, for the moment, his interest did not lie there. 'Tell me, troubadour,' he said conversationally, 'have you ever seen a heretic burn?' Guerau's breath was whistling through his lips. He couldn't speak. Satisfied, Girald returned to the table.

Now Yolanda climbed right underneath Brees for comfort

and after a bit, though Girald sat in silence, she heard the knights begin to speak amongst themselves. Somebody threw more logs on the fire. With warmth at her back, four legs tucked round her and her head in Brees's flank, some of her cheerfulness returned. Surely it was ridiculous to be so scared. If Uncle Girald did start rounding up all the Cathars in Castelneuf, they would just pretend they were Catholics. After all, how could God possibly care about that and nobody would betray them. Girald could set up his court, but nobody would be condemned. Soon he'd get fed up and go elsewhere.

She sat beneath Brees until the meal was quite over, then she watched her father lead her uncle out of the hall, the lamps picking out the bones of Girald's sunken cheeks. He carried not one ounce of spare flesh and the small drops of blood from his torn feet left red stains, like a skeleton who had stepped in a paintbox. As she left the hall herself, however, she knew one thing with every fibre of her being. Girald must never get his hands on the Blue Flame. That, she knew instinctively, would signify the end of everything.

IN THE RAIN

Despite Yolanda's optimism, the atmosphere at the château altered at once. Now that Girald was here, scouting parties were sent out from dawn to dusk to find the Flame and Aimery spent hours closeted with his father as Girald set up his courtroom. Doors were closed in the château that had never been closed before. Aimery's voice was loud, Berengar's weaker and weaker. In the face of Catholic wrath, the count felt powerless. He didn't want to go to hell, and this, so Girald assured him, would be his certain fate if he didn't support the Inquisitorial court. Nor did he want the Occitan to be lost to King Louis, which Girald assured him would also happen if the Cathar stain was not bleached out. Why was Louis coming in the first place, Girald constantly asked. Because as a Catholic Frenchman, he could not tolerate Cathar heretics on his doorstep. Aimery always looked at the ceiling at this point. Berengar, so unused to arguing, was out-argued at every turn.

Yolanda prowled about. She wanted to go to Raimon, but then again, she felt Girald's eyes on her and was nervous.

She had never really thought of Raimon's family as Cathars before, but it troubled her now. Even so, it still seemed quite impossible to her, despite Girald's arguments and his threats, that the Inquisitor really was going to do anything but talk. That was our tradition here within my boundaries. When necessary, the count issued a few warnings that were no sooner issued than ignored and forgotten. He would mutter for a day or two, then forget them too. That was his way and the way things had always been, so this atmosphere would last a few weeks at most and then Girald would move on and it would lift.

Yolanda managed to fool herself for several days, mainly because though she missed Raimon very much, Aimery was being far more pleasant to her this time than on his other visits home. He even consulted her on household details, asked her to show Hugh the mews and the kennels, normally his favourite preserves, and sang with her in the evening. It was true that some of the servants disappeared and others were so jittery they constantly dropped things, but most remained in their posts, as inefficient as they had ever been. She did not like to think that this was because they had nowhere else to go.

But then she learnt from Jean that Raimon's mother had died and the steward seemed unduly shocked. He'd heard she was getting better, but she'd died all the same. Forgetting everything else, Yolanda grabbed a shawl, and with Brees at her heel, hurried down the hill. She should have gone earlier! Now she must get to Raimon at once. She knew how much he loved his mother. This would be dreadful for him. She could have no idea how dreadful.

She arrived at the Belots' house with another mourner, which made Adela's reaction all the more shocking and humiliating. Instead of being welcomed in, Yolanda found the door slammed in her face. Not only that, but as she walked slowly back to the main street, she met Beatrice making her way up the hill. They spoke, but Beatrice was so nervous that she didn't comment on Yolanda's newly combed hair, or say anything at all about the bailiff and her wedding. As soon as she could, she walked off and didn't look back. Yolanda stared after her. Only now did she begin to understand that she had been living in a world of make-believe. Castelneuf's innocence was already polluted. Girald's very presence was causing poison to seep into the town like mercury down a well.

She made straight for the lake. If Raimon was anywhere apart from his home, he would be there. At the town side of the river bridge, she found two guards had been set. It was troubling and reassuring in equal measure to find both were very familiar to her. Fat, burly Pierre, with his red face and ham hands, had served an apprenticeship with the Castelneuf armourer and Sanchez, leaner, with the look of a terrier about him, did seasonal work with the sheep. They greeted her but they were busy cobbling a shelter together and showed no interest in where she was going. Nevertheless, once over the bridge, she called Brees to her heel and ran until she was out of their sight, their very presence making her feel like a criminal.

By the time she was out of the meadows and had broken through the trees into the valley proper, the day had turned into one of those where the clouds are a hanging blanket. It could have been winter again and she was glad of her shawl. It was not hard to find Raimon, but when she got near him, she found herself tongue-tied. From his dishevelled appearance, it was clear he had not been home and she had no idea if he knew his mother was dead or not. He didn't greet her and she held onto Brees tightly, suddenly afraid of Raimon, or for him, she was not sure which.

He gripped his belt in a way she had never seen before. 'Have you news?' His eyes flicked up and she knew that he had noticed her newly brushed hair. She wished she had left it matted. She took a deep breath. 'Do you mean about the Flame?'

'No,' he said. 'Not about the Flame. About my mother.'

She clasped her hands together. 'She's gone, Raimon.'

'Gone? You mean dead?'

Yolanda dropped her eyes so as not to see his. 'Yes, dead.'

'Thank God.'

Yolanda was shocked into looking at him straight. 'You're glad? How could you be glad?' Then her face cleared. 'Was she suffering? I thought she just had the wasting disease. I didn't know she was in pain.'

He didn't respond. He looked over her head, remote and unreadable. Brees jumped up and licked his cheeks. Still Raimon didn't move.

'Come! Come here, Brees.' Yolanda pulled him back but Raimon caught him at the same time, and sank to his knees, forcing Yolanda to hers. The grass was still soaking from undried early dew but she didn't care. It hit her harder than anything had ever hit her before that over the last few days she had been playing games when his life was shattering. She hated herself. 'Oh, Raimon, I'm so sorry.' It seemed such a hopeless, useless thing to say, even if she meant it from the bottom of her heart.

He would not allow himself to weep. Instead, he pinched great hanks of Brees's fur between his fingers while the dog beat his tail in a steady, sympathetic rhythm.

The clouds grew heavier. It began to drizzle and then to rain. Yolanda's face was awash with drops, not dazzling drops as they had been the day of the kiss. These were dull splashes, like poor-quality wax. Sometimes the rain felt like that. 'Raimon,' she said helplessly. It was hard to find any words at all apart from his name.

He shook his head at her, a shake of such misery that Yolanda, quite instinctively, wanted to wrap her arms round him, but he did not invite it so instead she wrapped her arms closer round Brees. Gradually his hand crept over the back of hers. She willingly turned hers over and when Raimon gripped it, she gripped his right back. 'You should go home, Raimon. Your father and sister need you.' Her voice was close to his ear. 'But you must be so careful. Uncle Girald has come and he's been made Inquisitor.' She felt him stiffen and held his hand harder because she didn't want him to pull away and then look at her as Beatrice had done. 'Did you see your mother before she died?'

'I went home,' Raimon said, 'I went home –' he found it hard to say any more.

'I'm so sorry.'

'You've been through it too – at least –'

'Yes,' she said, remembering the day her mother had died. It hadn't made her cry for ages but it made her cry now. 'I'm sorry,' she repeated, suddenly sobbing quite hard. 'How can I be crying? I don't want you to have to comfort me.'

'That's how it works sometimes,' said Raimon. He felt safe here, in this huddle, with Brees and Yolanda. Thank God for the rain. It made the huddle just a natural thing, washed away the awkwardness of that stupid kiss. Then his jaw tightened. Why was he thanking God? He didn't deserve any thanks at all. He thrust away all images of the White Wolf, and all images of his mother as he had last seen her. He tried to imagine her only as she had been before she was ill, before the Cathar Perfectus had cast his spell over her. The image wouldn't come. He saw only her parchment skin, the dewy sweat, and that terrible, terrible smile of acceptance as the White Wolf pronounced her sentence. He held Yolanda's hand so tightly that he knew he must be hurting her, but he couldn't let go. 'The Flame,' he said rather desperately, 'what are they saying about the Flame?'

'Your mother —'

'No, Yolanda. I can't speak of her right now. Please, just tell me about the Flame.'

'Uncle Girald thinks it's come for him. He's setting up his Inquisitorial court in the château. But it won't come to anything, will it, Raimon? Any Cathars can just pretend they're Catholics. Isn't that right? That's what your father and sister will do, if it comes to it? And the Flame will be used by us all together against King Louis?'

He wanted to reassure her. He wanted to tell her that she was right, that Cathars would renounce their faith without a qualm, that nobody would take Girald's court seriously, that

King Louis would be beaten by an army of Occitanians in which there was no difference made between Catholic and Cathar and that life at Castelneuf would resume, unblotted even by so much as a cross word. Once, even a few days ago, he could have pretended. But no longer, not after what he had witnessed in his own home. And an added cruelty was that he couldn't tell her about the White Wolf. For the first time, he would deliberately keep something from her. He hated the thought. Yet, though he had no experience of Inquisitors, all his instincts told him that she must know nothing that she could be forced to reveal to Girald. It was not that he didn't trust her: over most things he would trust her with his life. But in this case trust was not enough. He must keep the worst thing in his life from her and bear it alone.

'Raimon?'

He had almost forgotten her question, and she had to repeat it. His answer was more clipped than he intended. 'I don't know, Yolanda.' At once, he began to get up, afraid that if she questioned him again, he might crack and then everything would come tumbling out.

It was more in an attempt to stop him from moving than for any other reason that Yolanda spoke of Aimery's return and, before she could stop herself, of Hugh. Raimon looked quickly at her hair again, and so bleak an expression settled on his face that Yolanda could have bitten her tongue. Why hadn't she been more careful? But then he would hear about Hugh sooner or later. No stranger could pass without comment in Castelneuf. She tried to make Hugh sound as unimportant as Aimery's new squire and she tried not to mention his name again but it didn't work. Raimon asked where Hugh came from and though she told him, and even told him something of their conversation, thinking that this would somehow make things better, she knew she sounded insincere. After a bit, she fell silent and when Raimon made to get up again, she didn't try to stop him.

'I think it's you who should go home,' he told her, quite gently.

'I don't want to go home.'

'Don't be stupid, Yolanda. You must.'

'Can't I stay here with you?'

'With me?' He gave a shrug, 'That's all over now, I think. You must go home. Your uncle will be expecting you, and I dare say this Hugh as well. Once Girald has the Flame, as his niece you'll be quite a catch for a knight and I've no doubt that Hugh will be very decorative at your party.'

He did not mean his words to cut. He just opened his mouth and out they came. But they had cut, he knew that, and he was too deathly tired to take them back or even to know whether he wanted to. She was standing now as well, both of them joined by one thing: the feeling of being infinitely older than when they had knelt down.

'Do you know when my mother's funeral will be?'

'Jean didn't say.'

'It will be tonight, I think.' He guessed that it would be done to convenience the White Wolf. The Perfectus would be anxious to leave even if he would not go far from the Flame, but would feel it impolite to vanish before Felippa was buried. Yolanda waited for some further explanation, but none was forthcoming. Then, because he didn't seem to want her there any more, she turned and began to walk slowly away.

Almost at once, Raimon longed, above everything, to call her name; to tell her how he'd seen the Flame and danced, and of the arc of fire she'd flung at him in his dream and how it had welded them together. But he could not do it. His mother was dead, murdered, or as good as, by a man of God and Yolanda had brushed her hair for a knight. Such a little thing, Yolanda, he thought to himself, but oh, how significant. She was soon invisible in the downpour.

He went and crouched under an overhang. It was there he thought about the other thing that sat like a stone in his stomach. He had taken part in a Cathar consolation. With no knife to his throat, he had placed his hands on the Gospels and muttered the words the Perfectus recited to him. He had done that and he would never deny it, for that would insult his mother's memory. It did, however, change everything. He could now be branded an active heretic and if any Inquisitor learned of this, it would mean his end. Thus, in the space of only a few days, Castelneuf was finished for him. As soon as his mother was buried, he would leave, offer his services to Raymond of Toulouse and fight against the Occitan's enemies until he was dead. Then, as if to seal his promise, he rose and held his face up to the rain. Standing like that, he could pretend he wasn't crying although Parsifal, watching from above, had a pretty shrewd notion that he was.

THE FUNERAL

Aimery laughed at Yolanda when she got home and Hugh smiled.

'A mermaid,' he said.

'Hardly that.' Aimery was still laughing. 'You're as dirty as a puddle, Yola. Where've you been?'

Yolanda did not reply. Aimery would already know that she'd been over the river. He didn't need to know any more. She sat with Brees in her room. It was not for some time that she noticed a new purse lying on her bed. With its rolled edging and mother-of-pearl clasp, it had all the hallmarks of a Parisian craftsman. She picked it up and passed it from hand to hand. Brees sniffed at it without interest. Yolanda put it down again. She also put away the comb Hugh had given her the morning after his arrival.

There was no singing at supper that night. With Girald's hawk eye upon him, Berengar had forbidden it and all meat until Lent was over. Yolanda sat stony-faced as Hugh cut up tiny pieces of fish for her and, when these were refused, cut up even smaller pieces of cheese. He never inquired what was the matter, or demanded a response of any kind, not even an acknowledgement of his present, and for that she was grateful. Girald, chewing his crusts like a living corpse in their midst, was turning his parchments this way and that, to get better light. The following day was designated for the first Inquisitorial court and he was marking out his victims.

In such weather it was dark by vespers and, unable to concentrate on anything, Yolanda went back to her chamber. Her fire had gone out, for the servant who kept it in for her had already fled, and although Brees leapt up and draped himself over her on the bed, she was cold. She could not stop thinking about Raimon's mother. It was true that she would most likely be buried tonight, for though such secrecy had never been necessary in Amouroix, it had become a tradition for heretics to be buried after dark. Yolanda had been to one or two such funerals before, with her father. She rubbed her feet and Brees pressed himself more closely to her as if he read her mind. An hour later, she was opening her chest and pulling out a pair of winter stockings. They were full of holes, but she rolled them on anyway and changed her dress, which had once been flame-red, for one of deep blue, with holes only in the elbow. Brees waited until she began to tie on the ibex-skin boots she usually wore only when it was snowing and then galumphed down and just in case his mistress thought him sleepy, began to leap about like a giant puppy. Yolanda hugged him. 'Come,' she whispered, throwing her thickest winter cloak over her shoulder, then 'no – not that way' when he headed for the main staircase. Tonight she chose the smaller spiral steps that led almost to the roof of the château and made her way through the little-used top rooms. It was here that stacks of swords and piles of cross-bows together with spare rings for chainmail and quarrel heads for arbalesters' bolts had been stored in dusty chaos for a siege that never came. In the corner of one attic, a large iron wheel for knife sharpening was rusting away, the leaking grain sacks humped around it giving it the demeanour of the last man standing in a bloodless but devastating battle. Everything had been just the same as long as Yolanda could remember although occasionally, when the weather was too bad to do anything else, the armourer would gather up dogboys, pages, squires and buckets of fine sand to give everything a bit of a burnishing whilst he bored them with tales of sieges past and how much braver and more noble people had been in those days. When Yolanda was little, she thought that so long as these rooms remained undisturbed, all was well. What a fool she had been, not to realise that danger can come from within as well as without.

She reached the end of the rooms, fumbled her way down a straighter staircase and emerged into the anteroom in which her mother had sat in the evenings. In her day it had been specially lit with hundreds of candles so that the needlework at which she excelled could be carried out winter and summer, day and night. The intense light and happy industry had made this room, rather than the grander hall, the château's heart, and to Yolanda it had always been filled both with music and the countess's voice gently scolding the servants' inattention as she tried to teach them to read or to stitch. Yolanda brushed past the chair in which, just before every Christmas, her mother had sat sewing a swan's feather into a new surcoat for her father in a private whisper of love.

Apart from the chair, the room was unrecognisable now for Girald, with his unerring instinct for particularly personal cruelties, had ignored his brother's pleas for it to be left alone and had turned it into his courtroom. With a tall lamp at each corner, shackles and chains in heaps and a large judgement chair – fortunately the countess's had not been grand enough – there was nothing of either her or the gentle life left. Rather, the room was like the stage-set that Yolanda, when hardly more than a toddler, had seen in Pamiers one Easter. A storyteller had pretended to put the devil on trial and when he had appeared, she had screamed and hidden underneath her mother's skirt. She fled again now, with Brees a heavy shadow behind her.

It was still raining outside, but she took no notice. Skirting round the wall, she came to a dense patch of garlic mustard, bouncing as the raindrops hit it. It was a useful patch since it covered an ancient hole in the wall. In moments, she and Brees were through and away.

At the river, Pierre and Sanchez were dozing in their shack, their brazier having hissed itself out. The wooden gate they had erected was closed but had no padlock. Slowly and carefully, Yolanda slid back the bolts. The hinges creaked as she pushed Brees through, the water sluicing off his coat as he scraped along the wooden jamb, and she was almost through herself when two strong hands grabbed her. 'Caught you, you rascal!'

'It's me, Sanchez, just me!' Yolanda squeaked like a mouse, and then struggled to shush the dog. He mustn't bark.

'You, Mistress Yolanda! Well I never. What on earth are you doing out so late in this weather?'

'Nothing! Really nothing!'

'Nothing!' The two men laughed together. Sanchez let her go and went back inside.

Pierre sidled a little closer, holding his blanket above both their heads for shelter. 'Nothing's a funny thing to be doing at this hour.' Yolanda shook her head, smiling tentatively and lowering her lashes. Beatrice had taught her this trick, saying it never failed and she seemed to be right, even in this deluge.

'Alright. Knock once and cough loudly when you come back,' Pierre said, 'then we'll know it's you. We're not supposed to let anybody out, but I don't suppose you count as anybody.' He laughed at his joke and leered a little. 'You girls! Nothing gets in the way of your love-life, does it? Who cares about this rainstorm, the Flame or King Louis when there are boys and gossip! Who's the lucky one tonight? If he doesn't turn up, I'll volunteer.'

Resisting the temptation to slap him, Yolanda gave a passable imitation of one of Beatrice's best simpers and disappeared over the bridge. It was slippery with mud and moss and the darkness coated her like treacle. She held tightly onto Brees.

The cemeteries were set on some flattish land, just above the river. The Catholic tombstones, sticking up as they did like broken teeth, were somehow less menacing than the unmarked grassy humps of the Cathar dead who lay in their own cemetery, directly adjacent, like a row of misshapen invalids throwing back the covers in a break for freedom. A few years ago, she and Raimon had come here at midnight to try and send a message to Yolanda's mother through the Messengers of Souls, those great phalanxes of spectres, according to Nan Roquefort, who hung about graveyards waiting to take messages from the dead to the living. The old woman claimed to have seen hundreds but they had seen nothing and Yolanda had been very disappointed. But she could feel the Messengers around her now and they were not waiting in silence, they were whimpering and bleating, just as Nan had described. She almost fell over the wall into the Catholic graveyard to get away from them and took refuge behind a large tombstone erected in memory of one of her father's favourite huntsmen. Peering through the soggy veil of her hair, her skirts saturated and water filling her boots, she prayed that the funeral party would arrive soon. She would not allow herself to entertain the thought that Sicart might wait for better weather.

An hour passed and Yolanda grew more desperate as she grew colder. How long should she stay? She would count to 100, once in Occitan and once in the French she had learnt from her mother, but now seldom used. If, at the end, there was still nothing, she would go home.

Barely had she begun when she sensed small movements. So quietly had the funeral party arrived that not even Brees had noticed. In her relief, Yolanda shifted and then wished she hadn't, for now she could feel an icy snake of water trickling down her backbone, the only part of her which had been dry.

The burial party spoke not a word. She recognised Sicart's shape, and Adela's, and was puzzled that the third person was not Raimon but a stranger. Surely Raimon was here? Sicart and the stranger put down what Yolanda knew must be the shroud and dug fast, although it was hard since the soil had turned to slop. Nevertheless, they were soon waist deep. Then, still without a word, they picked up their precious bundle and carefully lowered it in. Adela muttered something, but the hammer of the rain made it impossible to hear what, and then began to help scrape back the soil with her hands.

The burial was nearly complete when there was such a clanking and clattering that Yolanda thought the dead really were casting off their chains. From behind her, like an army of raindrops, dozens of glistening shapes arose. Except they were not raindrops, for they were encased in chainmail and leather and their breath was heavy and foul. The Inquisitor, as suggested in the list of instructions issued by the General Council and which he had read several times, had stationed soldiers at the Cathar burial ground. It was an excellent place in which to catch heretics rendered a little careless by grief. Yolanda couldn't keep silent. 'Run!' she screamed as loudly as she could to Sicart and Adela. 'Run! run!'

She tried to run herself, but there was nowhere to run to, and anyway, her feet were gluey in the mud. The soldiers came upon her from behind. Brees did his best to protect her, launching himself upwards, legs splayed and jaw open, but he had no chance against so many. As Yolanda was knocked flat, her dog was seized and removed. At once she thrust out her hand, calling his name again and again, but instead of his familiar hairiness, her hands were caught by other hands, eager and rough, and she could not beat them off. Pressed down, always down, her nostrils were quickly filled not with Brees' familiar must but with the much ranker animal smell of soldiers used to finding their own freedoms in the dark. They had her at their mercy, leering over her and whispering in her ear terrible distortions of the words of love that in the light were sung to other tunes.

Through the thick horror, one hand stood out. Pale as moonlight, it reached down and pulled her through the maelstrom. There was no voice, but the soldiers fell away at the sight of it, for it was not one of theirs. Pulling mantles over their faces, for they were not unashamed of the licence they had hoped to take, they fled, and the next Yolanda knew, she was at the bridge again, alone. Her cloak was gone, but she was unharmed.

At once she began to run back towards the cemeteries, from where she could still hear shouting. 'Brees! Brees!' She couldn't go home without him. Frantic, she called again, and again, and then very nearly called Raimon's name, certain that he must be there and that he would come to her if he could. Just in time, she clapped her hand over her mouth. What was she doing? She mustn't call for Raimon. She mustn't call for anybody. They were living in the Inquisitor's world now, not her father's. She fell to her knees, and Pierre, running at the hullabaloo, virtually stumbled over her. 'Mistress Yolanda! For goodness sake, go home! Go home now! God knows, we shouldn't have let you through in the first place.' He picked her up and forced her back over the bridge.

'Brees!'

'The dog'll be waiting for you at the château. Sure he will. Go home. You're bound to find him there.'

'No, don't you see, they –'

'Mistress Yolanda, I'm telling you. You can't go out again. Go home. Go home now.'

She was never going to get past him. All she could do was

pray that he was right. Somewhere, Brees would be waiting for her. She stumbled up the main street, now almost a river itself, and got to the château gate. Brees was not there. She picked up her skirts and struggled to find the hole in the wall. He was not there. Panting with distress, she hauled herself through, across the courtyard and back through the small door. She could hear the slap of the rain on the roof tiles and knew there would be a trickle to her right from a leak high above her. Were there paw prints up these steps? She couldn't see because there was not enough light but her bedroom door was ajar. He could be there, he really could! He was, he was, he must be.

She flung open the door. Yes, surely! That shape on the bed! That lump by the chair! That shadow by the window! But there was nothing, only her room, only her things, only Brees' smell, his hair, old dirty paw marks on her coverlet, everything, in fact, but the dog himself. She ran to the window, dragging off the linen that kept out the draughts and cried out her dog's name, again and again, like a ship's siren in the fog. 'Brees! My Brees! Brees! My Brees!' Nothing, except, in moments, Aimery in the passageway.

'What a din! Is the Flame found? What on earth's going on?'

She ran at him, thumping her head against his chest. 'They've killed Brees. They've killed Brees. I just know they have.'

'Who's killed Brees?'

'The soldiers at the graveyards! Who else?'

Aimery grasped her shoulders. 'What soldiers?'

'Soldiers sent by Uncle Girald. He's a wicked man, Aimery.'

Aimery shook her. 'What on earth were you doing down at the cemeteries at this time of night and in weather that could drown a duck?'

She shook her head and buried it back in his chest.

He peeled her away. 'Yolanda, you must tell me.' His voice was harsh as his grip tightened.

'You're hurting me. Let go.'

'I'll let go when you tell me. What were you doing by the graveyards?'

'What do you think I was doing? I was at Mistress Belot's funeral. You should have been there and so should Father. She was our friend. I'm going back right now. I should never have left without Brees.'

'Don't be so stupid, Yolanda. You're going nowhere.'

'You can't stop me.'

'I think you'll find that I can.' He began to shove her back into her room. 'You shouldn't get mixed up in any of this.'

'"This"? "This", Aimery? What on earth do you mean? When did our friends become a "this"?'

'You know exactly what I mean.' She was wriggling and struggling and he was pinning her arms by her sides. 'Leave things to do with Uncle Girald to Uncle Girald.'

'Never,' she cried. 'Never, and nor should you.'

'Let go of her, Aimery.' A deeper voice cut through, and Aimery whizzed round so fast that Yolanda lost her balance and fell straight into Hugh's arms. Rather more gently than Aimery, he half carried her to her bed and set her down. 'You look as though you've had a mud bath! And you're soaked to the skin again. That's not good for you.'

'What do I care? I just want Brees. Find him for me. Get

him back.' She held onto Hugh's hand, which was warm and reassuring.

'We'll go and look, Yolanda, I promise.' He soothed her and petted her and listened to her outpourings, agreeing and nodding until she ran out of words. It was he who told her that a search party would be sent. It was he who ordered hot water and eventually persuaded her to get out of her wet clothes, scrupulously waiting outside the door as she did so. It was he who arranged for a posset and sleeping potion to be brought and who sat with her whilst she drank it. It was he who was holding her when, though her tears continued to fall and her chest occasionally heaved, she fell quiet. It was he who laid her down, smiling a little at the bits of old tansy and lavender and other girlish fripperies muddled into her sheets amidst the detritus of dog. And his smile, usually only a half-smile, widened into something quite whole. This had really been much easier than he thought. When he finally left her, he leant against the door for a moment, then sauntered back to his own quarters with the confidence of somebody who has got what he came for.

PARSIFAL AND RAIMON

No search party was sent out for Brees, and even if it had been, it would have found nothing, not unless it had looked far beyond the cemeteries. It was not to Hugh that Brees owed his life, nor even to Raimon: it was to Parsifal.

He had watched Raimon for a long time after Yolanda had left him in the rain, wondering if he might go down to him. The boy's grief stirred him deeply. It was like looking at himself in the years after Chalus Chabrol. But, as had become his way, instead of advancing, he retreated, returning to the cave under the scree. The Flame seemed very heavy today, even though, when he put it down, he saw that it had sunk to a pinprick, more white than blue. 'A pinprick of lead,' he murmured. It seemed to sit on his conscience. He turned his back on it and tried to light a fire in a hollow at the side of the cave, in front of the dangling tree roots, but had trouble because the kindling was wet, and though he struck his flint again and again, the spark just died away. So intent was he that he did not notice his visitor, at first.

Raimon went to the cave with barely a thought. He needed

somewhere to wait before going to the graveyard that night and though he had not forgotten the Knight Magician, he did not imagine that he would still be hanging about. It was a shock to find the cave so openly occupied. When he saw Parsifal still there, he drew his knife and all the emotions of his heart suddenly hardened into one vast bubble of anger. Whoever this man was, be it a friend of the Perfectus, scout for King Louis or a bandit knight, he shouldn't be here, not in this cave, not where Raimon wanted to spend the time before his mother's funeral and his last night under my skies.

It was something about Parsifal's utter inability to light the fire that stayed Raimon's hand. Again and again, as Parsifal fumbled and gently cursed, Raimon could have killed him. But though his anger still bubbled and frothed, it was impossible for him to kill somebody who seemed so helpless. The man had a lantern. Why didn't he use that? Nevertheless, remembering that Parsifal had floored him the last time they'd met, Raimon crept up behind him and seized him round the neck.

Parsifal choked as he struggled and they rocked together until Parsifal hooked his leg under Raimon's and tilted them both over. They hit the filigree box as they went down and the Flame, like an affronted snake, unrolled into the kindling, then rolled back again. At once the kindling caught and the fire was lit.

Raimon and Parsifal parted and picked themselves up. Parsifal watched Raimon but Raimon, absolutely transfixed, had eyes only for the fire. Though it was fast turning smoky yellow, it had not been that to start with. His arms were up, to ward off his adversary but he was slowly turning his head from fire to lantern, back to the fire and again towards the lantern. Only now he came to look at it, it was not a lantern, it was a box. 'You —' his voice was a breath, '— you have the Blue Flame.'

'Yes,' said Parsifal, for there seemed little point in denying it. 'I have the Flame.'

There was a very long silence, then Raimon repeated again, 'the Flame, the Blue Flame.' He did not know if he was talking to himself, or Parsifal or the Flame itself. At last, and with a supreme effort, he frowned, broke his gaze and took out his knife again. 'Are you a Cathar?' he asked, his voice very shaky, 'or are you a Catholic?'

Parsifal stared at the fire, the box, at Raimon and finally at his hands. 'I am Parsifal, son of Sir Bernard de Maurand,' he said, 'and I believe I am just an Occitanian.'

Raimon lowered his knife a little. 'You haven't answered my question.'

'I don't know any other answer.'

'Sir Parsifal de Maurand. I've never heard of you. Are you a brigand knight?'

Parsifal almost laughed. 'Just Parsifal, please. No "sir". A brigand knight? In truth, with no armour, no sword and no battles to my name I'm hardly a knight at all. Although,' and his voice became wistful, 'sometimes I think that being a brigand of any kind might have been a less lonely fate.' He moved one leg, then the other. Raimon's knife remained still so he moved cautiously all the way to the fire. 'That large dog left a rabbit a few days ago. It's a bit old, but still edible I think. I was going to cook.' The boy looked half starved, his face made even more pallid by the blackness of his hair.

'I can't eat,' Raimon said abruptly. He could see his mother again.

'But you could sit.'

Raimon shook his head and hovered. It was impossible to tell if Parsifal was friend or foe, the Flame's rightful guardian or a lucky thief, and all the while he was unable to tear his eyes from the Flame itself for more than a moment or two. It was so small, so much smaller than he ever expected. How could that tiny lick of blue have lit up the whole county? And could it really be true that he, Raimon Belot, was so close to it that he could touch it? He wished, very fiercely, that Yolanda were beside him. It was where she was meant to be.

'You're trying to work out whether I'm a good person or a bad person,' Parsifal said, passing the rabbit from hand to hand.

Raimon jumped. He didn't deny it.

'The thing is,' said Parsifal slowly, 'I don't know myself. I only got the Flame by chance.' He would have to get out his own knife, if he was to cook. He wondered if Raimon would let him.

'How long have you had it?'

'Oh, a while.'

'And what have you been doing with it?'

'Nothing.'

'You've had the Blue Flame and done nothing?'

'What would you have done?'

'I don't know, but something — lots of things.'

Parsifal nodded. 'Yes, I expect you would.'

'And I don't understand. If you've done nothing all this time, why did you choose to show it now?'

'Oh, that's easy,' said Parsifal. 'I didn't choose. It chose.'

'Flames can't choose.'

'This one can.'

Raimon looked at the Flame again. It flared a little and he heard it hiss.

Parsifal quickly took out his knife and set about the rabbit without further ado. It was strange, to be cooking for somebody else after all this time and he could feel Raimon's eyes boring into his back. 'When, exactly, did you get the Flame?' the boy asked again. 'I mean, how did it come to you? Why you?' He was still highly agitated, but he put his own knife away.

There was nothing to be gained by evasion so Parsifal told the unvarnished truth. 'I got it at Chalus Chabrol, the day King Richard the Lionheart met his death.'

He could almost hear Raimon's astonishment, and waited for the response although when it came, it was not quite what he was expecting. 'You must be very old indeed,' Raimon said.

It broke something between them, and, rather haltingly, for he had never told it before, Parsifal told Raimon his story – or most of it. Over forty years easily condensed into four minutes. Parsifal was brought face to face with his own short-comings in the most graphic way possible.

But even as his story unfolded, Raimon heard less and less of Parsifal and more and more of a voice coming from himself. This man had had the Flame and done nothing with it. Raimon would not make that mistake. Fate must have drawn him here, here to where the Flame was waiting for him. And he certainly knew what to do with it, now that he had found it. He would not waste this extraordinary opportunity.

He would take the Flame to the cemetery tonight and set the White Wolf alight. The Flame would make the White Wolf suffer as his mother had suffered. He moved towards the box, hardly aware of Parsifal any more, hardly aware of himself, aware only that the perfect means of revenge was right in front of him. And had he not earned it? When the Flame had called to him in the dawn, he had danced for it. Now it could do something for him.

Parsifal had already stopped skinning the rabbit. He had known the exact moment that Raimon had ceased to listen, and when he saw two spots of colour brighten the boy's cheeks and saw his knuckles whiten, he knew what was in his mind. When Raimon moved, he moved himself. Raimon should not take the Flame. It was not his Flame to take. Before Raimon even noticed, he dropped the rabbit and his knife, snatched up the box and held it tightly. Raimon gave a sharp gasp and whipped out his knife again. Parsifal was now the enemy. They glared at each other.

'Give the Flame to me, Sir Parsifal. I have a use for it.' Raimon stood.

'Just Parsifal, please. And I will not. I'm still the Flame's guardian.'

Raimon continued to glare. 'But you had no use for it. I have a use for it. Give it to me.'

Parsifal held the box even more tightly but now the Flame snaked out again, away from him and towards Raimon. Though Parsifal tipped the silver salver backwards, he was powerless to control it. Yet he stubbornly clung to the box, willing the Flame back, and as he clung, a new feeling almost stifled him. It took him more than a moment to identify it and when he did, he could hardly believe it. He was jealous! And so jealous. The jealousy crackled beneath his skin, in his ears, under his eyelids and hardened the skin on his white hands. How dare the Flame leak out towards this boy? How dare it desert him after he had tended it all this time? *How dare it abandon him now?* Though he had hardly brandished it like a hero, he had at least nurtured it and kept it safe. And with his jealousy came fear. What on earth would he do without it? He could see his future – a vast hole with nothing to fill it. A blast of temper, quite equal to anything that had ever risen in Raimon, blew through him. How could the Flame be so capricious? He gathered himself up just as Raimon lunged at him, and the two of them found themselves entangled in bizarrely careful combat, with neither wanting to damage the Flame but neither wanting to give it up.

Eventually, the inevitable happened. The box fell. At once, Parsifal froze, horrified. Not so Raimon. He bent down and seized it, running his fingers over the chips in the filigree and biting his lip. He backed away from Parsifal as he peered inside. Nothing. Then a spark. Then a flicker, and finally the Flame was burning like an angry firefly.

Parsifal, wiping the sweat from his brow, was at the front of the cave and Raimon near the back. 'Well,' Parsifal said, 'here's a sight. Now you have the Flame, precisely what are *you* going to do with it?'

'I know exactly,' Raimon replied, his voice hard and triumphant. The spots in his cheeks were very bright. 'First I am going to the cemetery to kill the man who killed my mother. Then I'm going to raise an army to see off King Louis and free the Occitan forever. Then I'm going to hunt down the

Inquisitors and all the Perfecti and then –' he stopped. Parsifal waited. 'And then,' he finished, his eyes glittering, 'then I'm going to get rid of God. If people must worship something, they can worship the mountains. The mountains don't have Perfecti or Inquisitors, they just are.'

'I see, I see,' Parsifal said. 'But the Flame was lit by God.'

'Who cares about that?'

Parsifal was silent for a moment. 'I suppose I do.'

'And so do Inquisitor Girald and the Perfectus called the White Wolf. Are they your friends?' Raimon felt quite reckless with the Blue Flame in his hands. 'Which one of them do you prefer?'

'I don't know either of them,' Parsifal said, trying to keep his voice at least a little measured, 'but I think you should remember that the mountains kill people as well.'

'Not on purpose.'

'How do you know?'

'They don't burn people or starve them. People die on the mountains, but the mountains don't do anything.'

'I have lived nearly all my life in the mountains,' Parsifal said, 'and I'm not so sure. I've seen men burn from the sun on the high slopes, and I've seen the corpses of those who have starved to death trying to cross the passes in the snow. The mountains show no mercy.'

'My mother was forbidden food by a Cathar Perfectus. She was getting better.'

'Would that be the White Wolf? You mentioned him earlier,' said Parsifal, and Raimon's tight, stricken expression told him the answer. 'Oh,' his temper was flattened with pity as he imagined the scene. He coughed to give himself a little time for though his anger was diminished, his jealousy still crackled. 'I must ask you this, though. When you've killed the Perfectus and raised your army, I suppose you'll know just how to deploy it, organise and feed it.' Raimon's face, though still shot through with defiance, lost some of its certainty. 'And you'll know how to stop a war once it has started and how to control men when the panic of battle closes their ears and clouds their eyes.' Parsifal could hear his father's voice echoing through.

'But I must do something, don't you see? I must go to the cemetery. The White Wolf is a wicked man. He deserves to die.'

'Yes,' said Parsifal, 'I can see how you'd think that and perhaps,' he said in more subdued tones, 'if I'd acted earlier, we'd have no White Wolves and no Inquisitors. I've completely failed.' He threw up his white hands, moved towards the fire, now merrily blazing yellow and orange, and sat down. 'I'm sorry for grabbing the box,' he said, shaking his head, 'it's just that I've had the Flame for so long, I can't think what I shall do without it, not that I've done much with it.'

Raimon hesitated, still suspicious, but then came to the fire himself. 'I'm sorry too,' he said. He was moved by the sagging of the knight's shoulders, and his apologetic uncertainty. It had never occurred before to Raimon that uncertainty could be so soothing. And the man was due some respect as the Flame's guardian. Raimon felt he should remember that. Keeping the Flame always by his side, he sat down. He was calmer now, but had still not given up his plan and in the long pause that followed, began to calculate how many hours until nightfall, how the burial party might approach the cemetery and, most importantly, when would be the best moment to catch the Perfectus. Raimon agonised over that, for he did not want the man to be unaware of his fate. He should suffer at least some agony. He shifted. He had never contemplated doing anything like this before and had never expected to. 'You do understand that I can't do nothing, Sir Parsifal, don't you?'

'Just Parsifal, please. Yes, my dear boy, perhaps I do.'

Silence again. Parsifal was glad to find his jealousy less crackly. It was sitting in his diaphragm now, but it had left his eyes and ears. 'It does occur to me,' he said to Raimon, with a look Raimon couldn't interpret, 'that maybe the Flame does want you for something special. I don't know. But I think it must, or you wouldn't be here. Perhaps it's fed up of me. I couldn't blame it. The real question, now that it has shown itself, is what we're supposed to do next.'

He got up. Raimon at once pulled the Flame closer to him. Parsifal put up his hands in a gesture of surrender. 'One thing I do think,' he said, 'is that it shouldn't be used to settle personal scores. If you take it tonight, I shan't help you, and I doubt whether the outcome will be as you desire.'

'I'll take my chance, Sir Parsifal,' said Raimon softly.

'Just Parsifal, please.'

The hours passed. Darkness crept in. Parsifal ate. Raimon did not, and when he reckoned it was time, he got up. He made little noise as he prepared to leave.

'Don't go,' Parsifal said, quite loudly, and kept on repeating himself long after he knew, from the silence, that Raimon had already left. He was never sure what made him change his mind and follow Raimon to the graveyard. He thought it was because without the Flame the cave was a cheerless place, just a hole in the ground in which a man with no friends and no further purpose might hide out. Whatever the impulse was, Parsifal did not wait long. Less surefooted than Raimon, and much less certain of the way, it took him a while to reach the cemeteries, hampered all the way by the rain. But he was there by the time the soldiers erupted. He heard Yolanda's shouted warnings and saw the burial party flee. He also saw Raimon struggling not with the White Wolf, but with two soldiers over the dog. The Flame was nowhere to be seen. He heard Yolanda scream as she was pulled down, an anguished answer from Raimon, unable to get to her, and it was without hesitation that he launched in himself.

After that there was only a vortex of mud and blood. He had no idea how he pulled Raimon out, nor the dog. He only knew that he had the strength of ten as he shovelled them towards the river, tumbled them in near the millstones and himself in after them. All he could hope was that when the soldiers realised their quarry had vanished, the rain would dampen their enthusiasm for much of a search and they would be soon gone. He was right, but even so, it was some time before the place was clear and Parsifal could pull everybody back onto the bank. Raimon, who had suffered only minor injuries, helped haul Brees out. The dog was badly wounded and still bleeding heavily, particularly from the neck. His thick collar was missing but it had saved his life.

'The Flame,' Parsifal panted when they were all lying face down in the streaming grass, Brees motionless beside them. 'Did you lose it?' It was hard for Raimon to hear, but he didn't need to ask Parsifal to repeat himself.

'I stuck it behind the wall. I saw them with Brees. I heard Yolanda, and I couldn't, I just couldn't –' He was completely stricken.

They found it, the box sodden but the Flame still lit, and this time Raimon made no complaint when Parsifal tucked it under his coat. Parsifal had saved them all: Yolanda, Brees and himself. The Flame seemed to have chosen rather more wisely in its guardian than Raimon had imagined. He helped Parsifal lash together a stretcher from branches and creepers and between them they carried Brees back to the cave. Though blood loss from many dagger wounds weakened him and one leg dragged badly, the dog's heart was strong. By the next morning, he was doleful but not dying and Raimon was determined to return him to Yolanda himself. He had not thought to quarrel with Parsifal again, but quarrel they did, for Parsifal thought this a very bad idea. The town would be in tumult after the night's events. Anybody who could be accused of being at the Cathar cemetery would be deeply suspect. They should leave Brees as close to Castelneuf as they dared and hope that somebody else would return him to Yolanda, or that he would hobble home himself. Raimon, for all his gratitude to Parsifal, obstinately refused to countenance this. Parsifal didn't understand, he said. He must return Brees personally, whatever the risk, and though Parsifal tried, he could not find the right words to dissuade him.

THE TRIAL

Girald's excitement, when he had learnt from surreptitious whispers that a Cathar funeral was to take place, had turned to fury when the soldiers he had posted crept, empty-handed, back through the château gate at dawn. His fury was also personal. He should have ignored the ache in his bones and the sickness in his stomach and gone down to the graveyard himself. He should have seized the whisperers and demanded a name. Apart from the Blue Flame, there was nothing he wanted more than a body, or a suspect, or at least somebody to parade in front of the people of Castelneuf so that they would know he was no paper tiger, but an Inquisitor with teeth and claws. So when the first Mass of the day was over and after he had given the last miserable soldier a tongue-lashing he would not forget, he wrapped himself in one of his brother's cloaks. An inch-by-inch trawl of the cemetery, up to his knees in mud, revealed nothing except a dog's collar, which he picked up on the end of a stick. He recognised it. Not quite a wasted journey, then.

A fresh batch of scouts searching for the Flame was setting

off as he returned. The serjeant tried not to meet his eye. Meeting an Inquisitor's eye seldom did you much good. 'God speed,' Girald said. The serjeant answered at once. Not answering an Inquisitor never did you much good either.

Once he had secreted the dog's collar in his pouch and changed out of his muddy clothes, Girald sat in his courtroom twirling his quill and scratching at blots on his parchments with his nails. He had learnt from other Inquisitors that patience, which he did not possess naturally, was often the most powerful weapon of all during a general questioning. He wondered how you practised keeping your temper. Perhaps, he thought, it would help that he knew exactly what he wanted from Castelneuf: he wanted the Flame, for with its help he could become Chief of the General Council of Inquisitors; he wanted at least a dozen successful convictions; and he wanted to be the generator of a large Cathar pyre. He did not feel that the list was in any way beyond him.

High above him, as the effects of the posset she had drunk wore off, Yolanda awoke. She was deadly stiff, for she had slept crunched up and she felt the loss of her dog as an amputee feels a missing leg. In her dreams she heard him whining at the door and sniffing under her bed. She saw him lumped under his blanket with a rabbit's skull, his maggoty mutton chop and one of her shoes. She was sure his wet nose was pushing under her arm. And then there were her other terrors. What had happened to the Belots? Easier to worry about them than hear those lecherous voices and smell that primeval smell. Where the saving hand had come from, she had no idea. It was not Raimon's, though. She knew that because she wished it had been.

She stepped over to her window and looked out. The rain had stopped and a watery sun was making an attempt to dry the earth, its dapples giving the untidy courtyard a romantic air it hardly deserved. Had it been an ordinary day, Yolanda would have crowed. Sun after rain was festival time. The whole of Castelneuf would have been singing. There was silence today and there seemed to be fewer servants than usual. Perhaps, after last night, they had finally all run away. She pulled on the first dress to hand and kicked the wet one she had stripped off the night before into a corner, then she made her way downstairs. For the first time in her life, she had no idea what she would find.

Dread can exert a magnetic force, and she was drawn against her will to the small hall. The doors were open and she could see her uncle sitting in the judge's chair with her father sitting unhappily in a smaller chair beside him. Simon Crampcross, his hands across his belly, stood behind Count Berengar trying to look as if he mattered. Aimery and Hugh were lounging on benches. Lining the walls was the answer to the missing servants. They were all here, dozens of them, Gui and Guerau included. Even some of the dogboys had been dragged in from the kennels and were scuffling about, many on all fours.

Uncle Girald, giving in to failing eyesight and reading his list through a wedge of glass, was taking a roll-call. Nobody moved, except to acknowledge their name until Guerau turned his head, saw Yolanda, and raised his hand.

At once Girald was alert. 'You. Step forward.'

'Me?' Guerau tried to make his voice jaunty.

'Yes. You.'

Guerau licked dry lips and though his eyes were insolent, there was a tremor in them too. Yolanda crept in and sat down.

'Guerau, isn't it?'

'Yes.' It seemed safe enough to admit that.

'Where are your shoes?'

'Under my bed, like the shoes of all good Christians.'

'Good Catholics or good Cathars?'

'I said, "good Christians" and that's what I meant.'

'Don't be sharp with me, man.' Girald's upper lip was bobbled with sweat. His feet and hands were cold, the rest of him feverish. He gave an order and Guerau's shoes were duly found, inspected and pronounced dry. They had clearly not been into the Cathar cemetery the night before.

Girald ground his ring round and round. 'Did you sleep in your own blanket in the hall last night?'

'Does any woman claim otherwise?'

One of the dogboys giggled, unable to help it. Girald bit his cheek. 'Did you see anybody leave?'

'I tend to sleep with my eyes shut.'

There was more giggling. The dogboys did not fear Girald, for they barely knew who he was. They feared only the huntsman.

Girald ignored them. 'You!' he barked at Gui. 'Gui, isn't it? What about you?'

'I sleep with my eyes shut too. Perhaps it's a musician thing.'

Girald bit his other cheek. The room held its collective breath.

But there was no explosion. Patience, patience. Girald allowed Guerau to sit down and asked several others to show their shoes. Some had to show their legs also. Others brought their cloaks and three brought the piles of outdoor clothes and wooden pattens for general use that sat in and on a chest at the back of the main hall. Not a drop could be wrung out of any of the cloaks, and the mud on the pattens was old. Yolanda knew she should have hidden her soaked dress. As for her boots, they were not only wet, they were ruined and she had no idea where they were.

But Girald seemed not to notice her. He moved on from clothes to prayers. Could the château's spit-turner recite the Lord's Prayer? Could the bird-plucker say the credo? Both spit-turner and bird-plucker could, with one or two mistakes. But these mistakes also seemed to pass Girald by. People began to relax. Perhaps, though the man looked like the kind of hawk they called the bone-breaker, he was really just a jay: lots of noise but no threat.

Yolanda began to slide out and Girald waited until she had nearly made it before his voice cracked like a whip. 'Ah, Yolanda.' She was tempted to flee but flew to her father instead.

Girald pushed back the folds of his habit and his skin was blueish, for though it was so chilly, no fire was lit. His voice was not raised but stood out anyway like the caw of a rook above the chatter. 'Last night, Cathar heretics were burying their dead. Soldiers witnessed this, but they escaped because somebody shouted a warning. I'm going to discover who it was.' He scrutinised her much as a vulture might scrutinise a promising carcass.

Berengar waved his arms. 'Oh goodness. Is this really necessary?'

'Do you wish to obstruct God's work?'

'Of course not, Brother, but really –'

'I'll do my job, you do yours.'

Berengar relapsed into silence. Girald whispered to Simon Crampcross, whose jowls shivered as he passed the order on.

Berengar held onto Yolanda tightly but Girald had not finished with him yet. 'You know, Berengar, you could save us a great deal of trouble by telling me yourself whose funeral it was.'

'Me? Oh, people die. I haven't heard of anybody in particular.' Girald's eyes narrowed.

Aimery cleared his throat and Yolanda's heart began to quake. Surely he couldn't betray the Belots. He wouldn't. Especially not to Uncle Girald. It was unthinkable. Yet she could see that he was going to say something.

'There is an old man called Guillaume,' Aimery began. 'His wife died the day I returned. Perhaps it was her burial. You could arrest him.'

Yolanda gulped, half relieved, half appalled. Guillaume was an ox-driver, an old busybody, certainly. He had once scolded Yolanda for spending fifty sous on a pair of fancy shoes she had never worn, but he was well-meaning enough and sixty if he was a day. She was outraged that he could mention such defenceless people to Girald. 'Leave Guillaume alone,' she said. 'He's done nothing.'

Girald turned slowly to her. 'Ah, Yolanda,' he said softly. 'Yolanda, Yolanda, Yolanda. I have something of yours, something rather precious, I think.' He showed yellow teeth, held up his hand and then stepped back to watch the effect. He was not disappointed. A cry burst out. 'Give it to me.'

'Tell me who was in the graveyard.' Girald made the dog collar swing.

'I won't,' she said, though her eyes went back and forth. It was like seeing Brees swing.

'If you don't, you'll never see your dog again.' There was no giggling now, and certainly not from the dogboys. Everybody shrank. To be small was not to be safe, but it gave Girald less on which to focus.

Yolanda found Girald's threat wicked but empty. Brees was dead. The soldiers who had threatened such violence on her would hardly have spared him and if he was not, he would have returned to her. She would not betray the Belots for a corpse.

Girald swung the collar round. 'I'll just keep this, then,' he said.

'Make him give it to me, Father,' she begged. 'It's all I have left.'

The count remonstrated. 'She's just a girl, Girald, not yet fourteen and what good is the collar to you?'

'You should keep a better eye on your daughter, Berengar.' Girald looked at Simon Crampcross, who nodded. A man came forward and gave Girald a sack, which he opened with distaste and turned upside down. Yolanda's dress and one wrecked boot slapped against the floor. 'Now, Brother, did you know your daughter was out in the Cathar graveyard last night?'

'I'm sure she wasn't,' Berengar said, not looking at the dress. 'You weren't, were you, Yolanda?'

'Father, I –'

A voice spoke up from the back. 'She was out with me, sir,

and I don't tend to take young ladies to graveyards.' Hugh's words were cool and confident.

'What, out courting in that weather?' Girald was openly disbelieving.

'The people of the Occitan are not put off by a little rain, sir.'

'Indeed. Well, Sir Hugh, all I can say is that if Yolanda really was out with you, that verges on the disgraceful.'

'Disgraceful, perhaps, but not heretical,' Hugh said evenly.

'But if you and Yolanda were staring at the stars in the rain –' Girald still pushed on although his tone was less aggressive – Sir Hugh des Arcis would have powerful friends – 'then why was that dog in the Cathar graveyard?'

'Dogs go where they wish,' Hugh replied. He seemed almost amused by the whole proceeding.

This gave the count a little confidence. 'Especially that one,' he chimed. 'He often gets into the flocks and causes trouble.'

'He was a good dog,' Yolanda said. She kept feeling that if she blinked hard enough, she would wake from this nightmare. Any minute now, any minute now. But all she saw was the collar swinging and she couldn't help herself: she jumped at it. Girald flicked it higher. She jumped again. He flicked it over his shoulder and she jumped again like a doll on a string. 'Give it to me! Please, give it to me.' The dogboys began to howl.

Girald's head throbbed but he was not for stopping now. 'Tell me who was in the graveyard.'

'Just give it to me!'

The hideous game was only stopped by a grunting, which cowed the dogboys into silence. Everybody turned and there, dragging his leg and with his head too heavy to lift more than a foot from the floor, was Brees himself.

Girald turned from grey to white and Yolanda from white to pink as she threw herself down the hall and collapsed with Brees in an untidy heap. The dog seemed to be alone. She scolded him and petted him all at once, asking where he had been and why he hadn't come home. Then she turned on her uncle, but he was neither listening to her, nor looking at her, and Yolanda's tirade faltered as she followed his gaze. Raimon was standing at the door and on one side of him stood Sanchez and on the other, Pierre. He was bound by both hands and feet, so that instead of walking his free, swinging walk, he had to shuffle. That shuffle was the most shocking sight Yolanda had ever seen.

She got up slowly, although she never let go of Brees. Even though the evidence was clearly before her, she couldn't believe it. Though Pierre and Sanchez had set themselves up as guards, they would not give up Raimon to Uncle Girald. Had they forgotten how Felippa had sat with Sanchez when he had come out all over in spots and his own mother had been too afraid? Or how Pierre and his father had helped Sicart and Raimon to build the new floor onto the Belot house? She clutched these memories as they began to fragment and darken.

'We found this one at the gates with the dog,' Sanchez said to Girald, looking uncomfortably round at the dozens of pairs of eyes fastened on him. 'He tried to get the dog through the bridge gate *by stealth*. If he was so innocent, and had come across the dog by accident, why didn't he just ask us to bring it back here?'

Yolanda didn't need to hear the answer to that question. She knew exactly why Raimon had needed to bring Brees himself. He was making his own kind of apology for the way they had parted, for his sending her home from the hill with his cutting dismissal still echoing. She couldn't smile at him, or thank him, or say anything, for fear that Girald would somehow use her against him. Instead, she put her hand up to her hair. She had not combed it again. The curious, hesitant exultancy he had about him, despite his shackles, she took for understanding and acceptance.

There was a movement behind Girald and she saw Raimon's shoulders hunch a fraction. Hugh was standing under the window. He had taken off an emerald ring and was inspecting it for flaws.

The Inquisitor didn't notice Hugh at all as he circled round Raimon. This was what he had been waiting for. One person on whom to focus. Now he could really begin. 'What is your name?'

Silence.

'His name's Raimon Belot,' said Pierre.

The Inquisitor inclined his head. He remembered Belots from when he was a boy at Castelneuf. Weavers. Easily broken, he thought. 'Raimon Belot,' he said, 'are you on good terms with God?' He hoped this might become a classic Inquisitorial opening, bearing his name.

Count Berengar intervened again. 'For goodness sake, leave him be, Girald. Let him go. The poor boy's just lost his mother.' As soon as the words were out, Berengar groaned aloud and reached out, as if he could wrest them back, but Girald had already pounced on them.

'Ah,' he purred, 'just lost your mother. So it's your mother who has died.' He circled faster, his finger on his lips, as if he was thinking, although he already knew exactly what he was going to say. 'I'm sorry to hear that, very sorry.' Eventually, he took his finger from his lips. 'I wonder, Raimon. When your mother was preparing for death, did she summon the priest?'

Raimon stood perfectly upright and perfectly silent. Girald raised his eyebrows. 'No matter,' he said, 'as fortunately we can ask the priest himself.' He addressed Simon Crampcross. 'Did you attend Madame Belot's deathbed?'

'I did not,' said Simon Crampcross. This was the correct answer, he was sure, not because it was the truth but because it was what Girald wanted to hear.

'Nevertheless, though you were not summoned, would you say that Madame Belot was a good woman, a pious woman, a holy woman?'

This was more tricky. Once he would have had no hesitation in acknowledging Raimon's mother as a good woman. Though a Cathar, she brought him soup when he was sick, and her husband had even woven a new tunic for him last Christmas and only charged half price. And she was pious too, in her way. At least she had a healthy respect for God. That was pious. And he had seen her out in the fields on her knees, praying, which also made her holy. Yet to the Inquisitor no Cathar could be good or pious or holy. His face creased and a pearl of sweat trickled into the folds of his chin. Then again this could be a trick question, for Simon Crampcross knew also that sometimes, and to some people, Cathars were known as Good Men and Good Women. Oh, it was so complicated! The pearl dripped off his pimpled chin and joined the other stains on his shirt as Girald waited for his answer. 'I would say she was a –' the silence shrieked '– er, I think she was a woman –'

'Yes, yes,' said Girald, his patience, despite his good intentions, beginning to fray, 'we all know she was a woman.' A ripple went through his audience. The priest was a buffoon. Girald didn't mind the ripple. 'She *was* a good woman,' he said. He would clearly have to help this stupid man all along the way.

'Indeed, a good woman. Just what I was going to say.' Another salty pearl dripped onto his chest, where it joined the other to make the small stain larger.

Girald grasped hold of his patience again and gave a meaningful smile. 'And such a good woman would want to make a good death?'

Here, Crampcross was on surer ground. 'Everybody wants to make a good death, Inquisitor,' he said.

'But good people in particular, wouldn't you say?'

'Oh yes, Inquisitor, I would.'

'Then, Raimon Belot, I ask you again, was your mother a good woman?' Silence. 'I must tell you that the choice is stark. There are only two types of women, the good and the bad. Let me rephrase my question. Was she a bad woman?'

Raimon would not answer and Yolanda had not yet learned that silence, too, can be a weapon. She interrupted and began to plead. 'Why are you persecuting us, uncle? We've done nothing and really, we're not important enough for somebody like you. You should go where you're really needed.'

'Not important? Castelneuf?' he said, raising his eyebrows at her. 'You are too modest, little Yolanda. If Castelneuf was not important, why has the Flame chosen it as the place to reveal itself? Even now, scouts may be bringing it to this very château and we must make sure we are ready to receive it by purging this whole place of those who distort the true word of God. The Flame expects it. No, I go further. The Flame demands it.'

Raimon didn't move but Yolanda raised her voice as loudly as she dared. 'The Flame's nothing to do with God's word or how people choose to pray! You know that, uncle. The Flame's to keep the French out! That's what it's for! It's the Flame of the Occitan and none of your business at all.'

'But tell me this, since you seem so well informed,' Girald's voice was dangerously icy. 'What's the point of keeping the French out, little Yolanda, if we are rotten within? God will hardly help us beat the French if we don't cleanse ourselves first.'

'This is all wrong.' Yolanda turned to her father. 'Tell him, Father. Tell him that's not our way.'

Girald gave Berengar no time to answer. 'And what is "your way", I wonder? Is it the way that allows the Cathars to inflict their foul beliefs on the innocent? Do you actually even know what those beliefs are, Yolanda? Well, do you?' He could tell by her face that she did not. He resumed grinding his ring round chillblained fingers. 'Perhaps I can tell you. You see, unlike you, I have made a study. You look surprised at that, but why? Know thine enemy is an old and very useful adage. But this is not the time for a lesson. I shall simply ask you one question: do you think it right that the dying should be denied food and drink?'

Yolanda was momentarily silenced. She had never heard this before but she, like Girald, noticed a tiny movement from

Raimon. Girald, who had been looking for it all this time, pounced at once. 'This is hardly news to you, is it, Raimon, because I'll bet that's what happened to your mother. Some bullying Perfectus told her she must never eat again after he had offered her what they call the "consolation". Consolation! She wasn't consoled, was she? She was starved. Needlessly.' He paused. 'Painfully.' His voice took on a singsong quality. 'Day by day. Hour by hour. Minute by minute. Second by second. And all at the say-so of some fraudster claiming to be "perfect". Perhaps, without this Perfectus, your mother would have survived and even now be baking bread for you at home.'

It was a happy coincidence for Girald that Raimon's last cheerful thoughts of his mother had been of her baking. It was an effort to keep staring fixedly ahead and he knew Girald could feel his effort. The Inquisitor's voice became like the stroke of a tiger's paw. 'Catholics, Raimon, do not believe such rubbish. Not at all. What we offer is hope. Now, throw over the Cathar nonsense and come to those who offer not starvation but comfort to the afflicted and your shackles will be removed at once. You will be completely free to go.' His voice was mesmerizing and, as he intended, was now the voice of reason in the room.

Yolanda's arms unclenched themselves a little from her sides. Uncle Girald must have mellowed, she thought. He was not quite so dreadful. All Raimon had to do was agree and this would be over. That would be easy. After all, what did he care about the technicalities of religion? And what Girald had said! Starvation. Madame Belot had starved to death. That really was worse than any penance Simon Crampcross could devise. Raimon should have told her. He surely did not imagine she would have told anybody else. Involuntarily, she moved towards him, wanting to comfort.

The Inquisitor did not stop her. The girl could be useful, for Raimon was still saying nothing. He waited for a moment then began again. 'There's another thing, Raimon. A boy like you, of an age to fight, will naturally be thinking of the Occitan herself. You'll be aware of her – our – present danger. Do you ever, I wonder, stop to examine the root of that danger?' Girald moved back now, to embrace a wider audience. 'The truth is that the Occitan is not King Louis's enemy. His enemy is only the Cathars. Without them, there would be no war here and no need for any bloodshed. King Louis doesn't want to wipe out the Occitan, he wants – indeed, it's his Christian duty – to wipe out the heretics. No true Catholic can stand by as they preach their evil doctrines. So if you care about the Occitan, if you truly want to help her, you must turn Catholic and denounce those heretics who threaten to destroy her.'

Much to Girald's satisfaction, there was a murmuring. Some servants were very pale but for many his words had struck home. Get rid of the Cathars. Live in peace. The Inquisitor would leave. King Louis would go back to Paris. It was a message many wanted to hear.

Raimon heard the murmurings, saw the faces and now chose to speak. 'Denounce the heretics? Hand them over to be burnt? Is this how we treat our neighbours in the Occitan? Is this how we treat anybody?' His voice was sharp and commanding. The murmuring ceased. The picture the Inquisitor painted became murkier.

Girald twitched. Blast the boy. Silence would have been better now. 'We burn to save, Raimon.'

'Burning, starving, what's the difference?'

'We burn with God's authority. The Cathars starve with the devil's.'

'They say the other way round.'

Girald's eyes gleamed. Success. 'So you know what they say.'

'You said it yourself. Know your enemy.'

Girald blinked. 'So they are your enemy too?'

'Everybody who kills for God is my enemy.' Raimon's voice rang out like a bell. Girald was not the only one who could address the whole room. 'Why do you listen to this man?' he demanded of everybody, sparing nobody. 'We are the people of Amouroix in Occitan. We know what's right and wrong. Let's not listen to this any more.'

People could not help paying attention, but though they nodded and even gave small cheers, when Raimon caught their eyes individually they looked down and shuffled their feet. The only people who persisted were Gui and Guerau, who stamped and clapped. Girald had them removed.

Raimon looked to the benches behind the Inquisitor's chair. Berengar was nervously admiring, Aimery was frowning and Hugh, so far as he could tell, was bored. Nobody was going to rise on his behalf. He had failed. His eyes briefly met Hugh's and Hugh allowed his to drop first.

Raimon was mistaken. Hugh was not bored. It was true that, to begin with, he had been watching the proceedings as a Roman senator might have watched his fiftieth circus: with a kind of bloodless detachment, but when Raimon had appeared, his interest had sharpened considerably. It was clear from Yolanda's reaction that this boy was no friend. No, indeed. Hugh realised something he had taken no account of before: he had a rival, and this made his intended, whose fascinations were already far above what he had imagined they would be, much more of a catch. Bored? Not a bit of it.

Yolanda herself, with Brees now pressed against her legs, was both thrilled and aghast at Raimon's outburst. It seemed so obvious to her what he should do. He should just say that he wanted nothing to do with the Cathars, which was true, and mumble something about Catholicism, which everybody would know he didn't really mean but which would satisfy Girald. Then they could be out in the hills again, swimming, or riding, or making chains of flowers in memory of his mother, or just sitting as they sometimes did, breathing and being. Yet the thought of Girald crowing was intolerable. She moved and Aimery was on her at once. 'Stay still, Yola,' he hissed. 'Can't you see this isn't finished yet?'

'But Raimon's right, Aimery. We do know what's right and wrong, and burning people must be wrong. You think so too. You must. You should say so.'

'Ssssh.'

Girald was waiting, tiny beads of moisture on his upper lip, his bowels beginning to churn as they often did when his stomach was completely empty. He needed to finish this and lie down. He crossed his hands below his belt for support. 'Are you saying that you, Raimon Belot, know what is right or wrong better than a king or an anointed priest?'

The room was silent again. Raimon knew at once that he had lost any final chance of carrying the room with him. However, he had not lost everything. He had seen the Flame, had held it. It had, in some way, chosen him. The thought stiffened his resolve. He was not going to back down. 'That's exactly what I'm saying.'

Girald's face convulsed as his insides lurched again. He dared not have hoped for such a good answer. He clasped his hands tighter as his bowels contracted. 'Do you hear that? The boy condemns himself.'

'And I'll do it again if you want me to.' Raimon lifted unclouded eyes to his interrogator.

'There's no need,' Girald said quickly. He turned and addressed the crowd directly again. 'Now, all those who wish to follow Raimon Belot, who is claiming to be the new Methuselah and the new Messiah all in one, step forward. Don't be shy! Didn't you hear him? He knows better than me, better than any king, better than the Pope himself or even a Cathar Perfectus how to get to heaven. He is Jesus Christ himself.'

'That's not what –'

'SILENCE! You have declared yourself. I am simply going to lay out how things are.' He grasped his hands together in the tunnel of his sleeves. He could feel bile in his throat. 'You are quite free, my friends, to follow this new Messiah. Do not let me stop you. I will only warn you that if you do, you too will be a heretic – not a Cathar heretic, of course, but a new species: perhaps we could call you Raimonians. Yes, that's a good name. So, you can burn with your new leader, or he can burn alone. Which is it to be?'

'Nobody's going to burn.' Berengar spoke up at last. 'I forbid it.'

Girald dismissed him with a contemptuous wave. 'Who wields the greater power, a count or an Inquisitor?'

'Well, an Inquisitor, naturally. The church always comes first, for the church is guided by God. I don't dispute that. But I —'

'The boy will burn this afternoon.'

'No, no, Uncle,' Yolanda could hardly breathe, 'you've misunderstood. Raimon's not saying he knows better than everybody, are you, Raimon? Tell him. Tell him.'

'My dear, that's exactly what he's saying and you know exactly how things work. If you have a diseased tree, do you leave it to infect others?'

'No, Uncle Girald, but men are not trees.'

'I agree. Men are not trees. Men have free will. They can change their minds.' He knitted his fingers. 'Let's see if we can make Raimon change his, shall we?' His bowels began a new agony of twisting just as he realised that he had got a little carried away. Berengar was right. Nobody was going to burn that afternoon because to light a pyre Girald required authorisation from a higher figure than himself. He was still too newly appointed. His fingers felt slimy. He was going to look silly unless — he turned to Aimery. Aimery would help him get Raimon exactly where he wanted him. They spoke quietly and then Girald coughed. 'I wonder if we should send for your father and sister.'

Raimon swallowed. 'Leave them alone.'

'That's not really possible, unless —' Girald used the pause to good effect '— unless we go back to the beginning. I shall ask you again whether your mother was a good woman, and if you say "yes" I will know that a Perfectus visited your house when she was dying. This information will be useful to me and I like useful information. It might even be useful enough for me to find mercy in my heart and leave your father and sister at home. But if you won't tell me, well, I shall send for them and see what they have to say.' This was a gamble for Girald. Raimon might remain silent, voluntarily turning himself into a martyr. Then Girald would have to concede that the pyre would have to wait. But what child would condemn his own flesh and blood? This was, Girald knew, the crudest form of blackmail, and Girald did not like anything crude. But his insides were crippling him. At his next trial he must make sure the accused had no opportunity to reply.

Raimon was aware of everybody in the room: the crowd losing sympathy; Yolanda sunk beside Brees; Hugh, sitting like an observer at a play; Aimery, looking at the ceiling; and the count with his head in his hands. He could not let his father and Adela burn, and they would burn, or at least Adela would because she would never give in. He was beaten and he knew it. He said it quickly. 'Yes,' he whispered, and then, because a whisper seemed an admission of a weakness he did not feel, he said it again, boldly. 'Yes. Yes. My mother was a good woman.'

The whole room groaned in pity and relief. Raimon only heard Yolanda.

Girald leant towards him and the questions, learnt from a list, came tumbling out. 'Were you present at your mother's consoling?'

'Yes.'

'Did you lay your hands on her with a Perfectus?'

'Yes.'

'Did you say the words?'

'Yes.'

'Do you know the name of the Perfectus?'

'Yes.'

'Well,' Girald barked. 'What is it?'

'The White Wolf.'

'And where is this White Wolf now?'

'I don't know.'

'But you know where all the Cathar hiding places are.'

Though nothing would have pleased Raimon more than the White Wolf's capture, he would go so far and no further. 'I don't know where he is.'

Girald considered, and then made up his mind. This was enough for his purpose. 'Finally we have it,' he said, and his voice boomed. Even his bowels gave him temporary celebratory respite. 'I knew you would eventually turn –' he chose the word as carefully as an archer chooses his arrow '– telltale.'

The taunt sang around the hall and though he had suspected it was coming, it still thumped straight into Raimon's gut. Telltale! What a sting that word had. He could see it written on the walls, murmured in the taverns, inscribed on his tombstone. Telltale! Telltale! He would have preferred 'traitor'. A telltale sounded so coy, so like a sneak and Raimon had always hated sneaks. It didn't matter that everybody knew why he'd given in. It was still terrible to him, and worse, that he had tried to rally the people of Castelneuf behind him and he'd failed. He had made himself a pitiable figure by not realising how often, except in dreams, even in a crowd fear trumps heroism. And all this in front of Hugh.

Only when, as a last insult, Girald produced the prescribed uniform of the outed and shamed heretic, a tabard of rough canvas garishly decorated with yellow crosses, and ordered him to wear it at work and rest for evermore, was he tempted to proclaim that the Flame belonged to him and that if people rallied behind him, together they could save the Occitan. But it would have been a lie. The Flame was not his. Parsifal had warned him not to come here and he had disobeyed him. So he said nothing.

Girald completed his triumph in a travesty of amiability. 'What a help you've been, Raimon,' he said. 'You've certainly earned the reprieve for your family, and as for you yourself, well, people, especially children, always wait for the first telltale and after that they all join in. Before the week's out I'll know every heretic and heretic's hiding place in Castelneuf. If anybody has scruples, they can say to themselves, "If Raimon Belot's helping Inquisitor Girald, we better help too".' His tongue was sticky. 'Help him put on the tabard, Sanchez, and don't forget, Raimon, that it will be the duty of anybody who catches you without it to report to me so that you can be dealt with in the appropriate manner.' Then he left the room because his bowels would wait no longer.

The tabard was forced over Raimon's head and when he re-emerged, he could not avoid Hugh. The perfect knight had taken Yolanda's hand, and the message Raimon took from both his glance and his clasp, was that he did not intend to let it go. In a morning of very bad moments, that was the worst moment of all.

THE BEAR HUNT

Fear compresses time and fear now engulfed my town of Castelneuf and permeated throughout my lands and amongst my people. No longer could they pretend to live in a cocoon, immune to what was going on elsewhere. The world had come to them and they had to decide how to deal with it. The fear they felt did not spread like a stain. It manifested itself in a sudden breathlessness, a sudden jolting as they walked down the street. There was no panic, such as comes with a natural disaster, just a leaden sense of foreboding interspersed with these jolts. People still went about their daily toil, but with heads bowed, like nuns. The most innocuous enquiries about health or shared duties were greeted with silence.

Girald's 'telltale' prediction came true. After Raimon had been forcefully paraded through the town, his yellow-crossed tunic hideously bright, Simon Crampcross sat in the small square in front of his church, wagging his finger and urging people to come forward and reveal the identity of all the Cathars in the district. His theme was very clear: if Raimon could help the Inquisitor, they could too. He was very persuasive. Singly and in groups, people trickled up to the château, some dragging their feet, others walking with determined strides, the quicker to get their betrayal over with. They betrayed longstanding neighbours. They betrayed friends. Some betrayed those against whom they had a grudge. Others betrayed anybody at all because the very act of betrayal, they thought, would make their own families proof against the Inquisitor. Slowly, the cellars, which had been used previously only for storage or children's games, were transformed into prisons. Sicart and Adela disappeared and Castelneuf became a town of living ghosts with Girald's black shadow king of them all. There was still talk of the Flame, for scouts went out to search for it every day. But since it never showed itself, just surviving and getting through became the most important thing in the minds of the ordinary people. If they could just hold their breath, then sooner or later this would pass and life would be normal again.

Not for Raimon. Life, for him, would never be normal again. After he had been released, he had thrown his tabard into the river and run back to the cave. As he neared it, he had recited, to the pounding of his feet, 'He must be there, the Blue Flame must be there.' He felt as though he had nobody and nothing else. Pushing back the tree roots, he couldn't see anything at first. 'Sir Parsifal!' he cried out, forgetting to be careful in his need. 'Sir Parsifal!'

'Just Parsifal, please. Really, I shall have to put up a notice,' came a voice from behind him.

Raimon spun round. He could hold on no longer. 'I shouldn't have – it was – I said – they wouldn't – I thought –

I lost –' He stood, trembling, in spasms that rocked him on his feet. Parsifal moved towards him tentatively. The boy's need of him was almost intoxicating, but also a little alarming. 'Tell me everything,' he said, and remained quite still until Raimon's flood had run its course and the boy was sagging, empty of everything. Only then did he bring the Flame out again from under his cloak, gave the box a little shake and held it in front of Raimon's face.

The Flame did nothing at first, but then something of the boy's despair seemed to touch it, deep in its fiery heart. It folded itself down, then slowly wound itself up, not smoothly, but jerkily like a clockwork toy and then, instead of shedding light, it began to draw what light there was into itself until Parsifal and Raimon could not see each other, but could only look at it. Gradually, it filled up the vacuum in which Raimon had been drowning, until his trembling ceased. It was hard to despair when the Flame was so alive, so mesmerising and so confident. It reached out to him, smoothing and soothing, until he felt as though he were looking at it properly for the first time. It was not just offering comfort, it was telling him something, he was sure of that. Perhaps, if he looked hard enough, he would under-stand, but when it died down and he found himself staring at Parsifal's blackberry bush of a beard, he was still wondering. 'Well,' Parsifal said, 'that was something.' Then he took Raimon gently by the arm, sat him down in the cave's most comfortable corner and gave him rabbit stew.

Yolanda was confined to the château by Girald and she did not dare to disobey. If she did, so Girald told her, others would be punished. She believed him. She kept herself sane by tending to Brees, having his leg set properly and bathing his wounds. She tried to imagine where Raimon was and what he was doing, but the pictures she conjured up were almost too wretched to be borne. As soon as Brees was strong enough, she decided she would send him out to look, but frightened by what Pierre and Sanchez might do if they caught him, decided against it. Hugh, careful not to press his advantage too obviously, sent his groom up with pastes and tonics for the dog and was glad to find that Yolanda did not turn them away.

The person most openly agitated was Aimery. It was unpleasant in the château with Girald's dreary courts, the servants skulking and whispering and the bread oven cold because the baker was imprisoned in the cellar. This was not the Amouroix he wanted to show Hugh. And he was nervous. Yolanda had stopped combing her hair. Perhaps Hugh would think twice about marrying her and then this fine chance to link Castelneuf to France would be lost. Moreover, Aimery was disturbed by news of the rebellion. Raymond of Toulouse, enjoying some small successes, had not yet sent for Count Berengar and his forces to bolster up his troops, but it could not be long until he did and then Aimery would be caught in a trap. It was one thing for his father to send a letter of support to Raymond, and quite another for Castelneuf troops to be seen in battle at his side. King Louis would never forgive that. And, so Aimery told himself again and again, there was no way at all that Raymond was ever going to win and the Occitan remain free. Small successes were only putting off the inevitable end, for the French war machine was relentless. It would ride over the Flame, ride over them all, and Aimery was not going to be crushed under the weight when, with a little judicious manoeuvring, he could enjoy life not as a powerless Occitanian nobleman but as a rich and powerful member of the French court. All the stuff about the Occitanian soul, all that nonsense encapsulated in the Song of the Flame was romance, and the days of such romance were over.

However, slumped in the main hall, unlit and stale-aired, the glory of the French court seemed very far away. For now he sat, feet splayed, flicking the top off a tankard of ale, staring at the moth-eaten bear's head and listening to the doleful tread of Girald's victims. He wished the Cathars at the bottom of the sea. Burn them, drown them, serve them up on toast, they were nothing but an irritant and his father should have done something about them years before. His father! Aimery could hardly think of the count without losing his temper. The man was like the bear's head: thread-bare and in urgent need of replacement. Then, with a sudden exclamation, he tossed the ale into the rushes and walked swiftly out of the hall towards the stables.

An hour later, his favourite horse was saddled and he was in the kennel courtyard giving instructions to the huntsman. Several hunt pages were already clutching nets and leather couples. The whinnying, anticipatory howling and low grind of spears on the sharpening stone were just what he needed to hear. This was what Castelneuf should be like: efficient and ready to do its master's bidding. He had changed his clothes and, warm in his red-sleeved woollen tunic, his feet encased in two layers of pigskin and his beard finely brushed, his spirits were rising. He sent a page for Hugh. Never mind the cold bread oven, he would show him something today that he'd never forget.

He hoped to get away quickly, but when the kennel doors were opened and the hounds burst out, Yolanda appeared. 'I'm coming too,' she said.

Aimery was dismissive. 'You know you can't, Yola, and we're only going to hunt for food. Besides, I don't think that old creature you usually ride could keep up with Argos.' He patted the arched neck in front of him.

'If you're hunting for the pot she can easily keep up. Please.'

Aimery regarded her quizzically. She was so transparent. She thought Raimon was in the hills and wanted to find him. 'No,' he said. 'You can't come.'

More men appeared. Yolanda frowned. 'Why do you need spears and crossbows?'

'You never know, we might disturb a bear!' Hugh was right behind her.

Yolanda looked at him and then swiftly back at Aimery. 'You're not going hunting for the pot at all are you! But you can't go bear hunting. It's too early. They'll only just have woken and some will have cubs!' She seized Argos's rein.

'Look, Yola, that's my business. Let go.'

'No, I won't. If you're going after bears, Uncle Girald should know,' she said in her most dangerous voice. 'Bear hunting has always been forbidden in Amouroix during Lent. You'd better clear it with him. You won't want to sin by mistake and go to hell.' She called to one of the pages. 'Denys, go and get the Inquisitor at once.'

Aimery gripped the pommel of his saddle. 'Come back here.' Denys looked uncertain.

'Go on, Denys. The Inquisitor.' Yolanda could sound just like her mother.

'Alright, you win,' Aimery said. 'If you can find yourself a decent mount, you can come too. But if anything happens to you, I take no responsibility and I'll tell Father and Uncle Girald that you tagged along without my permission. Oh, and you can't bring Brees. He'll just get in amongst the hounds and upset them.' That would surely put her off.

'Brees is in no fit state to go anywhere,' replied Yolanda at once. 'I've put wine in his water so he's sleeping. He won't even notice I've gone.'

'Well then,' said Aimery, still determined, 'it's just a pity you haven't a proper horse. Bad luck.' He kicked Argos and made him jump.

'I'll find one.'

'We can't wait any longer. Come on, Hugh. Alain, where are my gloves?' His squire handed them to him.

'Just one minute!' cried Yolanda.

Aimery laughed at her. 'How will you conjure up a horse in a minute?'

Alain made a sympathetic face, but shrugged.

'I'll lend you a horse, Lady Yolanda.' Hugh was once again her saviour. 'Would you allow me?'

Yolanda threw a glance of fiery triumph at her brother. 'Allow you? I'd be very grateful.'

He swung easily off his horse. 'Come,' he said, 'you shall choose.'

Aimery tried not to smile. This was turning out well.

All four of Hugh's spare mounts moved in their stalls when their master approached, but Hugh spoke to only two, a grey with a lean, rather sorrowful face, its mane and tail sparse and almost white, and a heavier black, with a Roman nose and a criss-cross of white-haired scars across its rump. 'Which would you like?' Hugh asked her. 'They've both seen a great deal of service. I shall retire them at the end of this campaigning season. Some men sell them for meat, you know, but I think they deserve better.' He didn't, really, and had always sent his horses for meat, but he knew it would please her. Courtship was not about truth.

Yolanda breathed in the horses' leathery smell and stroked their noses. 'What are their names?'

'The grey's Galahad and the black's Bors.'

'I'll take Galahad,' said Yolanda at once. 'I'm sure they're both as gallant as their namesakes, but Galahad was the Perfect Knight.'

'The Perfect Knight? Oh, yes! Of course.' Making a mental note to brush up on Arthur's blessed Table, Hugh called for the grey to be saddled and helped Yolanda to mount himself. When they returned, Yolanda raised her eyebrows at Aimery and he doffed his hat and grinned. She knew just what his grin meant and it made her smart.

The mounted huntsman, noting only that everybody was now ready, blew his horn and the hounds tumbled over themselves like children anticipating a picnic, a mixed pack today, led by sad-faced, long-eared Farvel, the count's best scenting bloodhound. Amongst the loose hounds, two sharp-eyed greyhounds and a few of the more impetuous running hounds were on leashes. With keen eyes and keener noses they all formed an undulating carpet of swaying sterns, flapping ears and dripping tongues. Hugh thought they looked a rabble.

Last to appear, like prize boxers before a bout, were the broad-headed, prick-eared alaunts and glowering mastiffs, their collars studded with the broken teeth of previous quarry. They were muzzled and wore their restraints not as badges of subjection but of pride as they surveyed the noisy scene, keeping their own sterns clamped tight between their hind legs. Now Hugh felt a prickle. A bite by one of those could take off your leg.

Aimery rode directly behind the pack with Hugh and Yolanda behind him, the horses scraping over slimy cobbles. Yolanda clung to the front of her saddle when Galahad, throwing off his years, kicked up his heels. As she crunched back into the hard-seated saddle, she missed the soft round-ness of her old mare's unsaddled back and the feel of Raimon's ribs where she was used to clasping her hands. 'Just sit tight,' Hugh advised. 'He'll settle when we're over the river.' His legs were shapely in leaf green and his jerkin, cleverly cut to disguise a thickening waist, was embroidered with yellow roses. No girl could be unaware that he was a handsome companion.

He stuck closely by Yolanda. She was pale, her face too thin and too shell-like for real beauty. He imagined her skin cool and slightly forbidding to the touch. Cool and forbid-ding! He was turning poet! Hugh was surprising himself. Though the girl was so unhappy and withdrawn and the dance she had danced on the night he arrived had never been repeated, increasingly he found her a drink of clear water after too much rich wine. In comparison with her, the women of Paris, with their capricious grace and self-conscious chastity, seemed cloying and contrived. Hugh was no romantic. He knew he would tire of any woman in the end, but by that time, with luck, the houses of Amouroix and des Arcis would be linked by legions of strong and pretty children. Meanwhile, he began to look forward to Yolanda adding glancing spring light to his grey northern castle, for she had a dazzle about her that her brother certainly lacked. As she relaxed onto Galahad, allowing him his head when he snorted as they passed a tethered pig, he laughed quietly. 'Hugh des Arcis,' he said to himself, 'you must take care not to fall in love.'

The whole party jostled joyfully out of the gate and streamed down the main road out of the town, apart from the alaunts and the mastiffs who padded with methodical aggression. Lumping along in their wake came the baggage wagon laden with weapons and food. The river was soon crossed and they were past the cemeteries, through the sunny meadows and into the woods. Amid the black poplars and the blossoming chestnuts some of the gaze-hounds made an unsuccessful foray after what, from their frenzy, Aimery was convinced was a lynx and turned out to be a passing shadow. Then they broke through the woods and headed down the valley and towards the mountains. The sky was not completely clear and the lower clouds were already smudging the mountain tops and threatening to descend farther. But Aimery sniffed the wind and was satisfied. The day promised reasonable light and good scent. Hugh would be mightily impressed. He let out a whoop, which startled a hare, and at once a wild hawk rose lazily over the easy prey, then plunged down, successfully binding the hare to her until one of the running hounds frightened her off and despatched it himself.

At the first blood of the day, Aimery's blood tingled. He kicked his horse. 'Come on, huntsman! Faster!' he cried and set off at a hard gallop. Galahad leapt forward and Yolanda's hair tumbled loose. She could feel the wind tugging at it and suddenly her spirits rose. She would find Raimon. They would find each other. Things would go well today.

The hounds poured on for mile after mile, up further hills, across ever more uneven plateaus and then plunging down into unseen and unexpected valleys until eventually they reached the steeper slopes of the mountains. Here the baggage wagon was unloaded. Spears, bows, arrows and nets would have to be carried now. After a short breather and a drink at a stream, they set off again, this time up true mountain tracks with Aimery talking and swapping jokes with Hugh until the paths grew too narrow to ride abreast. Then, in single file, often hardly visible to each other under trees clustered and bent from the wind, some with snow still wedged in branches never touched by the sun, they spoke only to their horses, encouraging them as they stretched their shoulders and puffed. After two hours, the slopes cleared as the thicker forests sank away. Yolanda, with Galahad now steady as a rock beneath her, felt as though she could ride into the sky.

The huntsman led them a circuitous, circling route, trying to save the energy of both hound and horse but the climb was inexorable, each peak higher than the last and each plateau more rocky. Everybody's ears throbbed to the boom of heavy water. On every side, the snowmelt turned winter's icy grottoes back into falls and cascades.

Deep in the shadows, and often having to make wide

detours to find cover, Parsifal and Raimon followed the hunt. The singing of the hounds had alerted them in the Castelneuf valley and Raimon had picked out Yolanda at once, on a warhorse rather than on the old mare they used to ride together, and with Hugh beside her. His heart grew hot. When he saw the boy's face, Parsifal had not even suggested that they should not follow. What harm could it do? He tucked the Flame away carefully. It did not object.

After two hours of heavy climbing, the hunting party rested again whilst Aimery despatched five archers to pick off mountain goats and ibex for the kitchens. Sitting on a tussock, Yolanda looked about her hopefully. Just a glimpse of Raimon was all she wanted, just a glimpse. Hugh watched her.

Aimery, however, had eyes only for the mastiffs and alaunts. All the other hounds had flopped down but they remained standing, only small drools betraying the strain of their exertions. He admired them greatly. After twenty minutes, he remounted. 'Remove the muzzles,' he said.

The huntsman blew the *prepare* and the air was quickly alive with expectation. Yolanda found herself swung expertly into the saddle. Galahad was tense beneath her, banging his head up and down to shake off even her light touch on the rein. 'He'll stop the minute we get going, and I'll be with you,' Hugh murmured. She nodded. In her head, she was already discussing with Raimon how quickly, with the music of the chase echoing from peak to peak, the terrible, beautiful hunt became the only thing.

Farvel was sent off first, pulling his kennel boy over the tufted grass, searching through the rocks, his nose working both ground and air. 'Don't crowd him,' admonished the huntsman as Aimery surged forward. Aimery reined in. 'Release him, boy,' the huntsman ordered. Once free, the bloodhound cast a wider net, sometimes vanishing from sight as he quartered the more open country seeking that scent for which he had been born. There was nothing. After twenty minutes, when tension had curdled almost into sickness, the huntsman gave three short dispiriting bursts of his horn, calling the bloodhound back. 'We'll move further up,' he said.

The horses, glad to be on the move, barged and jostled. Yolanda clutched Galahad's mane.

They moved round the hill, a wide, straggling group, and onto the next plateau. The sun was higher but the cloud had increased and the temperature was dropping. They halted. The bloodhound was sent off again. Again he circled, patiently and deliberately, his heavy jowls swaying. He knew his job and would not be hurried. He disappeared for what seemed like hours. Nothing. The running hounds, whose excitement had flattened into boredom, were sitting facing in every direction, some scratching. One sloped off and had to be whipped back.

Aimery was getting impatient. 'We must go higher still, huntsman,' he cried angrily. 'We should have brought more bloodhounds and sent out several parties. What were you thinking?'

The huntsman raised his hand. 'If anybody can find a bear, Farvel can,' he said with his slow wisdom. 'Don't you worry, sir, the day has hardly started.'

Aimery muttered under his breath. He was not good at tension.

They moved off, winding their way ever closer to the snow-line. The ground was stippled white, the hoar frost turning transparent underfoot. To their right, behind a break of trees peeping from a sheltered dip, they could hear a muffled boom and see plumes of spray.

In the end, they were rewarded. On the edge of the trees, Farvel was standing on a flat rock, quite rigid, his tail stuck out like a weathervane. 'Soft,' whispered the huntsman to Aimery, who was crowded up beside him, eyes straining. 'Wait a moment, sir. Let him get properly fixed.' Aimery was breathing heavily, the huntsman hardly at all.

The bloodhound crept forward, always going straight. The huntsman began to coo like a lover to his beloved. 'Oh, Farvel, my beauty! Oh, Farvel, my clever! Keep on, my lovely.' An ear twitched back. When the old hound reached the next flat stone, he stopped again, but this time he couldn't help himself and lurched forward, bellowing his triumph. A bear! A bear! At once, boredom utterly forgotten, the running hounds were wild and furious. 'Let us at him, let us at him,' they bayed as every instinct compelled them. Behind, the prick-eared alaunts and mastiffs strained and sulked and scowled, licking their teeth because they knew it was not their turn, not yet. Their keepers kept away from their heads.

The bloodhound ran a hundred yards and the huntsman was hard after him. 'Keep the coupled hounds behind. We'll need them to be fresh,' he threw over his shoulder as the loose hounds streamed onto the scent and he after them, his horn a peon of pride and exhortation. Nobody was tired now.

For horse, hound and man the terrain was wicked,

speckled with hidden rocks only visible if touched with snow. It was mad to gallop, but gallop they did. Galahad tossed off the restraining rein and Yolanda, her mouth half open, was carried to the front, Hugh on one side, Alain on the other, with Aimery always up with the huntsman.

The bear's scent was strong and the hounds, expecting any moment to find their quarry at bay, did not spare themselves. For the first hour, they ran like fury, only occasionally stopping to reaffirm the scent. It was overpowering. But where was the bear? It was impossible to keep up such a pace and as they scrambled further into the maze of rising slopes, the pace settled a little. By midday, they had had a glorious chase, but still the quarry was unseen. They had to catch their breaths. The hounds plunged into a stream, slurping up water and shaking their ears and Aimery flung himself off, exhilarated but disheartened. They could not return home empty-handed, surely. The huntsman, beckoning him over, pointed to a far hillside beyond a hidden valley. The lie of the trees was broken. Caves. 'You reckon he's heading there?' Aimery asked.

'Not he, she,' the huntsman replied with a crooked grin. He ran his hand over an imprint in the grass and smelt it. 'Look,' he said. Two sets of smaller prints were invisible, but experienced eyes had noticed where the top of the sward had been brushed by stomachs very close to the ground. 'Cubs.'

Yolanda exclaimed at once, 'Oh, Aimery, let's stop then. You know we shouldn't be hunting bears so early anyway. The hounds are tired and we've had such a run. Let's turn round and leave the bears be.' She felt guilty. She had not forgotten Raimon, or only for a moment, but she could not deny that she had not wanted the run to end. She could see obstinacy in Aimery's shoulders before ever he spoke. She cajoled. 'If we leave the cubs, there'll be more bears to hunt later on.' It was a clever, though hopeless, ploy. Aimery wanted what he wanted and he wanted it now.

'Don't be silly, Yola,' he replied crisply. 'We'll sicken the hounds if we give up when they've worked so hard. Farvel has found us a bear and will expect us to get it.'

'Farvel can find something else.'

'Isn't that just typical of a girl,' Aimery called out so that everybody could hear. 'They don't seem to realise that hunting's not a pastime. We don't just give up because cubs are furry and have nice faces. Come, huntsman. We'll wait until the leashed hounds and the spearmen appear, then we'll go on.' He was back on his horse, leaving Yolanda to Hugh. Hugh looked sympathetic. 'Do you want to go on?' She shrugged, frowning. He lifted her into the saddle and then spurred his horse up the hill. Even he was overtaken by the excitement of the day.

The huntsman issued his orders to the hound keepers. 'We'll need you soon enough,' he said. 'Spread wide and keep those caves as your centre point. Steadily now.' This was a crucial moment of his day. The bear was near, but not quite near enough for certainty. Should the leashed greyhounds be released now, or kept for later? He called to his favourites. 'Come Baron, come Salter, come Belle, come Elegance.' They raised their heads like trusted generals at a council of war. The huntsman made a gesture. They were unleashed.

This time, as they set off, though Galahad still felt game beneath her, Yolanda felt no thrill. Any moment now, the bear and her cubs would break cover. Her throat was tight as Galahad's hooves scraped and thudded over grass and granite. The air had turned very cool and though rays of sunshine were still pouring molten gold lances onto distant plateaus, the clouds hovered, as if undecided whether to rise or fall. The hounds ran fast into the next valley and the riders all followed, holding their breath. When the huntsman's triumphantly blown '*I see bear*' finally came through, they cheered. They had galloped enough. They were ready for the next stage.

Blurred as an inkstain and unworried as yet, the bear was moving swiftly downhill towards the water spread over the valley floor. She knew just what she was doing for she knew this country well. The banking undergrowth would shield her until the cubs were ready to make a leisurely dash for the caves on the far hill. The clouds, if they just sank a little lower, would help. The cubs themselves were invisible to the hunters for their mother was pushing them on in front of her. But they were slow. She knew the moment the greyhounds had a glimpse of her, could sense the air shifting and beneath her paws, with her fine instincts, she could feel the vibrations of the heavy alaunts now lumbering into top gear. When they began to howl their ancient howl, she glanced behind her and at once changed course, pushing her cubs along the water instead of over it, to the steeper end of the valley and thicker trees. There were caves there too, not as safe as the far caves, but they might have to do.

The hunt now took on a kind of delirium. The spear-carriers and pages, forgetting their weariness, nearly killed themselves in their anxiety not to be left behind. The huntsman himself was gripped with terror, not only lest he lose the bear, but lest his hounds reach her prematurely and be mauled before he could help them. Aimery, lips scarlet in his beard, felt the same breathless suspension as he felt just before the flag went up at a tournament and even Hugh was leaning forward, his half-smile now the grimace of real effort. He was amazed at what he was witnessing. This was hunting like no other. Behind him, Yolanda, her lips as white as Aimery's were red, was silently urging the bear to hurry, hurry and every time the hounds' music hesitated, she prayed that the scent was lost and the animal escaped.

It was not to be. Had she been alone, the bear would have exhausted the hounds. However, the cubs would not be rushed and she would not leave them. She reached the undergrowth and pushed her way up its side. The land steepened very quickly, clumps of undergrowth interspersed with bare rock eroded by the weather, and the river falling in an uneven silver ladder of thunderous cascades, often disappearing completely. The bear forced her cubs up. There were flat stones at the top. They could cross the river there without losing any pace.

But inexorably, the distance between herself and the hounds narrowed. Even as she was climbing, she could hear them gaining on her until she knew that she must resort to her last option. She pushed the cubs nearly to the top of the fall and then took refuge on a high ledge with an overhang above and a hollow behind. It was not a good hollow, for the open back was too small for a quick escape for a large bear. Nevertheless, she could stand at the front, a snarling sentinel.

The hounds, in their determination, had scrabbled up the

climb using nooks and crannies for footholds. After them, having abandoned their horses, came the hunting party on all fours, like the hounds but rather less swift. In moments Yolanda's skirt was torn beyond mending as she hung onto treeroots and grasped at unsteady rocks. She was agile and fit, but it took her half an hour to reach where the hounds were now gathered, with Hugh panting as his squire pulled down branches for handholds, some way behind her. When Yolanda finally made it, she was grabbed by Alain and yanked to the side. Then she gasped.

The bear was scarcely twenty feet away, the hounds in a semicircle around her. It was hard to say who was keeping whom at bay. From their places in the semicircle, the alaunts and greyhounds made constant swift and highly focussed forays, with the running hounds diving about in their wake. Occasionally a greyhound would make a successful snap and draw blood, but the bear, with her heavy claws and unflinching courage, would roar and slap out, gouging deep scratches on rumps and flanks. Blood mixed with blood. One running hound, unluckier than the others, was swept up in a crushing embrace and then dropped underfoot. Another was raked all the way down one side, and fled, skin flapping. When she saw the human beings, the animal reared right up and Yolanda caught a glimpse of the cubs' beady eyes, staring out in bemusement from behind their mother's bulk.

Bows and metal-headed arrows were quickly distributed. Aimery took a spear and tested it on his shoulder, ready to throw.

'Wait! Wait, young master!' cried the huntsman. 'She's a big one, and, with those cubs, she'll not be for giving up. Throw that, and she'll be out and after you and I doubt we'll be able to stop her in time. It'll take two of you.' He called his pack back, ordering some of them re-leashed and leaving only two mastiffs and two alaunts loose to bring her down if things turned out badly. He spoke to Farvel, who would pick up the bear's scent again if, by mischance, another pursuit had to be made.

Aimery was irritated by the huntsman's peremptory tone. He knew as much about bear hunting as anybody, probably more. He fingered his spear. He could throw true, he knew he could, and this was the best chance he might have to get what he had come for: a bear's head of his own to replace his father's, and a pelt to give to Hugh. And what luck about the cubs. He could send them to King Louis as a gift. Twin pelts would certainly mark out Castelneuf as a place on the map. He balanced the spear on his shoulder, weighed it up and threw.

The force pitched him forward, and though the throw was true and pierced the skin above the bear's heart, it failed to kill her. With no hounds in front to protect him, Aimery stumbled straight into his wounded quarry's path and she was ready for him. Snapping the thick spearshaft as if it were an old twig, she lurched out, baring her yellow teeth and caught Aimery between forelegs outstretched in a deadly welcome.

The bowmen had no time to set their arrows before she had dropped back on all fours, Aimery underneath her, her small black eyes full of murder. Only one thing could save him and only Yolanda was quick enough to use it. She had listened to her father's stories more carefully than her brother. She began to yell. Noise alone might confuse the bear enough to make her glance back at her cubs and give Aimery an opportunity to crawl clear. Accordingly, she began to holler and caterwaul, singing, screaming, anything to get the bear's attention. Hugh, standing by her, jumped away thinking she had lost her mind, but the huntsman knew what she was doing and applauded, and so did somebody else. On the top of the overhang directly above the bear, Raimon was whirling, beating his arms against his sides. Not knowing from where she faced the biggest threat, the bear twisted away. In a trice, Aimery was pulled to safety.

At once three crossbowmen knelt, drawing back their strings with iron claws and aiming at the bear's unprotected belly, but Aimery, upright again, and knowing nothing of Raimon, ran in front of them. Now it was he who was shrieking. 'Death to any man who looses an arrow. This bear's mine!' He grabbed spears and threw a bundle to Hugh. 'Quick, here's a chance you'll seldom get again. Throw off your sword or she'll grab the baldric. We'll launch these in turns, first me, then you. That's how it's done! Hurry! Hurry!' The rush of adrenalin had made him wild. 'If anybody interferes, and that includes you, huntsman, I shall have them flogged, you understand. Ready, Hugh? This is just for us.'

Yolanda, wide-eyed at Raimon but desperate for the bear, grabbed Hugh's arm. 'Don't, Sir Hugh, don't. It's not right. She's fighting for her cubs! Stop it. Stop it now.' But Hugh, swept away by the smell of the beast and the biggest thrill of his life, was already preparing his first thrust.

The huntsman pulled Yolanda back. 'It's too late for that, lady. Your brother's set and if Sir Hugh doesn't play his part, that bear'll have Sir Aimery. Do you want him mauled to death?' She bit her fingers.

Within seconds, Hugh, Aimery and the bear were involved in a macabre dance. The two men dived towards her as she dived towards them, feinting first at one and then at the other. The loosed spears jabbed and cut. She retreated and batted the spears, first one way, then the other. The oil in her coat and Hugh's inexperience with bears proved a stout defence but she was all the time hampered by fear for her cubs. She fought hard but as if fettered on a chain, for she dared not leave the hollow.

'Loose the mastiffs,' Yolanda implored the huntsman. 'At least they'll kill her cleanly. Do it now!'

But the huntsman hesitated. A thick wet cloud was descending and soon sight would be hampered. If he sent his hounds in, they would be fighting blind. As huntsman, his first duty was to them.

From his perch above, Raimon heard Yolanda and he had no hesitation. His blood was hotter than either Aimery's or Hugh's but his goal different. He would not kill the bear, he would save it, and not just for Yolanda or for the cubs but for himself and me and for the whole of the Occitan, and for the Flame. The bear became, for Raimon, the symbol of every-thing he loved and those intent on killing her of everything he hated. For the first time for weeks, his head felt absolutely clear.

Straight away he leapt from the top of the crag and seized Aimery's discarded sword. He did not know what he shouted, but Aimery whipped round, his eyes wide with surprise. 'Raimon!' Then his teeth were gritted. 'Get back. This is nothing to do with you.' Raimon answered with a thrust that drew blood from Aimery's shoulder. Aimery parried with his spear, fearsome with temper and adrenalin. But even with all the temper in the world, he couldn't fight both Raimon and the bear simultaneously. 'Get away!' he cried. 'Don't be such a fool. Get away! Get away!' He turned to jab at the bear, but missed and Hugh, unsure what to do, retreated.

The bear hunkered down on all fours, bleeding and grunting and the hounds, sensing weakness, began to bay and strain. It was hard for the huntsman to keep control. Aimery swung his spear. The bear roared and then, as if somebody had snuffed out the sun, the light vanished. One moment everybody could see everything, the next moment, nothing. One of the drifting clouds that had threatened all day had finally swallowed them all up.

Aimery whirled round and round. 'Where are you now, Raimon! Are you defending the bear? She doesn't need a telltale like you, you know. She'd be better off defending herself.' He peered through the mist, his fury growing rather than diminishing as he realised that without Raimon's inter-ference, he would have had his bear's head by now.

'Put the spear down, Aimery, and I'll stop.' Raimon's voice was muffled and distorted as the air thrust his words back in his face.

'I certainly won't.' Aimery was unable to tell if the bear was advancing or retreating. He felt Raimon at his back again. 'Grab your sword, Hugh, and let's see off this self-confessed heretic.'

At once, Hugh dived for his weapon and felt Yolanda kick it away. Never mind. The Occitan was certainly living up to its riotous reputation. He would have quite a story to tell the king. With his spear tucked under his arm, he advanced on

Raimon from behind — at least he hoped that was what he was doing. Fighting in the mist was like fighting underwater. He didn't want to kill the boy, but if the boy was intent on killing Aimery, he would do what he had to do. Then he felt a thud on his back. He was round at once, and now there were two thickenings in the mist, one surely Raimon and the other so formless that he might have been part of the cloud itself. Only his steel was not cloudy, and his hands shone strangely white. Hugh felt a stinging in his thigh. In seconds he heard Aimery exclaiming. He had encountered the grey shape too.

Then, just as quickly as it had engulfed them, the cloud sank, leaving them stranded in a world above the world. Momentarily disorientated, Aimery stumbled and when he looked again, there was no grey man, only Raimon.

The hounds knew before the humans that the bear and her cubs had slipped away and that with the sun beating strongly again in this new-washed world, her scent would evaporate quickly. Farvel was up and ready but no order came. He stood, disconsolate, as the running hounds, back in picnic mood, snapped at butterflies and the greyhounds stretched their thin muzzles. At last, the mastiffs and alaunts sat down. Their day was ruined. The dogboys would suffer later.

Raimon was poised. 'You've never called me a heretic before.' He didn't care. He was still full of the bear and the Flame.

'But that's what you told us you are, Raimon.' Aimery gripped his spear anew.

'I'm a loyal Occitanian. Is that what you are?'

'Oh, we're all loyal Occitanians,' said Aimery, highly irritated at Raimon's deliberate affront. Every moment he had to spend in this silly conversation gave the bear more opportunity to escape, for the land beyond the river was flatter. She would be half a mile away by now and the horses were at the bottom of the climb. Cursing silently he turned back to Raimon. Here was one quarry he could dispatch. 'I care about the Occitan just as much as you do.'

'But about yourself first,' Raimon said.

'Are you accusing me of being a traitor?'

'There are lots of ways of being a traitor.'

'And there are lots of ways of being a fool. Come on, Raimon,' Aimery dropped his spear, 'if you really want the Occitan to survive, you must do more than save bears.'

'And you must do more than arrange marriages.'

'Ah,' Aimery paid more attention. 'Now we're getting to the crux. This isn't about the Occitan at all, is it, it's about Yolanda. You want to prove yourself, don't you, and win her, with all the dowry she'll have. Then the Belots would be rich, eh, Raimon. You might even be able to buy a knighthood for yourself. I mean, even Cathars like money and it's not as if Yola is unattractive.'

Raimon kept himself steady. 'You're going to sell her to a Frenchman and then perhaps you'll sell the Amouroix too.'

There was a noise from the hunt followers as Raimon's accusations rang out. Already frustrated, some were spoiling for a fight. They looked at Hugh with new eyes, and at Aimery himself. Aimery threw back his shoulders. 'That,' he said very clearly, 'cannot pass. Give me your sword, Alain.'

Yolanda sprang forward. Hugh blocked her. 'My dear, you must let them fight it out.'

'But it's quite unfair,' she cried, not stopping to think.

'Raimon's never learnt to fight with a sword. He's just a weaver!'

Aimery lowered his sword at once. 'Oh, my goodness, thank you, Yola. That's a very important reminder. Of course I can't fight "just a weaver". It would defile the whole notion of knighthood, a bit like fighting a woman. What shall we do? Wait! I've an idea! Somebody send for some spindles and we can fight with them. Yolanda would like that, Raimon, because then the advantage would lie entirely with you.' The effect was just as he intended. People laughed and the mutterings ceased. Now this was just a fight over insults.

Raimon, though, was not looking at Aimery, he was looking at Yolanda. 'Just a weaver'. He couldn't believe she'd said that. 'Just a weaver'. It was like that laugh all over again, except worse. Knowing what she'd done the moment she'd done it, Yolanda had her hand over her mouth, tears streaming down her cheeks.

Aimery saw at once. Yolanda really was helping his cause today. 'Look, Raimon,' he said so that everybody could hear. 'You're finished here. Leave Castelneuf. Leave the Amouroix. Your life lies elsewhere. Go on. I'll not pursue you. I'll not even tell Girald you're not wearing your heretic's tabard.' He waited, and when Raimon didn't move, he shrugged. So they would fight and Aimery would win. It was a pity, in one way, but then, so many things were.

Raimon began to circle. It was quite true that he'd never fought properly with a sword. However, he did not need teaching that hot anger is less useful than cold strategy. He wondered, as he tried to balance himself, about the Flame. Would it suddenly decide to help him? Would Parsifal? He prayed not. The Flame was for the Occitan. This was for himself. He would show Yolanda that he was not 'just a weaver'. And he would show Hugh.

There was limited space in front of the hollow where the bear had been and Aimery stood more or less stationary as Raimon launched his first assault. Their weapons thudded dully against each other. Raimon circled again. Again the weapons thudded, and then again. Nobody made any headway. At the bottom of the slope the horses moved uneasily in the everchanging shadows.

Aimery warded off the blows with lazy ease as he calculated how best this could end. Should he simply kill Raimon outright? That would be very simple. Or should he beat him down and force him, at swordpoint, to crawl away? He glanced at Yolanda. No. That wouldn't do. He knew his sister. Perhaps the best outcome was to kill Raimon, but purely in self defence. Yes, he could manoeuvre that. He began to spar.

But it was not as easy to direct the fight as he thought, for Raimon quickly understood that he had one major advantage. Against a trained man, Aimery would have been confident, for the moves each made would have had a certain predictable choreography. Against the untrained Raimon, there was nothing predictable at all. Nor, which was not helpful, did Aimery know if Raimon really wanted to kill him. It took him quite a few minutes to realise that Raimon did not know himself.

Thud, clash, and always the rush of the river.

Thud, clash, and the river singing the chorus.

When no progress was made on either side, the squires and pages began to whisper amongst themselves and the hounds to whine. Rain threatened, and the day which had started so brightly soured further.

The two combatants galvanised themselves. They couldn't go on like this for ever. Raimon's strokes became wilder swipes and Aimery began a steady onslaught to press him towards the hollow. A quick, underarm thrust and blood was drawn on both sides. The pages stopped whispering.

Raimon had to move back, but would not be pushed towards the hollow. Instead, with the same instinct as the bear, he moved towards the water, step by step, blow by blow, forcing Aimery to follow. At last, he could feel the edge of the bank. The river ran flat here for a short length before abandoning itself to the rocky pool about forty feet below. On the boulders set at crazy angles across the top of the waterfall, the prints of the bear and her cubs were still clearly visible. Raimon leapt onto the first. Aimery lunged at him and missed, then leapt himself. His landing was inelegant for the surfaces were very slippery. Raimon was slithering too, onto the next boulder, and then the next, until there was no more water, only the forest forming an unyielding barrier behind him. Raimon knew he had to kill Aimery now, but knew as well, with a sudden sinking of his heart, that he didn't want to. Killing Yolanda's brother might well kill something in Yolanda herself. But how to stop now?

Aimery sensed Raimon's reluctance to punch home a final blow almost before Raimon himself, and he relaxed. At once the water, weighty and powerful, took action of its own. For a long second Aimery stood, feeling his feet lose their purchase. Had he let go of his sword, he might have saved himself, but he would not. Like an unsteady skater holding a precious object, he leant forward, arm out, then back, fell once, tried to rise and fell again, this time more awkwardly and where the current was strongest. Only as the river picked him up like a piece of driftwood and slid him inexorably towards the edge of the cascade like a body riding a sled in the snow, did he realise he had a much more implacable foe than Raimon. After all, the river was not even deep. It was only when he was right on the brink that with a sudden blind movement, he let go of his sword and thrust out his hands.

Raimon didn't have to think. Dropping his weapon, he plunged in, his own hands outstretched for Aimery's. It should be easy, surely. Their hands joined. But the water was relentless and Aimery beginning to panic. From the opposite bank, others plunged in to help. One seized Aimery's tunic just as a branch, whipping over the fall itself, smacked hard against Raimon's chest, knocking him flat. Aimery, safe now, after only a second's hesitation, let go of Raimon. Let nature do what it would.

It was a strange sensation, going over the edge. Raimon felt nothing to start with, except that the deafening world of the hunt, the riverbank and the duel had been suddenly and very completely turned off. Nor did he feel any fear as he dropped, head first like a diver, until just before he smacked against the hard bright surface beneath him. Then he felt a fear so pure it almost stopped his heart. *I'm going to break into a thousand pieces* he thought. After that, everything was black.

Yolanda screamed and strained over. She shouted his name. She begged him to surface, but all she saw was heedless spray and white vapour drifting from earth to heaven.

AFTER THE HUNT

Easter passed in a daze. Yolanda could not and would not believe that Raimon had gone, but searches down the river proved fruitless and she knew from other drownings how long water can hold onto its victims. She had nightmares about that. Her father sat with her as she rocked, her eyes tightly shut to block everything out, but he could not sit for long. I could not help. My waters and meadows, my trees and my winds simply served to remind her of her loss.

Girald's courts, at which the count's presence was obligatory, were gathering in intensity. The road to the château had become a kind of Via Dolorosa, a path to Calvary, with many trudging up — woodcutters, joiners, cooks, the bailiff's mother, artisans, shop-keepers and a small, moon-faced messenger-boy who had been lame since birth — and fewer trod back down. Girald's stomach, settled better since the Lenten fast was over, allowed his Inquisitorial skills to bloom. He himself had become less cadaverous and was more like a baleful magpie. He had employed a full-time scribe to record his genius at tripping people up and the château's cellars were gratifyingly full. It would soon be time for him to present his evidence to the Inquisitor General and gain permission for a fire. When Berengar protested, Girald threatened to try him as well. Blood loyalty came after loyalty to the Catholic Church and anyway, Girald had a feeling that the Blue Flame itself was just waiting for the burning day. As the pyre rose, it would reappear and the Occitan would be claimed completely for the Catholics. Berengar should be pleased, for a completely Catholic Occitan should be safe from King Louis. He'd have no excuse to invade. For his work at keeping the Occitan free, Girald could see himself hailed as one of my greatest heroes and also a hero of the Church. He trusted that Berengar would make sure that due recognition was given.

This made Aimery laugh, although not in front of Girald. How deluded these churchmen were! Well, let Girald believe what he wanted to believe. For Aimery, things were turning out well and he defended himself firmly when Yolanda railed against him about Raimon. 'For goodness sake, I didn't pick a fight with him, he picked one with me. What could I do?'

'You shouldn't have let go. You shouldn't have let go.' It was all Yolanda could say.

'I didn't let go on purpose.' This was almost true. When Yolanda went on and on, he lost patience. 'Look, Yola. If you hadn't called him "just a weaver", he'd never have got so angry. If it's my fault he's drowned, it's yours as well.'

She had no answer to that, as Aimery knew she wouldn't.

A week went by and Aimery began to press his father about arrangements for Yolanda's party. Berengar was horrified. There could hardly be a more unsuitable time for a party. Aimery disagreed. A fourteenth birthday was important. It turned a girl into a lady who would need no reminding that, if she was not going to be left a despised and lonely maiden, it was time to secure her knight. Berengar must think of the future, not the present, and not just Yolanda's but Castelneuf's too. He did not dispute that Yolanda was highly distressed by Raimon's demise, but she could not mourn forever. He was very persuasive. When Yolanda was told, she reacted first with horror and then with a kind of appalled indifference.

Hugh watched and bided his time. He was pleased about the party. It would provide the perfect opportunity to secure this southern prize and then leave. He was not growing impatient with Yolanda, although the tight, tense figure who now sat on the dais eating nothing was hardly the wild bird he had found so charming, or even the cool shell-like creature from the hunt. Far from it. He hoped that he might succeed in bringing some light back to her eyes and heart. He did not, however, find the household knights particularly friendly or his quarters particularly comfortable and there would be no more bear hunts for a while. What was more, Girald, to whom Hugh was always scrupulously polite lest he find himself on the wrong end of that rasping tongue, was insufferable at dinner. All in all, it was time he went home.

Three weeks before the party Hugh judged her ready to receive small presents. He began with a soft doeskin collar for Brees, then another comb, a silk belt and a set of hairpins decorated with small fragments of jade – 'to match your eyes,' he said. Yolanda showed no interest in the gifts and he did not press them on her, just made sure that Brees wore the collar and that the rest found their way into her chamber.

That was not his only line of attack, a strange metaphor for a lover, perhaps, but apt, for it began to please Hugh to view this new, closed Yolanda as a citadel to be breached. Slowly and carefully, he began undermining her defences, as a miner undermines a castle's walls. He kept people away from her, particularly Girald, and when Aimery grew angry with her silence, he protected her. It was he who, in the absence of the troubadours, now in the cellars for singing the Song of the Flame with an added verse that poked fun at the Inquisitor's dignity, told her stories, not caring whether she was listening, just seeming content to sit quietly beside her. He tried, too, to make sure that she never saw the lists of prisoners and when he failed, was with her when she begged that Beatrice be released and argued that Adela should not be imprisoned for returning to the town to shout insults at Simon Crampcross. He played his part without a fault. He only had to bide his time. Soon Yolanda would love him because it was the easiest thing to do.

Parsifal supposed it was luck that had pushed Raimon up behind the waterfall rather than in front. He had climbed down through the trees as fast as a man half his age, and after more terrible minutes than he would ever like to relive, had seen something in the blackly shimmering backdrop that didn't quite belong. Stones and water had done quite some bruising and battering but Parsifal hitched Raimon onto his back and half staggering, half walking, made his way back down the mountain, through the valleys and over the rivers and hills until, three days later, he regained the refuge behind the scree. He was more than determined that the boy wouldn't die. He was not so sure, however, in what state he would live. He seemed sodden as a sponge all through. Without thinking, Parsifal used the Flame to light a fire, risking the smoke, then he patched Raimon up, placed him on his side and sat down to wait. If the boy did die, he would take his body to the cemetery and bury him with his mother.

It was days before Raimon stirred, days more until he put his hands to his head and demanded to be untied.

Parsifal was with him at once. 'My dear boy. You're not tied up. I've just wrapped your cuts in spiders' webs. It's an old trick my father's groom taught me. Cobwebs tie up the poison. Spiders are very clever fellows.'

'Sir Parsifal. Thank God.'

'Just Parsifal, please. Are you hungry? You've had almost nothing except river water. I'm afraid it's rabbit again. I tried dormouse but there's not much on a dormouse.'

Raimon rolled over and went back to sleep.

Two days later, he eased himself painfully into a sitting position. 'How long have I been here?'

'A couple of weeks. You've been quite ill.'

Raimon didn't think he was hungry at first, and picked at the food Parsifal gave him. Two weeks? What had happened in two weeks? He ate a bit more, and was suddenly shovelling it in.

'Steady on,' said Parsifal, 'you'll make yourself sick.'

Raimon slowed down for a little. 'I can't remember very much,' he said.

When Parsifal began to tell him, his face darkened. He remembered now. *Just a weaver*. 'The Flame?' he asked. He would concentrate on that.

'It's here.'

He put down the bowl and lay back. There was silence for a while. Then he spoke again. 'We can't just do nothing any more.'

'It seems to me that you've done quite a lot and not all of it very wise.'

'You know what I mean. We can't do nothing. We've got the Flame and we've got to use it. Aimery is going to betray the Occitan. I know he is.'

'Yes,' Parsifal said, 'but it's so hard to know how to use the Flame for the best.' He took it out of its box. 'I mean, why did it show itself when it did? What good has it done? I'm supposed to know and I don't.'

Raimon wiped his mouth. The air of the cave was clammy which made his head still feel full of water. The Flame today was in dull mode, its blue unmemorable. He was silent for a long time. 'Perhaps,' he said in the end, 'perhaps it wanted to draw everything to one place. I mean that's what's happened, isn't it? The White Wolf was already here, but after the Flame showed itself, the Inquisitor arrived. And Sir Hugh.'

'And was that a good thing?'

'It doesn't seem so,' said Raimon grimly.

They both regarded the Flame, although it did not seem to notice them at all.

'I feel I should be able to answer questions rather than ask them,' said Parsifal, 'but I'm always very confused and the Flame doesn't even try to help me.'

'You knew how to rescue me,' said Raimon, 'and Yolanda at the cemetery, and Brees.' He said Yolanda's name with a twist of his mouth that Parsifal pretended not to notice.

'Oh, I think I prayed, and God did that,' Parsifal said.

Raimon shifted and his cheeks hollowed. 'What, the same God who allows the White Wolf and the Inquisitor to live whilst my mother dies?'

'Men killed your mother.'

'In God's name. If God didn't like it, why didn't he strike them down?'

'Men have free will, Raimon —' he paused. 'Do you know, I've been trying to remember, whilst you were sleeping, exactly what my father told me about the Flame. I've always thought that one of its roles was to keep the Occitan free from invaders. That's what my father thought.'

'And that's right. The Song says so.'

'But what if it's not right. What if it doesn't mean just keeping the Occitan free from invaders like King Louis?'

'What other invaders are there?'

'Well, there's Inquisitor Girald and the White Wolf.'

'But they're not really invaders,' said Raimon. 'The only thing they have to commend them is that at least they both want to keep the Occitan free.'

'Free?' Parsifal absentmindedly filled Raimon's plate again. 'Does the White Wolf make people free? Does Girald make people free?'

'No, but that's different. At least they still want the Occitan to be a place on its own.'

'Yet still, according to them, to be a true Occitanian you must be Cathar or Catholic. It's not really freedom, is it.'

Raimon said nothing.

'I've been thinking,' said Parsifal carefully. 'What if we're all wrong about the Flame? What if it's got nothing to do with King Louis at all? I mean, what if the Flame stands not for freedom in the paths of righteousness, as my father told me, but freedom *from the paths of self-righteousness*? Could it be, and I'm only saying could it, but could it be that over the centuries people just substituted the original words for words that suited them better? Righteousness sounds good, and thinking you are righteous means you can claim to be right. Both the Inquisitor and the White Wolf think they're righteous. But they're not really righteous, are they? They're self-righteous, which is a false kind of righteousness and their self-righteousness blinds them to the truth, which is that they're just men who know nothing much at all.' It was a very long speech for Parsifal and he felt quite breathless.

'But when I stood up at that – that trial, and tried to say that, or something like it, nobody stood with me,' Raimon argued. 'Nobody. They were all completely dumb. Even if I'd shown the Flame I don't think people would have shouted Girald down.'

'They were all frightened, Raimon, terrified. You can't blame them. When people are frightened, they just agree with the person who seems strongest, and that certainly wasn't you.'

'It will never be me.'

'Perhaps not,' said Parsifal carefully, 'except that you're brave and seem to know what freedom really means. That's a kind of strength. If there is a reason that the Flame showed itself here, in this place and at this time, could it not be you?'

'But I'm not a knight, I'm –'

'Just a weaver? You don't believe that, do you?'

'It's what Yolanda said, and anyway, never mind about me,

what will happen to the Occitan if the Flame won't help against King Louis?'

Parsifal shook his head. 'That I don't know,' he said, and felt his old fears and insecurities returning. 'Perhaps I'm wrong about you, wrong about everything. Maybe I'm just getting old. Old men clutch at things, you know, particularly old men like me who've spent most of their lives running away and hiding.'

There was a splutter at their feet and they both looked down. Parsifal's sudden garrulity seemed to have cheered the Flame up. It had been smoking, but now its blue was the blue of the midnight sky, changing suddenly to turquoise before sparking into the colour of an Amouroix summer evening. 'What's it saying?' Raimon asked, for the Flame's show seemed completely random to him.

'I've no idea,' said Parsifal rather gloomily. 'Absolutely no idea at all.' Raimon looked disappointed. 'Come,' said Parsifal, 'sleep again. If you don't get your strength back, we can do nothing, even if the Flame itself were suddenly to write a book.'

Raimon obediently lay down, and Parsifal lay down too. He was soon snoring. Not so Raimon. He rested his chin in cupped hands. What a strange thing this Flame was, and what a strange man this Knight Magician. When he finally felt sleep creeping over him, he hoped he would dream about himself saving the Occitan. Instead he dreamt about Yolanda and it was not a dream, it was a nightmare, for she was next to Hugh, with her hair brushed like a halo, in a way she never brushed it for him.

THE DARK

He woke with a start. He was being dragged. His arms flew up as his spiders' web bandages trickled off like skeins of tickling threads. 'What —'

'Quiet! Quiet!' Parsifal stopped dragging him and urged him onto all fours. 'There are people.' He was crouched right down beside Raimon, the Flame's box in his hand because he'd had no time to get it into the pouch. 'I don't know what they're doing.'

This soon became clear. Like the syncopated barks of a dozen sore-throated foxes came the ruff-ruff-ruff of two-handed saws. Timber was being felled, cut into small logs, rolled down the scree and stacked at the front of the cave, behind the piles of collected stones but in front of the fringe of roots. Parsifal and Raimon squashed at the back expecting any moment that the protective curtain would part and they would be discovered. The dark of the cave would work in their favour, but the forester had a lantern. When the curtain had remained unmoved for more than ten minutes, they began to breathe again. They could hear the forester cursing.

'The Inquisitor said logs small enough to catch quickly, you imbecile. And hurry up, it's cold in here.' He appeared to throw the timber that offended him back out of the cave.

'Oh Lord in Heaven,' said Parsifal. The boy moved closer. 'Logs for pyres.'

Raimon swallowed hard, his legs, still weak, suddenly weaker still. 'Sir Parsifal —'

'Just Parsifal, please.'

More shouts. 'What's that thing doing here?'

Now the root curtain did part and through it, all tongue and paws and the thrills of greeting, bundled Brees. He nearly knocked Parsifal down before hurling himself at Raimon. The boy took hold of him anywhere he could get a purchase, unsure whether to drag him back or push him out. Brees just licked and licked. Then the sound Raimon both longed for and dreaded: Yolanda's voice, high and anxious, and tired. She called the dog's name again and again, as if she couldn't think of anything else to say. Raimon felt Brees open his mouth to bark, to tell her what he'd found and gripped the shaggy throat so that what should have been a roar turned into a squeak.

'I can't see him, mistress.' The forester's voice was suddenly uncomfortably near. 'But he shouldn't be here and nor should you.'

'He came in.' Yolanda's voice was nearer still. She was stepping towards the curtain. 'I'm not leaving without him.' She found herself in front of the roots, murmured a small 'oh' of surprise when she felt what they were, pushed them aside and found herself staring at the whites of two eyes with deep dark holes in the middle.

Though he could see almost nothing, for she blocked out all the tiny light there was, Raimon knew she was frowning, knew just the way her forehead would fold, with the little vertical crease in the middle, and how the muscles round her mouth would create a tiny dip in her upper lip. He didn't know, any longer, if he was glad to know these things or not.

Yolanda couldn't think at all. She dropped the roots so that they swung down but left her arms still through. With very careful precision, as though touching paint that might turn out to be wet, she extended two fingers. Raimon knew it would be wiser to draw back, but he didn't. Her fingers found his cheek and traced, with almost unbearable delicacy, the path into the dimple in the middle that she and his mother had always loved and he had always hated, and then further down towards his chin, still clear of a man's stubble. Her fingers stroked round the smooth oval and up. When they found the edge of his lip they hesitated, then resumed, gliding over the soft ridges of his ears, and then into his hair. Her fingers stopped here and her other hand crept up until she had his head between her hands. He let out a long breath. Her hands pressed together. He could feel the pressure, feel her fingers spreading, keeping his head carefully gathered between them, as though if she didn't, bits might disperse and she would lose them.

The forester, halfway between the curtain and the cave's mouth, was peering. The girl seemed to be standing in a very peculiar way. 'Is there more cave behind?' He began to move towards her.

It was agony for Yolanda to let her fingers drop, but she did, trying to keep what she had felt on their tips. 'No,' she said. 'There's nothing behind here except wall. I was just feeling in case there was a wolf hole or something that Brees could have got through. That's what must have happened. He's certainly not here now.' Her voice was nothing like her voice of a moment before. Now it was the voice of a sleep-walker or somebody reluctant to wake from a dream. The forester didn't notice. He noticed very little that was not to do with trees and anyway, in the damp and dark, most voices are distorted.

'Come along then, mistress, out you come.' He moved back, heard his men arguing, clicked with irritation and returned to the cave opening.

Yolanda turned to the root curtain once more. Once more she pulled it aside. The face had gone, but something else transfixed her. Beyond where she could reach, two pale hands shimmered. She recognised them at once. They were the hands from the cemetery. They came forward, low as her waist, part of them hidden, with a panting noise. She found herself clutching Brees' collar. Then the hands vanished. That was it. There was nothing more. Yolanda left the cave, telling the forester that Brees had, all the while, been hiding behind the finished logpile eating the remains of a badger's dinner. She did not let the man see her face for in it he would have seen such a fierce joy that he might have guessed she had seen something that was nothing to do with Brees at all.

The log-chopping didn't flag until sunset and then the forester called his weary men together and paid them with bronze at which they grumbled and spat because they had expected silver. 'We could do with that dog to guard this lot,' he remarked to nobody in particular. The men quickly dispersed in case they found themselves 'volunteered' to do guard duty. The forester, remembering his wife, shrugged and left the cave alone.

Even after the men had gone, Parsifal and Raimon did not emerge for fresh air, for they had no idea there was no guard and it was too dangerous to discover.

'If she comes again, don't tell her about the Flame,' said Parsifal.

'She won't come.'

Parsifal grunted.

It was nearly midnight when she appeared, or rather was heard. Brees, naturally, came first and this time he got the welcome he expected. Raimon buried his face in the dog's fur. Then Yolanda was speaking softly, her arms outstretched. Now Raimon drew back a little, finding that although he wanted to hold her as tight as he had held her on the steps of the great hall on the day this nightmare had started, his pride had not yet forgiven her for 'just a weaver'. But she was there, fumbling forward, barely realising that she was breathing his name with every breath she took, both in and out. He could feel her despair as she pushed aside the roots and this time found nothing. Now she was no longer breathing, but panting, like a small animal searching for safety. Parsifal, crouching in the furthest corner with the Flame behind him and praying that it would not choose this moment to set the world alight, could feel her agony. *Go to her*, he silently urged. *Go to her.*

And Raimon, shoving the thornbush of his pride aside, did. He found her hands and this time, she was not delicate. She hurled herself into his unseen embrace and he could feel her tears, not gentle tears, but the hard, bitter tears of self-reproach. 'I'm so sorry . . . I never meant . . . I didn't think . . .' She finished no sentence, for whatever words she chose seemed inadequate for the task of repairing the hurt she had caused. Yet she still gathered them up in jumbles and hurled them at him, willing him to catch them and turn them into the healing apology she could not frame herself. As Raimon caught what she threw, hardly even hearing what she said, he found himself full of gratitude for the dark, for it allowed him to murmur to her, to stroke her hair and find it gloriously matted and, finally, to stop the words with a kiss. He knew she wouldn't laugh now, not even if his kiss went slightly awry because he could only sense and not see her mouth. Brees, finding himself not wanted, went to Parsifal and they sat in patient communion, each thinking thoughts that had absolutely nothing in common with the other.

At last, from Yolanda, there were small whispered questions. She cared deeply for the answers one moment and cared nothing at all the next. What did it matter how Raimon got here? He was here. It was enough.

But he answered, though with caution. 'You remember the Knight Magician of the Breeze?' Of course she did. Raimon told her as much as she could know, and when he spoke of Parsifal's pale hands, she asked only one question. 'Where is he now? I should thank him.' She clutched Raimon harder, remembering the cemetery.

'Not here,' Raimon lied, although it pained him to do so. 'He's gone.'

They sat down, never leaving go of each other. Her tangled mane was against his cheek and he could feel smooth patches in her dress where the velvet was rubbed away. The lumps of mud at the sleeves and hem gave him a pleasure as fierce as Yolanda's earlier joy. It was not dirt to him, it was the bond of earth.

In answer to his questions, she began to tell him how it was at the château. She told him how her uncle had filled the cellars, and how they had caught Adela and imprisoned Beatrice. She told him his father had vanished.

'Alone?' Raimon asked, before he could stop himself. 'Do you think he was alone?'

'I don't know,' she answered, finding this a curious question. 'I suppose so.' She told him too that Girald was leaving soon, heading for a town called Avignonet, where he was to meet the Inquisitor who had the power to sign the death warrants. 'The evidence has already gone in a cart,' she said. 'There were two chests stuffed to the brim. That's why the woodcutters – the woodcutters –'

'Yes,' Raimon told her, holding her even closer. 'Yes, I know.'

She told him that the first pyre would be lit in two weeks. Raimon's throat constricted. That it had come to this. An Occitanian burning Occitanians. He could not help himself. 'Girald has no business here, no business anywhere. I'm sorry he's your uncle, Yolanda, but he's no business to be alive. I should like to kill him myself.' The acrid stench of the road from Limoux was once again in his nostrils.

'Sssssh! Ssssssh!' Yolanda put her hand over his mouth. 'Ssssssh!'

He collected himself. 'Is that foreign knight still at Castelneuf?' He could not bring himself to call Hugh by his name. Yolanda hesitated, thus giving him the answer.

They moved fractionally apart. 'He'll think us barbarians,'

Raimon said shortly. He moved further away and she could already feel cold air seeping into the space where before there had been none. She wanted to push the air out, but when she leant over, there was only emptiness. Raimon was standing up, and now he was purely practical. The cellars must be emptied before Girald returned. There must be no burnings at Castelneuf. He asked her who held the cellar keys, how many exits and entrances – he couldn't remember exactly. He wondered if they could do this, or perhaps that. What did she think?

She stood too, and made a few tentative suggestions, then stopped him with one phrase. 'The night of my party,' she said. 'We might do it the night of my party.'

'Your party?' She did not have to see his jaw to feel it drop. 'In amongst all this, you're still going to have your party?'

She felt hot in the cold. 'Aimery insists. He won't hear of calling it off. He's made my father dispatch the invitations and carry on as if nothing has changed. I didn't want it, Raimon. You couldn't think I did and the worst thing is that people will come not because they want to but because they are frightened to refuse. But that night,' she said rather desperately, 'there'll be so many people coming and going and so much noise that everything will be in a muddle. That would be the best night to get everybody out.'

Raimon tried to see only that she was right, but somehow, the vision of her dancing with Hugh was the only vision he could conjure up. He stood and, for distraction, called to Brees. The dog came willingly. Raimon bent over him. It was a minute before he felt something different. 'The collar's new,' he said. 'A present?'

A terrible half-guilty, half-angry blush suffused Yolanda's face. Now it was she who was thankful for the dark. 'It's nothing, Raimon. He was just trying to be kind.'

'Ah,' said Raimon, and his voice was quite flat, 'by "he" you naturally mean the man who's certainly not "just a weaver"?' Pride and jealousy prickled him again.

'Please, Raimon.'

He struggled with himself. She caught his hand. He half pulled it away but she wouldn't let him because she wouldn't let what they'd had only moments before dissolve like a dream. It had not been a dream. It was real, real as Castelneuf, as real to her as I was, real as the Occitan, real as the Flame they both believed in. Even in his jealousy and pride, she would not let him forget that. So she held onto his hand, refusing to let it go. They stood in a silent battle, each determined not to give in until Yolanda, moving her hand to take his whole arm, began to sway, and forced him to dance. At first he was stiff and unyielding but she would not be thwarted and then they were moving together. They did not need music. Round and round they moved, tracing familiar patterns, their limbs always in rhythm, never having to guess where the other's feet were. They were stopped only when Brees pushed between them, wanting to join in, and that made both of them laugh.

Parsifal, still crouched and very uncomfortable, raised his head, rigid with alarm. What on earth were they doing? He shook his head. He didn't suppose he would ever understand much about that side of life now.

When, finally, Brees made it impossible to continue, Raimon and Yolanda talked and this time there was no awkwardness. Yolanda was right, Raimon said. They would use the night of the party. Her part would be to make sure the guards had plenty to drink and to keep the celebrations loud and busy. With Girald away by then, and if she seemed at least a little happier, Aimery, who was Raimon's chief worry, would relax and a relaxed man is not a man who notices much. With a catch in his voice, but wanting to prove something to himself and to her, he told her to dress with care and, clenching his fists, told her to brush her hair. That, more than anything else, would please her brother, because — well, because. She touched his cheek. It was the nearest they got to speaking of Hugh again. He told her to leave the rest to him.

It was only when a pink dawn striped the mouth of the cave and the chorus of birds forced them to raise their voices that they realised they were now sitting in grey damp rather than black damp. Raimon got up at once. Yolanda must not see Parsifal. She must go. With his heart in his mouth, he crept out to make sure no early woodcutters or axe sharpeners were hovering in hope of extra work. He could see none, so he came with her out of the cave to the bottom of the scree with Brees nosing about at their heels. In the brightening light, neither Raimon nor Yolanda looked their best, even to each other. The magic of the night was past. It was not until Yolanda bid him a final, slightly shy, goodbye, that Raimon caught her and held her so hard that he really did hurt her. 'Just this one thing before you go,' he said. 'Never, never interfere on my behalf again. Do you understand? Never.'

'Not even if your life depends on it?' She tried not to flinch.

'Not even then. I'd rather die than have you plead my cause.'

'Why? Are you ashamed of me?'

'No, can't you see? It makes me ashamed of myself.'

He let go of her then and she scrambled away through the woods.

An hour later, with the day truly begun, she reached the meadows. Brees was padding silently beside her, her guard and her uncomplicated friend. On impulse, she leant down, removed the collar and threw it away. She would find another. When she reached the river, she found the wet clothes she had discarded on her way out, tied her dry ones in a bundle above her head and swam back over. Creeping in through the hole and the little door, she made it, unnoticed, to her bedroom.

That night, at dinner, she was just as silent as usual. Only Hugh noticed that a slight sparkle was rekindling itself and he was almost vain enough to believe that it was for him, except he noticed also that Brees was no longer wearing the collar with the mother-of-pearl clasp. Then he looked at the girl he now thought of as his, and he wondered.

The Theft

It was the waiting that Raimon could not stand and after a week of Parsifal nodding his head, unable to be of much help since he'd never been inside the town, Raimon threw down the stick with which he had been drawing a rough plan of Castelneuf's streets and defences and scuffed it into the dirt. 'I can't do this any more,' he said. The forester and his woodcutters had gone, leaving only sawdust and six raw treestumps behind. The Flame burnt solidly, with no tricks now, and they kept it before them as they deliberated whether they should take it with them and hope that its appearance would be enough to have the château servants and at least some of the knights, possibly including Berengar, rally behind them, or whether to keep it hidden. Yolanda did not return. In his head, Raimon knew there would be good reason for this, but still. Surely she could have crept out just once more?

Parsifal tried to divert him, with no success until he produced two coarse swords from his pack and began, rather absentmindedly, to polish them. They were rough things, not swords any knight would have wanted, but they would need them. Raimon picked one up. 'I didn't know you had these. Where did you get them?'

'The bear hunt. I suppose they pulled them off when Sir Aimery was in the river and forgot them. Somebody'll have got an earful.'

Raimon held the weapon out, feeling its weight. 'Teach me.'

Parsifal concentrated on his polishing. 'It takes years of practice. Not much point in starting now.' In truth, Raimon's suggestion panicked him. In his whole life he had had only three lessons in combat, given to him by the old de Maurand armourer because Parsifal had pestered him so badly. The lessons had started as a joke, for Parsifal had been much too small for a sword, but the armourer had been impressed by the little boy's determination. Nevertheless, though Parsifal knew he had shown promise, three lessons a lifetime ago hardly qualified him to teach somebody else.

However, Raimon was as determined now as Parsifal had been then. 'I wish I'd kept Aimery's sword,' he said. 'That was much better balanced. This one is too heavy at the hilt.'

He threw it over and Parsifal automatically caught it.

'You're right,' Parsifal said. 'Very poor smithery.' He tried to put that one away too, but Raimon was too quick. He snatched it back and held it flat against Parsifal's stomach.

'Hey, hey,' Parsifal protested.

'Defend yourself, Sir Parsifal. Come on.' Raimon gave the sword a jerk.

'Just Parsifal, please.' He had little choice. Gripping his hilt with both hands, he swung up, knocking Raimon off balance. Now he had the advantage, and setting his feet as the old armourer had taught him, he deftly turned his blade so that Raimon was helpless and Parsifal could have run him through in a second. 'Forgive me,' Parsifal said, pleased with himself, 'but if my memory serves me, the first lesson of the sword is anticipation. What am I going to do next?'

'I've no idea.'

'Think, boy, think.'

'Step back, having made your point?'

Parsifal threw back his head and snorted. 'A very good answer,' he said. His panic receded and an excitement he hadn't felt for years took its place. 'Now, let's begin.'

For the next hour, Parsifal was the ghost of the old armourer, hopping and nodding, darting in and darting out, prodding arms, nudging legs and poking ribs. 'Think ahead,' he instructed. 'That's the secret. That and your grip. My father's sword was longer and heavier and only built for two-handed swinging when mounted. I often wondered how he didn't swipe off his horse's head. These are lighter. You still need two hands, but you could thrust with one if you had to. Now, up and round and up and round again. That's right. Once more. Up and round.' They fought on until Raimon, by a lucky strike, tripped Parsifal onto his knees. Dropping his sword at once, Parsifal bowed his head. 'I beg of you mercy, Sir Knight,' he said.

Raimon, hot and flushed, put down a hand to help the older man to his feet. 'Hardly,' he said, but he did not hide the fact that he was pleased.

The following day, he woke Parsifal at dawn. 'I'm going into the town,' he said, his face set. 'I need to see.'

Parsifal wisely didn't ask what it was that Raimon wanted to see. 'And if you're caught?'

'I won't be.'

Parsifal took his hand and held it for a moment. 'I'll be waiting right here,' he said. 'God be with you.'

Raimon gave a peculiar smile. 'Will I be better off with God or without him, I wonder?' he asked. Then he was gone and Parsifal was left to ponder the question alone.

Crossing the river was easy. Raimon chose a spot much further up than the mill, further up than Yolanda had chosen, because even though the river was wider, it was more discreet. He stripped quickly and bundled his clothes onto his back. The river was cold, but not as cold as that first dip he'd taken in what seemed another life. He swam without a splash and then, avoiding all but the vaguest of goat paths, he headed for the sheer rock on the east side of the château and began to climb. It was hard work, for the finger- and toe-holds were tiny, and several times he slipped. But at least he did not have to worry about being seen. Nobody ever looked down this side of the valley because people had called it impregnable for so long that they never stopped to wonder whether it really was.

It took him three hours to reach the cavity in the château wall, a journey that on the normal road would have taken barely twenty minutes. His limbs ached as he glanced down and saw the familiar patterns spread out below. He could even pick out the roof of his own house. No smoke curled above it. It looked quite dead, but now that he could see it, he was filled with an unexpected desire to see inside it again. Perhaps, even though her bed was empty, if he stood by it, he could say the kind of goodbye to his mother that he'd like to have said. Once he'd had this thought, it wouldn't go away. It wouldn't take long. He covered his head with his cloak.

The main street was busy with traffic but the side streets were nearly deserted. Only the goats and chickens wandered without restriction, and though the day was fine, most shutters were closed, or nearly closed, like the eyes of old men at the seaside. Those few people who were out had shawls over their heads just as he had and slunk rather than walked. The slinking was catching and by the time Raimon got to his own front door, he was slinking himself.

In contrast with everyone else's, the Belot door was wide open, or so Raimon thought until he saw with a shock that the door was, in fact, not there at all, and nor were the shutters. He peered in, expecting chaos, but the place was perfectly tidy because every stick of furniture in the house, every chest, every trestle, every bench, had been turned into neat bundles of kindling. Raimon could see the remains of his mother's chair, the spinning wheel, Adela's pallet and his father's weaving machines, all smashed and stacked. Even the staircase had been dismantled and the pieces stored in piles small enough for one man to carry under one arm. Raimon walked round and round, almost unbelieving. Girald meant Adela to burn with wood from her own bed. He said not a word, just walked faster and faster. He could feel an explosion arising, right from his toes. He would wait until it reached his throat and only then would he give vent. He opened his mouth. He had no idea what he would roar. He had no idea afterwards what he had roared. He only felt himself consumed by a fury so great that he lost all care for his own safety. Nothing would stop him rushing at the bundles, kicking them over, scattering the pieces and then running round, legs flailing, and scattering them again. Had he had a flint, he'd have burned the house down himself. Then, with a final blast, he was gone, running up the street, careless of everything. Only when he reached the château wall again did he appreciate the enormity of the risk he had taken. His fury was still with him, but he lay on his front, his face crushed into the soil until he could hold onto it and distil it into a tiny burning stone lodged even deeper inside him than his heart. Only when he was sure that it would not flare out and make him roar again did he drag himself into the courtyard using the spring growth of weeds as cover.

In contrast with the town, the château was full of movement. Already, guests from all over the Occitan and even further afield had begun to gather for Yolanda's party. To house the plethora of horses, temporary stables had been knocked together. Grooms, squires and pages were chattering, comparing and boasting. Under Berengar's vague direction, workmen were busy repairing bits of the roof deemed unsafe and cleaning the uncleanable. The place was heaving with unfamiliar faces and in his unremarkable clothes, Raimon hoped he would just be one amongst many. He chose a moment to rise and then walked swiftly under the small bridges and up the linking stairways. When he saw somebody who might recognise him, he turned his head away but he had no difficulty approaching the small door up the turret stairs. He was hoping to get to Yolanda's room, when out of the door came Berengar and Girald, heading straight for him. Girald was dressed for travel. Swiftly, Raimon turned to the side and ran down several different sets of steps towards the main barn, where the Castelneuf horses and those of their more permanent guests were housed. Skirting the door, it was a familiar climb onto the roof, one he and Yolanda had done many times, and a familiar drop through the trapdoor where there would still be enough of last year's hay to cushion him.

The stalls were full, with the Castelneuf horses set apart from the visitors', five of which, coursers and warhorses, caught Raimon's eye at once, for their flanks were protected from the dust by fine coverlets of yellow silk embroidered in each corner with two crimson crossed lances and a Latin motto Raimon couldn't understand. Hugh's horses. Raimon was sure of that. He waited until the grooms went out for some refreshment and then dropped onto the floor.

Galahad, standing with his rump to the manger, whickered. Raimon recognised him at once as Yolanda's mount at the bearhunt. He ran his hands down his neck, but his eyes fixed on the surcoats emblazoned in Hugh's colours draped carelessly on the wooden partition and the saddlery banked up against the barn wall. So intent was he that he did not at once hear the tread of feet and when he finally dived under the manger, he didn't know whether he'd been seen or not. He tensed right into himself as the feet stopped and Aimery leant over the partition, continuing what had clearly been an earlier conversation.

'I think she'll like that,' he said.

'What girl wouldn't,' Hugh replied. 'Gallant old warhorses appeal on every level and they don't come much more gallant than these two.' He patted Galahad, but dismissively. He had had the best out of both him and Bors and was happy to give them to Yolanda for her own. He had three new ones waiting for him in the north, all of which were proving to be worth the money he had paid. 'Galahad gave her a good ride on the bearhunt and where Galahad goes, Bors goes too.'

Aimery laughed. 'I must say, it hardly seems necessary to give her another present. She's yours already. Your stories about

Paris have quite turned her head. If you'd asked her to ride there with you last night, I think she'd have done it. Does the city never sleep?'

Hugh ignored the question and Aimery found himself scrutinised in a way he found very disconcerting. 'Yolanda does like me, I think,' Hugh said at last, 'but at this moment, I'm more curious about you.' Aimery blinked. Hugh did not. 'Why do you offer the Amouroix to King Louis?' he asked. 'I doubt whether I would, in your place. I mean, if I were Occitanian and my father was Count of this place, I doubt I'd want to be thought a traitor.' He stroked Galahad's neck in exactly the same place Raimon had only moments before although he never took his eyes from Aimery's. 'And the Flame. I've heard the Song and what everybody says about it even though they've yet to find it. Does it mean nothing to you at all?' He gave one of his characteristic half-smiles.

Aimery was sure this was a test and fiddled with Galahad's mane as he answered. 'Is it disloyal to want to minimise suffering? We both know that the king won't be stopped. The Flame's all very well, but even it can't produce fighting men out of nothing. Unlike us, King Louis has an endless supply of troops. I understand that even if nobody else wants to. And really,' he stopped. 'Frankly, Hugh, it's time the Flame was snuffed out. That's what I'll do if I get hold of it. There's no room for such things any more. Look at this place and tell me truthfully. Is it not time we became part of something bigger than ourselves?'

'I don't think Yolanda sees it quite like that.'

Aimery gave up with Galahad's mane and pulled splinters from the partition. 'Not at the moment maybe, but she will in time.'

Hugh leant against his horse. 'You underestimate her, Aimery.'

'Oh, I don't think so. Yolanda's not a fool. She may be a bit dismal right now but with the weaver out of the way, I don't think she'll be too reluctant to join her fortunes with yours. Haven't you noticed? His skeleton won't even be washed clean yet and already she's more cheerful.'

'Indeed,' said Hugh, narrowing his eyes.

Aimery was encouraged. 'Look. I think you should take her away directly after the party. There's no need for her to be here when Girald returns from Avignonet with the death warrants. This Cathar stuff has been upsetting for her.'

'Don't you care about the pyre? You must know all of those destined to burn.'

'What else can be done with people who persist in error?' Aimery said with a piety both knew was entirely insincere.

They broke off when the door opened and Brees pushed his way in. Raimon curled himself into an even tighter ball. If the dog came to him, he was finished. But Brees had rolled in stinking fox droppings and Aimery quickly pushed him out again. Hugh watched. 'That dog will be miserable in Paris,' he said. 'I think I'll find your sister a small greyhound. They would look very pretty together.'

'Oh, I don't know,' Aimery was uncomfortable. 'Yolanda does love him.'

Hugh was saved from answering by the appearance of Yolanda herself. She had come in to avoid being stared at by more prisoners being transported to the cellars: her old nursemaid, two elderly sisters who sold love potions, and six children, all caught making a circular rather than straight sign of the cross over their bread. Like an expert fisherman, Girald had reeled them in, a last batch before his departure.

'My dear girl,' said Hugh smoothly, seeing at once that she was upset. He took her arm and sat her down on a heap of hay as if she were an irreplaceably precious object. She withdrew her arm and addressed only Aimery. 'How can you say nothing when our friends are being rounded up like sheep?'

'Hysteria makes you ugly, Yola.' Aimery spoke fast and with unattractive glibness. 'The Cathars all believe they're going straight to heaven anyway, so really, what does it matter how quickly they arrive there.'

'You don't like it any more than I do,' Yolanda cut straight through his nonsense. 'Why can't you and Father stop it between you?'

'Do you want us to burn too?'

'Uncle Girald would never do that.'

'Oh, he would, Yolanda, he would.'

'Perhaps it would be better to burn than to help him burn others.'

'No, I don't think so,' said Aimery, with feeling.

Hugh thought it time to change the subject. 'I'm glad you've come here, Yolanda, I've got something I'd like to give you.'

'No more presents, Sir Hugh.' Yolanda pulled Brees to her.

'I wish you'd stop calling me "Sir",' Hugh said, steeling himself against Brees's smell. 'Don't we know each other well enough for just "Hugh"?'

She didn't reply and he returned to Galahad. 'This old warrior gave you a good ride the other day,' he said. 'Would you like to have him? And where he goes, Bors goes too. Two horses for you, as part of your birthday present.'

'I can't think of having presents,' she said. 'I can't think of anything.'

'Don't look on them as presents, then. Let's just say the horses are yours because I've no more use for them. Could you accept them then?'

She shook her head.

'You shouldn't be so ungrateful,' Aimery told her. 'You'd be the only girl in the whole Amouroix with two warhorses of your own, to do what you like with.'

He was gratified to see that these words did have some effect. He had no idea what Yolanda was thinking, but Raimon did. Two warhorses would certainly be useful. He would have smiled but he dared not move a muscle. There was more conversation, more persuasion and finally, from Yolanda, a reluctant acceptance before Aimery steered them all out of the barn and told Yolanda that she should dunk Brees in the water trough.

Raimon uncurled himself at once, hesitated, then slipped on one of the des Arcis surcoats. Oat dust from the manger had speckled his hair, lightening its darkness, and he didn't shake it off. He patted both horses, settled the surcoat and then left the barn himself. He gave up any idea of going to Yolanda's room and this time made his way down to the bottom of the château, to the wide gap which led the way to the cellars. He walked casually, keeping to the shadows where he could, and when he reached the entrance he walked straight down the jagged steps, looking neither to right nor left, for all the world as if he were a des Arcis flunkey sent with an important message. He stopped only when he got to the gate at the bottom, once rusted but now polished and firmly locked.

Carved into the bare rock, with domed roofs and bars instead of wooden doors, the six individual cells, each measuring roughly fifteen feet across but going back much further, were opposite him, set in an uneven line amid the rubble of the château's foundations. Half a dozen guards were huddled, cooking over a smoky brazier in front of the middle cell, but otherwise the only light was from a series of tallow flambeaux and the only smell was of animal fear. In all their long life, the Castelneuf cellars had never had a sinister air about them but they were horribly sinister now, for though they looked no different than they had when they held sand or wine or wood, they were filled with the whispering echoes of hopeless prayers and with the worst sound of all: the hapless and unsuspecting gurgling of a baby's laughter.

Amongst those praying in the middle cell, Raimon saw Beatrice. At first he mistook her for her mother, for her buxom comeliness had leaked away like bran from a sack. He also saw Gui and Guerau wedged side by side, and then could have listed everyone else, for he knew them all. It was like seeing his childhood incarcerated. Then he saw Adela. She was sitting upright, her lips pressed as tightly as if somebody had sewn them together. She had a mad look in her eye.

Raimon held himself taut against the wall and tried to think. The way he had come down, though the quickest way out, was too exposed for such a large group of people to use in a hurry, even if the gate was open. The prisoners would have to go a different way, through the foundations' myriad passages which came out in several different places. The drawback there was that every passage led directly or indirectly into the château courtyard system and since each courtyard had its own gate and its own lock, anybody emerging from the cellars that way could be caught like a rat in a trap. Even if he could get all the keys, and all the guards were otherwise occupied, it would take too long to match key with lock. They would have to come this way. He would have to get the key and they would have to trust to luck and the distraction of the party entertainments.

In the end, it was ridiculously easy at least to get the key. One of the guards let himself out of the gate, locked it behind him and began to climb the steps, hooking the key loosely into his belt. Raimon pressed himself into the wall and kept his eyes fixed in front of him. In the dark, the man might pass him without comment, believing him just to be a curious squire. Raimon had no sophisticated plan, but he hardly needed one. The man came abreast, saw the surcoat, made a comment, nodded and walked on. Raimon then waited for a moment before quite openly following him closely, unhooking the swinging key when the narrowness of the passage pushed them together, and then sliding it inside one of his boots. As they emerged into the light, he turned smartly left as the man turned right. And that was that.

He wondered whether he should push his luck further and, unwise as he knew it was, the temptation to steal from right under Hugh's nose proved too great. He walked quickly back to the barn. The door was wide open and the place filled with servants of both high and low degree preparing horses for exercise. He took a deep breath and strode in amongst them, walking confidently over to Bors and Galahad. Nobody looked at him very carefully. The horses were fidgeting and pushing, anxious lest they should be left behind when all their fellows went out. Raimon picked up two bridles but then, since the sight of a squire bareback on a destrier would have certainly excited comment, he took two saddles also and when he was ready, led the horses into the courtyard. Gritting his teeth against the hard leather and harder wood, he mounted Galahad, gathered up Bors's leading rein and took his place in a chattering group. His luck was going to hold. He was sure of it. Nobody challenged him as he clattered through the château gate, nor in the main street, nor at the bridge, where the whole party turned upriver. He rode with them for a while, then began to lag behind until a bend in the bank meant he was on his own. 'Come on,' he said to Galahad, and both horses were too well trained to disobey, even if they did whinny as their friends vanished. Raimon urged them into a canter, and pushed them on until they were well away from the château and within the disguising shelter of the trees. He was almost laughing now. It was a beautiful day. He had the cellar key and two horses. Quite a haul to show Parsifal.

Had it been raining, he would have paid more attention. As it was, when two people leapt at him from the thicket, he didn't even catch a glimpse of their faces. One moment he was on top of the world, the next the world was crushing him, tying him up and pulling him, blindfolded, somewhere he did not want to go. He resisted with all his might, but was easily overpowered and when he was finally allowed to stop and the blindfold removed, he found himself face to face with his father, and behind his father, in a group of about ten others, stood the White Wolf.

Such was his shock, that Raimon could think of nothing to say. All he noticed was that although everybody else was filthy, the Perfectus's hair and beard was still the colour and texture of swansdown. Sicart, on the other hand, dazed by this vision of his son, seemed to have lost half his bulk, and his mouth had developed a twitch. 'They told me you were dead,' he said.

'They were mistaken.' Raimon waited for his father to express some relief, but none came. They might have been distant cousins, or even acquaintances who met occasionally. It struck him that he had no idea what he thought of his father any more. He wanted to hate him but he hardly seemed worth hating. It was shocking how much he had aged. 'Adela,' Sicart said, and his voice, like his limbs, seemed to have lost all substance. 'She's in the cellars. She's going to burn, Raimon. I don't think I can survive that.' He glanced back at the White Wolf, half fearful, half apologetic, before turning back to his son. 'Have you come from the château?' He clutched his arm. 'Are they lighting the pyre today? Will it be today?' He was a pitiable figure.

Raimon disengaged his arm. He could not bring himself to comfort his father, but he would reassure him as best he could. 'No, no, of course not,' he said. 'They're not going to burn today.'

The White Wolf interrupted, his voice still as pleasant and even as Raimon remembered. 'I'm sorry for your uncere- monious greeting,' he said, 'but we're short of information and we didn't want you to gallop off. What can you tell us about the timing of the pyre, for I won't desert God's martyrs in their time of need.' His eyes were quite calm, even warm. He might have been asking the hour a shop opened or a market stall would be ready for business.

'Timing of the pyre? God's martyrs?' Raimon felt the key in his boot. 'Only a madman would call them anything but terrified people facing a hideous death.'

'And I shall face it with them,' the White Wolf said almost gaily. 'You may think me a madman for being prepared to die for what I believe, Raimon, but I assure you I'm not. I shall help them, and we shall all be in heaven together.'

'If you want to die, that's your business,' Raimon said, his lips curling with utter disgust, 'but it's the devil's work to force others.'

Sicart was beginning to crumble, and despite the White Wolf standing so close, he began to plead. 'She can't burn, Raimon, she can't.'

It was terrible for Raimon to see his father cry. 'Perhaps she won't, Father.' He wouldn't say anything about Yolanda's party or the key but he wanted to give his father some kind of hope. 'Perhaps the evidence won't be good enough for the Council to sign the warrants.' This was impossible, as Raimon well knew, but it was all he could think of to say.

Sicart shook his head. 'Any evidence will be good enough.'

'Maybe something will happen and the Inquisitor will never get to Avignonet.'

'Avignonet. Avignonet.' Sicart repeated the name. 'Is that where he's going?'

Raimon nodded. 'That's what I hear.'

His father was on his knees. 'Perfectus, it's not so far to Avignonet. Could we not get there before him and destroy the evidence so that he would have nothing to show?' He did not disguise that he was begging.

The White Wolf looked faintly contemptuous. 'Do you

not want your daughter to go to God, Sicart?'

'Of course I do.' Sicart was no longer begging, he was breaking down. 'Only not like that.' His voice was rising. 'Was my wife not enough, Perfectus, was she not enough?'

Raimon looked at his father, there on his knees, his back bent, his pride dissolved, his health broken and his whole body shaking with distress. With quiet deliberation, he spoke again. 'You know that the Blue Flame's been seen in Avignonet too, Father? Had you not even heard that? It's why Girald has gone himself. He's determined that the Blue Flame is his.'

At once, just as Raimon hoped, intense anxiety permeated the White Wolf's whole being. 'The Blue Flame? Are you sure?'

'I'm only saying what I've heard.'

The White Wolf's eyes flickered over to the horses.

Raimon was careful to say nothing more.

There was a pause. The Perfectus moved towards Bors. 'The Blue Flame,' he repeated. 'You're certain of that?' Raimon shrugged. It was enough. 'Come, Sicart,' the White Wolf said, 'perhaps you're right. Maybe we should go to Avignonet. We can go together.' He took Bors's rein and, not ungracefully, mounted. Raimon helped his father to mount Galahad. Sicart was gabbling. 'Yes, yes, thank you, Perfectus. We'll get to Avignonet and destroy the evidence and then Adela will be safe.' He kicked Galahad, who grunted.

'Wait!' The Perfectus looked at Raimon, who was still holding Galahad's rein. 'Avignonet, you say?'

'Avignonet,' Raimon repeated, his face betraying nothing.

Sicart was in an agony of impatience. 'Come ON,

Perfectus.'

But the White Wolf held his reins tight and dallied still further. 'I'm not sure.' Was that a twist in the boy's mouth?

Raimon looked the White Wolf directly in the eyes. It was cobalt meeting steel. 'The Blue Flame is to be found at Avignonet,' he said loudly, making sure that everybody could hear, 'just as salvation is to be found in your consolation.'

'You see!' cried Sicart. 'Why are we still waiting?'

The White Wolf lingered for one more second, and then, when Raimon let go of Galahad, he drove his heels into Bors and followed.

When Raimon eventually returned to the cave, Parsifal had never seen him so exultant. He had seen Yolanda, stolen the key and, best of all, sent the Perfectus on a wild goose chase. It was a fair trade for the loss of two warhorses. Let the Inquisitor and Perfectus fight it out in Avignonet. By that time, the prisoners would be free. 'Uncover the box,' he begged Parsifal, and when Parsifal obliged, and the Flame flared brightly, Raimon became almost dizzy.

It was Parsifal who noticed that the Flame's centre, instead of being blue, was as black as Raimon's eyes. He didn't say anything, because he didn't want to spoil the boy's elation, but long after Raimon was asleep, he was still sitting up, fingering the swords. The Flame was dancing, but not as Raimon, or any human being Parsifal had ever known, might dance. This dance had no joy about it, and it occurred to Parsifal that the Blue Flame was not dancing the dance of freedom but dancing the dance of death.

THE PARTY

The disappearance of the horses caused a small stir. Yolanda at once guessed what had happened and Aimery frowned and fumed and grew very suspicious but could do little. Berengar made no comment. The squires, when questioned, told how somebody in a des Arcis surcoat had taken both horses. Perhaps, some suggested, the man had taken them back to Paris. After a day or two, when neither Yolanda nor Hugh seemed anxious to pursue the matter, even Aimery had to let it drop, although he did not forget it, not for a minute. But the party was looming.

For everybody at Castelneuf, this was the oddest time, for even the clatter of platters, flap of tablecloths and the smells from the kitchen, all growing louder as the day drew nearer, could not disperse the tension. Nobody could forget that deep in the château's belly sat those who should have been guests. Nor could they forget that their hopes had been raised by the apparent appearance of the Blue Flame, only to be dashed again – and worse than dashed. Since the Flame's appearance, nothing but ill had happened. It was hard to accept.

Three days before the party, more friends of Aimery's arrived, clearly not from the Occitan. The servants and household knights were fearful of these northerners at first, but since the guests did nothing but laugh and josh and tease the maidservants, it was hardly possible to believe they meant any harm. Aimery noted all this with some satisfaction. When the time came, I was to give in gracefully to King Louis and the king would be suitably grateful.

Shortly after dawn on the day of the party itself, Yolanda was hunched into a ball in her chamber, Brees at her back, watching baskets of decorative blossom and great fans of hackle feathers being carried into the hall. She alternated between high anxiety, terror even, at the thought of the evening and all that could go wrong, and the joy of reliving again and again her reunion with Raimon. Out of all the dances they had ever danced, she would never forget the one in the cave. Sometimes she closed her eyes and stretched out her hands, pretending that she was once again pushing aside the root curtain, and that any moment now her fingers would reach his face.

The hardest bit of all, however, was pretending that she was going to enjoy herself. She had contemplated trying to send a message to Beatrice, to tell her what was to be attempted. It was very hard to think that her friend believed her to be callously celebrating. But although there were still people in the château Yolanda could trust completely, she didn't want to place them in danger. And she couldn't go herself. Aimery's friends and servants were everywhere.

Suddenly stifled, she leant out into the clamour of the courtyard below. Through the gates over the last few days had rolled an untidy train of brightly coloured carts, all sprouting a motley collection of singers and dancers. The count had been encouraged by Aimery to spare no expense and the list of entertainments to liven up the late afternoon and evening would have thrilled Yolanda in other circumstances. There was to be a dart-throwing contest, a mock battle with oranges from Valencia, acrobats and, from Catalonia, an Imaginator to tell fortunes. Yet these seemed as nothing when Gui and Guerau's instruments still hung silent in the hall.

Across the river, at the top of one of the paths cut into the forest, Raimon perched in a tree and waited for Parsifal's whistle. When it came, he braced himself, then dropped. There was a brief struggle, after which Parsifal apologised to the victims and advised them to return to their homes. Their clothes and their horses would be put to good use. When they began to quarrel with this courteous thief, he and Raimon drew their swords. They fled. 'God go with both them and us,' Parsifal said fervently as he pulled on a multi-coloured tunic and helped Raimon to do the same.

And so they all waited, and the château waited too.

At last a slow dusk began to fall and the smoke from the kitchen chimneys thickened. Now a great rumbling was heard, and after the rumbling, a cheering. Fifty barrels of ale and as many casks of wine were rolled from their place of storage and up a makeshift ramp into the great hall. They were cracked open and now the entertainments in the court-yards began. Though it was not yet dark, with reckless extravagance new candles and freshly made torches were lit and the small boys designated to tend them scurried about clutching baskets of flint and steel and the all important buckets of sand and water in case of accident. Though Yolanda had specifically asked that there should be no bonfire – how could they, when its roar and rush would be torture to the prisoners? – her request had been ignored and within minutes a huge pile of straw and old wood was spewing sparks and ashes into the twilight.

In the other courtyards, as the night deepened, smaller fires were also lit so that eventually, from the valley, the château seemed peppered with small volcanoes and in between the fires, like capering devils, men and women juggled and span wooden platters, performed somersaults and did handstands on each other's shoulders. It was certainly a spectacle.

The Imaginator set up his tent in the herb garden and soon had a steady stream of clients as first the servants and then the knights lined up. Some came out frowning, others forcing themselves to laugh. The French knights wished they had never been tempted, for the Imaginator whispered of miserable death and eternal damnation. Hugh, in a tunic of unostentatious but expensive blue silk, emerged silent and thoughtful. Though the Imaginator was heavily veiled, he had a familiar look about him. He searched for Yolanda but couldn't find her. Instead he found Aimery closeted with his father discussing last minute details. He called Aimery out, and for the first time, Hugh had a look of impatience about him.

Yolanda, lingering in her room and expecting Aimery's furious summons at any moment, was staring at herself in a beaten-up silver plate. She had nothing new to wear and without Beatrice it was no fun painting her eyes, brushing chalk on her cheeks or rubbing rosemadder onto her lips. She toyed with the comb Hugh had given her, remembering what Raimon said about her hair. Brushing it still felt like a betrayal. One minute boiling and the next clammy with nerves, she had no idea what the evening would bring. She could not think beyond it. Slowly she started with the comb and after she'd done her own hair, did Brees's as well.

At last Aimery banged on her door, but instead of being furious at her tardiness, he was hovering with a sheepish look on his face. When he saw her hair, he visibly relaxed. In his arms lay a long, sleek sheath. 'It's a dress, Yola. It came from Toulouse. If our mother had been alive, she'd have made you one, I know, but she's not and I know how you feel about having a party at the moment, but it is your fourteenth birthday and you are my sister, so –' He handed it to her. They stood together. 'Come on, you must be quick,' he said. 'The feast is starting. We're both going to be late. Get it on and we'll go down together. Father's waiting.'

She grabbed the sheath and, a moment later, reappeared, shutting Brees in behind her. Dogs were banned tonight, to make more room. He whined briefly, then settled down to scratch. He missed his dirt.

Aimery held up a torch to see her and made small, admiring noises, for the dress tumbled in clever silver folds that gave his sister's elusive beauty an unwarranted sophistication, and her hair, loose and unadorned, added the perfection of simplicity. They walked down the steps together, neither knowing what to say to the other. When she appeared in the hall to a shower of compliments and gifts, Aimery was proud, and when he handed her over to Berengar, already standing on the dais, he was unsurprised to find tears on his father's cheeks.

Yolanda was dazzled. Never had she seen so many candles, although it was bitter how few faces she recognised in a hall supposedly full of friends. The Occitan knights were clustered together by the fire, as if under siege, all their swords piled in a corner as was customary. The only person who had kept his was Aimery. The knights acknowledged Yolanda, but many of the servants would not meet her eye. Nevertheless, without a sound, she took her place of honour, her father on one side and expecting Aimery on the other. But it was Hugh who was her neighbour.

'Sit, sit,' said Berengar.

At once, two troubadours Yolanda did not know and who did not know her leapt with a great flourish out of two empty waterbarrels, and sang with sly smiles. Their music was fine, finer than anything Gui or Guerau could have produced, and the lyrics cleverer. But though both birthday songs were greeted with wild applause, they were, in fact, quite empty, for they sang of a girl who was not Yolanda. It was, however, very easy to choose a winner. She just stuck out a finger and pointed.

After that, it became for her a party in a story. She was there, but not there, eating but not eating, drinking but not drinking, speaking but not speaking, just as you do in dreams. Her real self was with Raimon. She knew he was here somewhere. She did not have to see him to be certain of that. She spoke too quickly and laughed too loudly, shining like a brittle star. Only occasionally did the weight of her anxiety overwhelm her and then she drooped like an overblown rose.

Hugh leant over. 'Drink some of this,' he said, pressing a goblet to her lips. Warm and spiced, the wine coated both her throat and her consciousness with its syrupy balm. She took three swallows, then three more before a drop of the wine fell down the front of her dress where it sat, a small red bead amongst the silver. Though Hugh quickly flicked it away, it left a tiny pink stain.

Course upon course arrived and the hall grew hotter and hotter as the company grew more rowdy. The servants did not fill individual goblets any more. They just left the men to dip their tankards in enormous jugs set on the floor beside the trestles, drain them and dip them again. Yolanda's tongue was sticky and her head fuzzy. Hugh was too solicitous, the food too rich, the air too thick. The masked jugglers made her dizzy. The hall's painted ceiling and the tapestries, garish now after being specially scrubbed for the occasion, closed in on her. She pushed back her chair. 'Let's dance,' she cried. 'Come, Father, I want to dance first with you.'

Aimery clapped his hands. 'The birthday dance!' he cried. 'We must all watch the birthday dance!'

Nobody took much notice but the troubadours struck up anyway and father and daughter moved together. Yolanda leant her cheek against her father's shoulder. It seemed so long since they had even spoken. He was shrunken in his festival clothes and she had to guide him through the steps. 'All will be well, won't it?' She didn't know what she wanted him to say, and when he squeezed her fingers, she was not reassured. They danced until the music stopped and then they parted.

Aimery, now full of liquor, called the hall to better attention. It was time. 'All of you, come on, silence, silence.' He banged his goblet on the table. There was some sort of hush.

It was enough. Aimery cleared his throat. 'Before we all join in the dancing and enjoy more of the outside entertainments, which, I can promise you, will not disappoint, I want to propose a toast. And as this is a very special day, and a very special toast, I want everybody gathered in here, and I mean everybody. We must do this properly. So get the squires and the grooms, the cooks and all the household. Go to the mews and bring in the falconers. Get the huntsmen and the armourers. I want even the dogboys.' His speech was distinctly slurred but the servants obeyed him. He raised a jug to Hugh.

Yolanda, highly uneasy at the looks between the two men, got up but then sat down. If the courtyards were empty, Raimon really did have a chance. She held herself very still.

It took some time for everybody to assemble and the hall had never been so full. There was scarcely room to breathe. Nevertheless, Aimery waited until he was satisfied that everybody was present, before planting his feet wide. Now he spoke, sending his words clearly into every corner of the room. 'I have two toasts to make. The first, naturally, is to my sister, Yolanda. It's her birthday, and for that we wish her joy.' He took a long drink and wiped his mouth on the back of his hand. 'The second toast, my friends, is to something even more important. The less drunk amongst you –' laughter at this '– may have noticed the dress Yolanda is wearing. This is no common dress. It's a dress that tells a story. Can you guess what that story is?' The knights stamped their feet. Yolanda could hardly understand. Aimery pulled her to her feet. 'My lords, you've guessed right. The story is a romance. The dress was the proposal and the wearing of the dress the acceptance.

My sister Yolanda is betrothed to –' The stamps from some of the knights turned to roars and drowned out the name. It didn't matter. Hugh was standing, acknowledging and smiling. The knights bearing my colours were less enthusiastic. Romance was all very well, but marriage between an Occitanian and a Frenchman was a contract. Some frowned. Aimery just opened his eyes very wide.

Yolanda did not look at Hugh or the knights. She was looking down at the folds of silver that fell so neatly to the floor. It was just a dress, surely. But she had put it on so quickly. What had she not seen? She gripped a candle and pulled up the spangled train. Then her face was ashen. 'No,' she said loudly, 'no.' The dress was indeed a romance for, if you looked closely, in its glittery tracings were united the fist of des Arcis and the bear's head of the Amouroix, interspersed with the letters H and Y coiled so tight together it was impossible to say where one letter ended and the other began. Thus was I, publicly and irretrievably, to hitch my wagon to the des Arcis star, and every person in the hall knew it.

Now Yolanda turned to Hugh. 'You tricked me.'

He was very calm. 'There was no trick on my part. The dress could not have been clearer.' She made as if to run from him, but he seized her arm and there was something more than romance in his eyes. He spoke quickly and quietly. 'Keep the hall full, Yolanda. This is the best chance there'll be.' He gave her a little shake. 'Smile, smile and sing. Nobody will leave if you sing.'

It was not possible to misunderstand him. His arm was now a support, not a restraint. She opened her mouth but nothing came out. People began to rise. Hugh shook her again. 'Dance then,' he said, 'dance for their lives.'

She hesitated for a moment. He nodded. Then she was on the table. Her steps were automatic at first, but then, as Hugh began to clap, more sure. She gathered herself up and he held out his hand and helped her to leap from the dais and through the crowd, from barrel to trestle to barrel, and then he let go so that she could hold out her hands to the guests, for each to take his turn. Now nobody thought of leaving and the brows of those knights who had frowned grew less furrowed for Yolanda's face was alight with something they could not quite grasp and they all queued up to lift her and whirl her round. The music joined with the dance and the pace increased. Faster and faster the troubadours strummed until Yolanda was being thrown from arm to arm, table to table, barrel to barrel, like a piece of gossamer blown on a rough wind, and in every throw, every whirl she saw not her momentary partner's face but the face of a prisoner tasting freedom. Only when she was so dizzy she could dance no more did Hugh catch her up and carry her back to her chair, where she sat collapsed, her hair a riot and the train of the dress no longer a smooth teardrop but now a frost of tatters from clumsy feet.

The guests were clapping, the French knights thrilled and amazed at this unexpected magic, and the household knights noisily proud of their count's daughter, so it took a little while for everyone to begin to trickle out, still applauding, still drinking, full and happy in the heightened atmosphere and ready to enjoy the further excitements that Aimery had promised. It took even more time for their chatter to turn to surprised silence. The courtyard below the great hall was completely empty, the gate into it swinging. The entertainers had vanished. The guests were suddenly suspicious, suddenly very conscious of the lack of their swords. Some turned back towards the hall, trying to remember exactly where the weapons were. Those who could not get back up the steps crammed together in defensive bunches. Others, still in full celebratory mood, laughed. This, they cried, was a ruse to add theatricality to some miraculous surprise. Aimery had promised them a spectacular party and this was a prelude to that spectacle. Aimery, at the top of the steps, shouted that this was indeed the case. There had been a small delay, that was all. He encouraged them to go back into the hall and carry on drinking. His father would open more barrels. The troubadours had a new epic with which to delight them.

He himself pushed through the crowd and ran with only Alain beside him from courtyard to courtyard. Each was empty of everything but the remnants of the fire for when Raimon had unlocked the cellars and the prisoners had bundled out, everybody had fled. Nobody wanted to be a witness to this. Witnesses, too, could end up in the dock.

The stragglers were at the main gate. Aimery could see them being urged along by Raimon. Alain thought he would shout and call for guards as soon as he saw them but instead Aimery slowed to a walk.

How fate spins on a moment. Had Parsifal been in the courtyard rather than down at the bridge seeing to Sanchez and Pierre; had the prisoners moved a little quicker; had Aimery kept his mouth shut; so much might have been different. But Parsifal was not there, the prisoners were hesitant and slow, suspecting a trap, and Aimery could not resist calling out 'Very brave, for a weaver,' just as Raimon was about to slip out of the gate himself so that the boy stopped, hesitated and then, disastrously, turned.

'What did you say?'

'I said, "very brave, for a weaver".' He made no move to stop Raimon from leaving. 'Go on now, back to your loom. You've got what you came for.'

'You knew?'

'You made a bad Imaginator and you don't think you could have got the prisoners out if I'd decided to stop you, do you?'

Raimon stared at him.

'You've Hugh des Arcis to thank for all of this,' said Aimery smoothly. 'He doesn't want my sister and his future wife –' he enjoyed saying that '– upset. So when he recognised you, he asked that you should be given a chance. I must say, you've done very well. When Girald comes back and finds the cellars empty, I shall blame the whole thing on my father. There. Now everybody's happy.'

'I want to see Yolanda.' Raimon had his sword in both hands. 'She's coming with me.'

'No, I think not. She's betrothed to Hugh now. Come on, Raimon, you can't have everything.'

'Send your squire for her and let her choose.'

Aimery was growing impatient. 'There's no question of choosing. She's moved into a different world.'

'I want to see her.'

Aimery spoke as if to an idiot. 'What you want is of no interest at all to me. Yolanda is going to marry Hugh des

Arcis for her own good and the good of the Amouroix. Exactly what about that statement don't you understand?'

Raimon raised his sword. 'You're betraying the Occitan.'

Aimery raised his. 'I'm doing it for the Occitan. If other places are wise, they'll think along the same lines.'

'You're doing it for you.'

Aimery began to edge forward. 'If you don't go now, Raimon, I'll kill you and this time I'll make sure I do it properly.'

'You'll have to kill me if you want me to give up either of the things I love.'

'Oh, love,' said Aimery comtemptuously. 'What has love got to do with anything at all?'

There was a brief silence and then, because there was nothing else to say, they were fighting, both in deadly earnest. They were better matched, to start with, than they had been at the bearhunt, but a few lessons from Parsifal did not make Raimon a difficult opponent for a knight of Aimery's greater weight and experience. There was no river this time, nothing to give Raimon any advantage at all and Aimery pushed hard. He would not be thwarted again. He wrong-footed Raimon, bore down, kicked out and dislodged his sword, then altered his own grip and lifted his arms for the final thrust. He hesitated only because he could not decide immediately whether to crush head or neck, and in that moment, the uneven hoof-beats of weary horses were heard piling in at the gate. For a second, Raimon thought it might be Parsifal. It was not.

There were three men, all swaying with exhaustion and their own horses, together with the two they were leading, dripped sweat onto the cobbles. Only one man spoke and when he had finished, he dropped the reins of the riderless mounts, turned his horse around and all three men rode away. The encounter took less than a minute but Aimery's shock at what they told him paralysed him for a moment. Underneath the poised sword, Raimon could not imagine what Aimery would do now.

Nor could Aimery. He again made ready for the thrust, then changed his mind, made Raimon get up and take the reins of the abandoned horses before hurrying them all into the cave in which the wine kegs for the party had been stored. He had to get Alain to hit the horses to make them move again, and once in the cave they stood, their heads between their knees and their knees buckling. With the rope that had bound the barrels together, he tied Raimon tightly beside them.

Ten minutes later, he returned to the hall. The guests were expectant. Aimery stood on a barrel. 'I'm sorry,' he announced. 'We were to stage a mock siege, with Greek fire and catapults, but the troupe hasn't arrived. It's too bad.' There were groans of disappointment. 'Never mind!' He was loud and bluff. 'There'll be other parties! Eat, drink! Troubadours, play up, play up.' He ran round, filling tankards himself, and after a few slow minutes, the party continued. Berengar was sitting down, totally bemused.

Yolanda, having got nothing from her father, was tugging at Aimery's sleeve. 'What's happened? Please, you must tell me.'

'The cellars are empty,' he told her.

'Empty!' she could not stop her smile.

'Empty.' He looked at her quizzically. 'Be thankful for that, Yolanda.'

'Oh, I am.' His expression was so odd. He should be furious. He kept looking at her but he would say nothing more.

When she could, she ran out into the courtyards. The quiet was eerie. She ran to the cellar entrance, but hesitated before descending the steps. She felt Hugh behind her. 'Do you want to go down?' he asked. 'They really are empty.' She shook her head. All she wondered now was when Raimon would come back for her.

It was dawn before the revellers, slack-jawed and mumbling, collapsed into the rushes and slept. A thoroughly frustrated Brees was waiting for Yolanda in her room, and when she took off the silver dress and threw it into a corner, he seized it at once. Yolanda wished him joy of it. She would never ever wear it again. As far as she was concerned, the dress and Aimery's toast meant nothing. It was only when she lay down that she remembered she had not said goodnight to her father.

When everybody was settled, Aimery went to Berengar, who was still sitting in the hall in exactly the same place, and told him what the weary rider had told him. He opened his hand and when Berengar saw what was enclosed, he let out a loud moan and his heart, strained to breaking point since the day Girald arrived, began to crack. He leaned hard on Aimery to get into his chamber, and bumped into the table as though, amid the light, his own world had suddenly turned dark. He fell onto his bed and Aimery had to lift his feet. Servants ran for the chateau's herbalist.

'Horrible, horrible,' the count was gasping, although Aimery didn't know whether at the news or the pain.

Nevertheless, he bent down and whispered something else into his father's ear.

This time, Berengar's moan made his hangings tremble. 'It's not possible.'

'I'm afraid so.'

Berengar tried and failed to grip his son's hand. 'I don't understand the world any more, Aimery.' His face was twisted in mortal agony. His left side was in spasm.

'I'm not sure you've ever understood it, Father. You have to be a part of it to understand it. You've just ignored it.'

The herbalist arrived, took one look and shook his head. 'You'd better send for Simon Crampcross,' he said. The servants began to wail and a momentary flash of pity crossed Aimery's face. He sent for Yolanda and then heard his name. 'Father?' He leaned over, close up, so that his father would be able to see him. 'Do what is right,' the old man said.

'I'll do what is best,' Aimery replied. It was, at least in his eyes, the truth.

AFTER THE PARTY

Aimery waited until the sun was high before, with a bell rung loudly and continuously, he forced the insensible partygoers to haul themselves up, hawking and spitting and regretting the wine. Pages ran with cold water and twigs with which their masters could pick bits of last night's dinner from their teeth. Aimery himself was already freshly laundered, as was Hugh. They sat on the dais.

Yolanda came, dragging one foot after another, her eyes hollow with sleeplessness. She had been with her father to the end. He had not recognised her, but it seemed to her that two expressions had vied for a last supremacy over his face: one of relief that all was over and the other of supreme regret. When, just as the candles in his chamber were being renewed, he drew his last breath, she was not sure which expression made her cry the most.

Aimery, nodded at her in acknowledgement of their loss. Then he turned to the matter in hand. 'My friends,' he said, 'I have something truly abominable to tell you. Earlier this morning, three messengers came here to Castelneuf. The news they bore is shocking.' He stopped. 'So shocking that my father's heart could not withstand it. A few hours ago, he died.'

There was a groan, and many of the knights fell to their knees. The servants were already openly weeping. Aimery gave a short and pretty eulogy, as was expected, then he paused and waited for the knights to stand up again. 'Now I must tell you what I told my father. Whilst we were celebrating my sister's birthday and betrothal, our uncle, Inquisitor Girald, and six fellow Inquisitors, were being murdered.' There was quite a different noise, a clatter as knights felt for their swords. Aimery held up his hand. 'My uncle lies at this moment in a pool of his own blood. He was dragged from sleep, and cut down whilst on his knees.' Some knights reached for their swords and gripped the hilts. Aimery waited for a few minutes. 'The weapons used were not just spears and daggers, but axes and maces. By the time the murderers had finished, our uncle was only recognisable from this.' Yolanda, who had heard none of this before, clapped her hands over her mouth as Aimery opened his hand and picked something out between two fingers. It was what he had shown to his father: a small object, blotted with blood and hair, but still unmistakeable. It was Girald's ring. When the knights roared, though his father lay dead only yards away, Aimery did not stop them.

Hours later, after the old count had been properly laid out in the hall in his best surcoat with candles head and foot and Simon Crampcross muttering by his side, Hugh told Yolanda that Raimon who had been arrested for Girald's murder. At first, Yolanda, in a state of exhausted shock, had laughed in a kind of hysteria. They were sitting in the small hall, still all set up for Girald's court but with its menace gone. Now it was simply dingy. Then she had cried and finally taken a deep shuddering breath. 'That can't possibly be true,' she said. Aimery came in. Hugh nodded at him and he repeated it. 'I'm sorry, Yola,' Aimery said.

Now she was angry. 'You know perfectly well that Raimon – that Raimon – that he was – was killed at the bearhunt. You saw for yourself.'

'Let's not pretend, not any more, Yola. Raimon wasn't killed at the bearhunt.'

She bit her lip.

Aimery sat down beside her. 'We know Raimon killed Uncle Girald because –' there was the smallest of pauses, '– Galahad and Bors were found at Avignonet, outside the tavern in which Girald was staying.'

'What?'

'You heard me. The horses Hugh gave you, and which you gave to Raimon, were found there.'

'But I didn't –'

'It's not the time for lies. We all know he took the horses, and anyway, –' he stopped again, for this was the last moment to change his mind – a glimmer, perhaps, of regret but he didn't change it, '– Raimon was captured riding away from Avignonet. The knights who brought Girald's ring brought him with them. Raimon had the ring in his pouch. I'm sorry, Yola. I didn't want to tell you, and certainly not today. But that's the truth.'

The shock silenced Yolanda. 'Where is he?'

'Come,' said Aimery quite gently, 'I'll show him to you.'

She followed blindly. She couldn't and wouldn't believe that Raimon was a murderer. He had been here, freeing the prisoners. He had. Who else would have freed them? Yet she had not seen him and she kept hearing in her head Raimon telling her that Girald didn't deserve to live. But she couldn't, wouldn't, believe that he had picked up an axe and killed her uncle in cold blood. Aimery was telling her how sorry he was. She wanted to scream.

Alain already had Raimon in the courtyard. Stiff and hunched, he staggered, much as a boy might who, unused to heavy riding, has been many hours in an unfamiliar saddle. Alain held him before them and though Aimery was quite genuinely sorry for what would now happen, he could not be sorry that this boy who had proved himself such a persistent nuisance, would, at last and this time for always, shortly be an obstacle no longer.

Yolanda tried to speak, but Aimery cut her off, and though she protested loudly, Hugh hurried her away.

That day Raimon was taken to Foix for trial and the judge hardly bothered to wait until the end of the process to pass sentence. There was no point. Raimon had been caught at the site of the Inquisitor's murder; he had admitted, in front of the late Inquisitor and witnesses, to having taken part, with a Cathar Perfectus, in his mother's consolation and, what was more, he had deliberately discarded his prescribed heretic's tabard. There was only one fit punishment: the pyre. Raimon was asked if, for mercy's sake, he would express horror or remorse at his crime. He would not.

In fact, Raimon said nothing at all throughout the proceedings. He turned himself into ice. Whatever he said could make no difference, except, perhaps, to incriminate his father. One of the witnesses swore he heard the name 'Belot' shouted at Avignonet. No doubt he had. It was ironic that he was the only witness who was probably telling the truth.

But though he could freeze out almost everything, he could not freeze out Yolanda and one image haunted him: the glassiness in her eyes when he had been dragged into the dock. True, it had been the day she buried her father, but the glassiness had not been from grief: it had been from uncertainty. She really thought he might be guilty. He could not allow himself to think about that, nor about whether, had he been with his father and the White Wolf when they came upon Girald, he would have added his blows to theirs. Nor about whether Girald's murder was his fault. He could not be sorry the Inquisitor was dead, but such a death! Not a clean thrust with a sword, but axes and maces. That was not death, it was butchery. He tried to banish all that and think only of Parsifal and the Flame. They were his last hope now. So quickly had everything turned to dust.

After he was sentenced, many cruel days were spent debating where he should be burnt: in Foix for convenience, at Toulouse as an example to all or at Castelneuf. Days turned into weeks.

Up in my hills, Parsifal waited too. The Flame told him nothing, but he knew what he must do.

It was finally decided, claimed indeed, as an act of mercy, that Raimon's pyre should be built at Castelneuf and he was transported back, bound and shackled, bearing a heretic's tabard once again and kept in a heavily guarded cart by the river on the town side of the bridge.

When the pyre was built – there had been no volunteers, so Simon Crampcross had had to threaten people with eternal damnation if they did not respond to the summons – Aimery went to inspect it. Children were playing round it, but Aimery backed quickly away. He had never seen anybody die like this and decided that he would watch it lit and then retreat. He ordered Hugh to keep Yolanda away. 'Take her to Paris at once and marry her. Nice clothes, a baby or two and all those Parisian amusements will help her get over it. After a month or two, she'll have forgotten us all. When things are better settled, she can come back to visit.' He fiddled with his beard and plucked imaginary pieces of straw from the cuffs of his tunic as he spoke, not even convincing himself.

Hugh had some sympathy. 'I suppose this is really necessary?'

Aimery stopped fiddling. 'You know it is, Hugh, and when you get to Paris, don't forget to tell King Louis that the new Count of the Amouroix knows his Catholic duty,' he said. 'This is not just a murderer but a heretic that we're burning.'

'He's already heard,' Hugh told him. 'As my wedding present, as a compliment to your sister and the county of Amouroix, he's made me Seneschal of Carcassonne. Your sister will be married to a man of real power.'

Aimery gave a grim smile.

Yolanda refused, point-blank, to leave before the execution was carried out. She had sent letters to the judge begging for a reprieve, and couldn't believe one wouldn't come. Hugh did not argue, just ordered her things to be packed up – not many of them, she would have her own seamstress in Paris – and frowned when he contemplated Brees, padding around like a sultry lion. Now was a bad time to get rid of the dog, although a clean break with the past might be best for Yolanda in the long run.

By the time the execution day dawned, Yolanda had almost stopped living. She watched her things packed up with no apparent emotion. What did she care about things any more? She had not eaten for days. She passed Hugh in the courtyard with Galahad and Bors, two luggage wagons and an armed escort in the des Arcis colours. They were waiting for her. They would have to wait longer. She would not go yet. She made straight for the château gate. It was closed and two soldiers would not move at her order. She turned to Hugh. 'Do you hate me?' she asked.

'What a question. You know I don't.'

'Order them to let me out.'

'I can't do that. Believe me, you don't want to go down there. You can't help your friend now.'

'Let me out.' She could feel a wail rising from within her and tried to strangle it, but could not strangle all of it. With a huge effort she turned it into words. 'He must know I'm there. Please. He's got nobody else. After that, I don't care what happens.'

Hugh considered and his tone was very reasonable. 'Look, I can't let you go. I promised. But I do have an idea. Send Brees. Raimon will see him and know you've sent him because you couldn't go yourself.'

'I need to go myself.'

'Don't you see that that would pain Raimon more than anything?'

'No, no it wouldn't. How dare you say it would. You don't know him.'

'No, but I know what I would prefer if I were him.'

Yolanda argued, but Hugh was unbending, and at last, in despair, and telling Hugh she would never forgive him, she sent Brees with a servant. The dog went obediently but reluctantly, straining backwards then forwards as he tried to understand what Yolanda meant him to do. After he had gone, acutely regretting handing him over, she began to beat her fists on the ground. She was beyond reason, although Hugh tried, and only when the bells began to toll, warning of a soul about to be sent to heaven or hell, did she stop. At once, Hugh brought Galahad to her. 'Mount now, my dear. It really is best to be away.' He lifted her into the saddle. The bells tolled on and on.

Hugh mounted himself, waiting impatiently until he thought the roads would be cleared. He didn't want to wait until the pyre was lit, for he thought the sight and the smell might cause Yolanda irreparable damage. They must be away before there was any sign of smoke. The whole cavalcade trotted out, with himself holding firmly onto Galahad's rein. Though the horses slithered down the hill, he pushed them on. They must hurry.

The streets were deserted and they saw nobody until the bottom of the hill, where there was a small logjam of people. Here they were delayed. Raimon was still crossing the bridge. He should have been well past by now, but the sight of the boy stepping forward with as much desperate eagerness as the shackles allowed, as if he were proud to die, had transformed him from piteous prisoner into heroic martyr. Everybody was trying to touch him, or at least touch the hem of his tunic and some women who had got to the pyre early to get a good place, tried to push back across the bridge to fetch pots so that after the fire, they, like their wiser neighbours, could gather up the warm ashes and keep them as relics.

Hugh exclaimed with annoyance and drew his sword, using the flat of it to forge a path. When that proved impossible, he tried to turn Galahad round and take Yolanda back to the château. The horse was willing enough, but in the press of people, he grew alarmed and lost his footing and Yolanda, sitting like a rag doll, was pitched off. Hugh grabbed her, missed, and she vanished under a rolling carpet of bodies. Shouting to his squires, Hugh leapt off himself and tried to fish her out, but she was now so firmly knitted into the carpet that she was as impossible to untangle as a small thread in a giant knot. At first, trampled and kicked, she lay prone and uncaring. It was only when she heard Hugh's voice calling her name that she was galvanised and began to fight using elbows and fists. First she got herself onto all fours and then upright. 'Let me through! I must get through!' Some people, when they saw who she was, tried to help her, others ignored her. Either way it didn't much matter for the crowd was so tight, she made very little progress. Crushed and bruised she nevertheless kept going. She would get to Raimon. She would. She didn't care if he had murdered her uncle. She just wanted him to know she was with him and would always be with him. Yet even fighting like a cat, she couldn't get close to him. The bridge was too narrow. There was no room to move.

At last, there was no option but to climb onto the parapet. It was narrow, the stones were damp and the river ran blackly beneath but she used the shoulders of the people below to steady herself. That was better. One foot then the other. One foot then the other. Now she was moving. Before the bridge end she was calling to him. 'Raimon! Raimon!'

But he would only look forward. He could not look round. If he did, his courage might fail him and that must not happen. He must think of nothing. That was the only way he could manage.

Yolanda stopped calling. 'Come down,' an old man urged, but she wouldn't do that either. Instead, she began to sing the Song of the Flame. She began in quite a small voice, but it would not stay small. The second time she sang the Song, it was much stronger and more beautiful and the third time it was too loud for beauty and too insistent to be ignored. She sang not to cheer or to comfort, she sang to gather up everything she and Raimon had had and everything they might have had and she sang not just for him and for herself, but for a whole world coming to an end.

In Occitan there hovers still
The grace of Arthur's table round.
Bright southern heroes yet fulfil
The quest to which they all are bound.
No foreign pennant taints our skies,
No cold French king snuffs out our name.
Though we may fall, again we'll rise.
No Grail for us, we burn the Flame!

The Flame, the Flame, the Flame of Blue,
Sweet Occitan, it burns for you.

When she had finished for the third time, she started again, and then again. And now she wasn't alone. A humming was heard, like a distant swarm of bees. Through tight lips, tens of throats vibrated, then hundreds, as the humming spread. At the pyre, Aimery's new French friends drew together, the hairs on the backs of their necks prickling. They looked to Aimery, but it was clear he was powerless to stop it.

As Yolanda sang, a path was cleared for her and she stopped singing only when, at last, she stood where she wanted to be. 'Look at me,' she said to Raimon.

'I can't,' he said, keeping his eyes on his feet.

'Look at me,' she said again.

He looked, and found it still there, that glow he had felt in the dark: intense, with no gaps into which doubts can creep or petty grievances take root. She was not here to try and guess, from his face, whether he had or had not murdered Girald. She was here because she loved him. That was all. He moved forward until their cheeks were almost touching. He did not have to speak. They breathed the same breath, just as they always had, but this breath was not the childish breath of that first bungled kiss, this breath was rich and deep, filling his veins just as he knew it was filling hers. But then he had to break the spell. He had to tell her. 'I've seen the Flame,' he said.

'Yes,' she said, through her tears. 'It will be there for you.'

'No, that's not what I mean. I've really seen the Flame. The Knight Magician of the Breeze. He had it – he has it. I told you he'd gone, but he hasn't, or at least he hadn't.' He didn't know whether he'd been clear enough for her to understand. She seemed bemused. She was looking round, as if Parsifal might suddenly appear from nowhere. 'Don't look round, just listen. The Flame's here. It's come to help us, I'm sure of that. Don't give up hope. The Knight Magician – Sir Parsifal – he'll work out what to do. He must.'

'But what's the point of Flame without you? What's the point of anything?' Her lips were trembling.

He lifted his shackled hands and took hold of hers. 'The Occitan,' he said simply. 'That's the point.'

'I'd give it all up to save your life.' She was gripping his hands, trying to mould them into her own.

His face darkened. 'Don't say that. Never say that. I don't want that. Do you understand? I could never want that.'

The crowd was getting restive. Yolanda gripped his hands even more tightly. She wanted to say something, to do something, that would carry his soul away now, before what was to come, but she couldn't think of anything. The crowd began to encroach again. Raimon was forced to move forward and she had to let go. As he left her, he turned, and for one blistering second, it was as if they were quite alone, just the two of them, ready to run into the wind. Then he was gone and the crowd, wanting to speed things up, pushed her aside.

She was alone and staring beyond the crowd at the hills behind when Hugh got to her. 'Come,' he said. Though he felt for her, she was still his prize and he was claiming her. She didn't argue when he lifted her, once again, onto Galahad and took the reins more firmly this time. As soon as the road was clear, he pushed both horses into a gallop. The Song of the Flame resounded in his head. No matter, the clatter of the horses' hooves would drown it out. He had had enough of the south for the moment.

In the heretics' cemetery, Raimon was soon strapped to the stake. The soldiers quickly piled brushwood at his feet and then set themselves as guards round the pyre. Aimery gave the signal for silence. There should be no delay now. He began a short speech that was expected and although his voice did not ring out with quite its usual authority, the gist was clear enough. Raimon was a murderer, he said, who had been lawfully tried and sentenced. It was a sad thing for the Count of Amouroix to preside over the burning of one of his own, but justice must be done.

The stake dug into Raimon's back and though nothing was yet lit, he could already smell the smoke. He refused the blindfold. If his eyes were bound, he would be on that road from Limoux, holding his father's hand, and he did not want that to be his last vision. He wanted to see the sky and the hills, and turn the clouds into animals again. Now that the moment had come he wondered how long he would take to die and was glad that soldiers hid him from the crowd. He already knew that nobody can face the flames without fear although he hoped very much that he could stay silent. When the tapers appeared, their flames invisible in the sunlight, he stared, with great concentration, at a red-tailed eagle sailing lazily overhead.

He could tell that the wood had been lit, not from any heat, but from the gasps of the crowd. It seemed a curiously long time before he could hear the gust and crackle as sparks teased round the straw. For moments more there was nothing but smoke, then a few rags ignited and their flames wavered, bowed, then sent out tendrils to meet each other, like a whole lot of friends shaking hands. The men with tapers retreated.

The pyre was not going to go out now. As the flames grew stronger, they also grew more adventurous. Now Raimon could feel heat under the platform and his eyes began to sting. It could only be a moment before the whole thing was ablaze. He breathed very quickly and then not at all. It was strange, but though it was almost unbearably hot on his feet and the back of his legs, his face felt deadly cold. The whole world began to turn red and yellow and he was struggling to keep his mouth shut. Any second, he would have to open it and when he did he had no idea what kind of a sound would come out.

There was screaming, which he was sure must be coming from him even though his mouth still seemed to be closed. He felt the wood beneath his feet give way. This was it. This was it. But instead of flames licking his legs, something was arising from the straw. Raimon choked. A human figure, almost a comic figure, for he was half man, half haystack, was beside him. And then the figure shook itself and Parsifal, his clothes smoking and his surcoat shredding, was holding the Blue Flame high above his head.

Afterwards, everybody swore the Flame was a towering inferno that rose from the heart of the fire like an angel rising from hell. In reality, it flared only a little taller than before but the colour it spread was so powerful that the other flames seemed to shrink before it. Parsifal sliced through Raimon's bonds and took his hand. 'Jump,' he cried, 'for God's sake, jump.' They jumped clam-tight together, and before these two blue human torches the soldiers fled, and then they were running round the circle of spectators, Parsifal brandishing the Flame, his hands white as chalk and flaking from the heat of the pyre. 'Do you know what this is?' he cried. 'I dare you not to know what this is.' They all cowered back.

A chink between the soldiers was all Parsifal sought but one would not appear. Nor did the crowd remain an astonished, paralysed mass. They were no longer interested in Raimon. At last! The Flame! They crowded in, holding out their hands and Parsifal had to raise the silver salver high above his head, higher than he thought possible, to stop it being ripped from his hand.

Then the Flame poured downwards like a blue fountain and people exclaimed and covered their eyes. Some had to pull back. A chink appeared in the throng. Parsifal dived through it. He could smell his own hair singeing but he had Raimon's hand in his and he would not let go.

Aimery stood, open mouthed. He began to run forward, then backwards, not knowing what to do, and by the time he had collected himself, Parsifal and Raimon were away, clambering through the cemeteries, then into the woods whilst the Flame's fountain dwindled to a trickle, then to uneven drops and then dried up altogether like a firework that has run out of fuel. People were shouting, searching and beating the undergrowth with sticks as if Parsifal and Raimon were a pair of foxes or birds to be flushed out. They divided up and beat in quarters. They pushed forward in a long line. But always sticking together, Raimon and Parsifal ducked and weaved, flattening themselves into holes and curling into trees, sometimes being missed only by a whisker. If they could just hold out for long enough, the searchers would grow disheartened and go back to Castelneuf to regroup. Meanwhile, still at the cemetery, issuing orders and sending for the hounds, Aimery fumed and the French knights did not disguise their disappointment as the pyre, with nothing to sustain it except Raimon's unused blindfold, eventually burnt itself out.

Hugh's calculations had been accurate. Yolanda never saw any smoke at all, let alone smoke that turned from sulphurous grey to Flame Blue. In her head, she went over and over what Raimon had said to her, and what she might have said to him. After an hour, she was quite cold inside and found herself thankful that human beings could only feel so much, and that afterwards there was nothing. Perhaps she would never feel anything again. She found, in this new state, that she was glad Brees was not with her. He was part of her old life, her feeling life. Now she would not feel. She would simply be. That was how she'd get through it. And she would find the Blue Flame. She made that vow, although she would never forgive it or the Knight Magician for not being there when Raimon needed them most.

It was long after sunset before Parsifal and Raimon dared to breathe easily. They could still hear the shouts of their pursuers and knew that though they were searching in quite the wrong valley, Aimery would be very reluctant to give up. Very quickly others would come to join him. This was not a chase to find an escaped criminal. The Blue Flame had turned it into a chase for the Occitan herself.

When he had watched the last of the scenting hounds turn into noisy streaks in the dusk on a hillside far away, Raimon tilted his face to the sky, pulling the evening air into his lungs, relishing the slight chill and prickle on his scalp where his sweat had dried. His hair was as matted as Yolanda's. He peeled it out of his eyes. It suddenly seemed important to count the stars. He felt he had never looked at them properly before. Parsifal was more circumspect, keeping his eyes skinned for the hidden scout, the hound dilly-dallying, the hunter left behind. They must find somewhere safe to rest. They began to walk northwards, deeper and deeper into the forests. After a little time, Raimon spilled out his thanks. Parsifal pushed the thanks away. 'You must thank the Flame,' he said. 'I was terrified.'

'So was I.'

They walked on. The moon only just penetrated the forest canopy here, and with the trees so tightly closed in behind them, it was almost pitch black. But Parsifal didn't dare to get out the Flame to use as a lantern. Their progress was slow.

'Sir Parsifal,' Raimon's voice was deeper than before, and more thoughtful.

'Just Parsifal, please.'

'What do we do next?'

'I would have thought we were going to find Yolanda.'

'Yes,' Raimon said, 'that's what I want to do. I want to get her back more than anything. But I keep thinking. She told me on the bridge that she'd sacrifice the Occitan for me and I told her I didn't want that, and I didn't. So –' he took a deep breath.

'I think I follow you,' said Parsifal.

'You see, Sir Parsifal, I just want to go to her. I can't imagine not going, yet I know that it's not the right thing to do because the Flame's not my flame. Do you understand me? It's the Flame of the Occitan. I've said that so often, I've forgotten what it means, but the fire, that heat –' he walked more quickly. 'I think I understand better now.'

'Yes.'

'I think Aimery will move very fast. If the Flame disappears again, he'll hand over the Amouroix to King Louis and other counties will follow. And you know how he'll do it and not be branded a traitor?'

'How?'

'He'll say that it was he who released the prisoners. People will be grateful. The Cathars will return to their homes. He'll tell them that he's acting in their best interest and that if only they do what he wants, everything will be just as it was before Girald came. And when all the hullabaloo about the Flame has died down, which it will if it disappears again, they'll want to believe him. He'll offer peace and quiet. That's what he'll offer them. By the time they realise exactly what the terms of that peace and quiet are, it'll be too late.'

'You think they'll want peace and quiet badly enough to bow to a king they've spent decades defying?'

Raimon stopped. 'I don't know,' he said. 'All I know is that good people often do nothing in the hope that bad things will just go away. That's what Count Berengar did. He wasn't a bad man, not at all, but to be a good man, you have to do more than just mind your own business. Yolanda is my business. She's everything. I would die for her. But it's not the time for the Flame to leave the Occitan. The people sang the Song of the Flame on the bridge and they saw it at the pyre. If it vanishes again, they'll lose all faith in it, and if they do that, the Occitan is finished. How can I let that happen?'

Parsifal couldn't see Raimon's face, but he could sense the

struggle going on as his love of the Occitan and his love for the girl waged war, one against the other. It was a heroic struggle, a struggle fit not for a weaver but for a knight, and though it was a noiseless struggle, it was more agonising than open battle, for at least in open battle a man can seize his sword or axe and howl as he swings it mindlessly. There could be nothing mindless about this. 'The Flame saved me,' Raimon said, 'and now it's my moment to try and do something for it. I must show what it really stands for, not Catholic or Cathar or even you or me, but all of us together.' He heard Parsifal sigh deeply. 'Am I right, Sir Parsifal? Am I right?' He could not afford to make a mistake.

'Just Parsifal, please.' The old knight found it hard to speak. He was thinking of the forty years he had wandered, never recognising his moment, or never wanting to. This boy put him to shame. But Raimon did not seem to think him shameful for he suddenly placed his own hands, the hands which had so recently been clasped so tightly inside Yolanda's, within Parsifal's white ones. They sought comfort and found it. Then Parsifal let go and took the Flame out of its pouch. No matter what the danger, they must see it now. It sat in its salver, just as it had when Parsifal had first set eyes on it and here, at this moment, though it did nothing special, it was more intensely the Flame of the Occitan burning for two of its own than it had ever been before.

A long time later, Parsifal returned it to the pouch and when he did, without a word, both he and Raimon turned round. They would go back to Castelneuf and they would offer not peace and quiet, but sacrifice and struggle. They would not hide the Flame, but display it openly for all to see, and with it they would confront the poisons of their time and lance them. And if they failed and the Occitan was swallowed up in blood and fire, history would never, ever be able to record that they had not tried their best.

After that there would be Yolanda. She would come back to an Occitan where they would dance and never have to stop. At least that's what Raimon hoped. No, he knew it must be more than a hope. It was what he had to believe.

I shall sleep now. This is a good moment to rest. Old countries, like old men, get tired you know. But when I wake I shall resume my tale, for there is a great deal more to tell.